Total-E-Bound Publishing

By Carc

CW01085867

By Jambrea Jo Jones

Wet Your Whistle
Gaymes: Rough Riders
His Hero: A Ring and A Promise
Unconventional at Best: Rough Awakening
Homecoming: A Detour Home
Feral: Pride and Joey

UNCONVENTIONAL IN ATLANTA ANTHOLOGY

SEEING HIM
CAROL LYNNE

BLOWN AWAY
AMBER KELL

HIS LAST CLIENT
T.A. CHASE

WHERE TOMORROW SHINES
JAMBREA JO JONES

SLIPPERY WHEN WET
STEPHANI HECHT

OUT OF SERVICE
DEVON RHODES

Unconventional In Atlanta Anthology
ISBN # 978-1-78184-632-2
Seeing Him ©Copyright Carol Lynne 2013
Blown Away ©Copyright Amber Kell 2013
His Last Client ©Copyright T.A. Chase 2013
Where Tomorrow Shines ©Copyright Jambrea Jo Jones 2013
Slippery When Wet ©Copyright Stephani Hecht 2013
Out of Service ©Copyright Devon Rhodes 2013
Cover Art by Posh Gosh ©Copyright July 2013
Interior text design by Claire Siemaszkiewicz
Total-E-Bound Publishing

Published in 2013 by Total-E-Bound Publishing, Think Tank, Ruston Way, Lincoln, LN6 7FL, United Kingdom.

SEEING HIM

Carol Lynne

Dedication

For Trevor, the extraordinary concierge at the Meliá.
Thank you so much for taking care of us in October.

Chapter One

With the office lights turned off, Trevor Sharp peered out of the window. From his position, he was able to see the broad-shouldered silhouette of the man he'd watched for over a week. He had no idea who the man was or why he slept in a nook of the Meliá parking garage, but there was something about him that continued to draw Trevor's attention.

Security would have run the man out had they spotted him on their monitors, so evidently the small crevice was one of the few places their cameras didn't reach. *Interesting.* Did his mysterious dark friend know he'd be safe in that particular spot or was it pure luck?

It had been a week ago that Trevor's ex — Dickhead Danny, as Trevor liked to refer to him — had actually shown up at the hotel and waited in the parking garage for Trevor to leave work. Danny had immediately started the same tired argument about why they needed to get back together. When Trevor told Danny he had no desire to see or speak to him, his ex had snapped. Danny wasn't articulate enough to fight with words—he'd always preferred to use his size and strength to win an argument. Danny had pushed Trevor hard against his car and had showered him with spittle as he'd screamed at him.

Then, from out of nowhere, a man wearing a faded, desert-style fatigue jacket had broadsided Danny, knocking him to the ground. Several punches had been thrown by both men, but it had been Danny who'd eventually run away with his tail between his legs. It had happened so fast, Trevor hadn't even got a good look at his mysterious protector, but Danny had called the man a freak before he'd run off. When Trevor had tried to approach the man to thank him, the stranger had quickly turned his face away and nodded before disappearing into the shadows.

Instead of driving home that night, Trevor had turned around and gone back into the Meliá. He'd spent each night since sleeping in one of the unused hotel rooms or on the sofa in his office. Although the security at the hotel was a nice bonus, he'd discovered his invisible man only moved around once dark descended on the city of Atlanta.

Trevor sighed. Earlier that evening, he'd taken a to-go box, containing one of the hotel's big hamburgers, Tater Tots and a bottle of water out to the garage and had left it near where he knew the man slept. He'd set the food in a spot just outside the shadows, hoping to get his first real look at the man he couldn't stop thinking about.

Unfortunately, his plan hadn't worked. The invisible man had stayed in the darkness of the nook that he'd made his home and had used his legs to retrieve the to-go that contained the food.

Why're you hiding? Trevor should probably be afraid of the obviously homeless man instead of feeling a sense of warmth that the man's proximity provided. He heard someone whistling and glanced over his shoulder. Keith, one of the security guards, was riding down the escalator that led to the Meliá offices.

"Mr Sharp?"

"Hi, Keith," Trevor greeted.

"Why're you sitting in the dark?" Keith started to reach for the light switch, but Trevor stopped him.

"Leave 'em off. I've got a migraine and it helps to sit in the dark." It wasn't the truth, but the guard didn't need to know that. Trevor glanced at the keycard in Keith's hand. "Where're you going?"

"I saw someone messing around your car in the garage, so I thought I'd take a look," Keith explained. "Don't worry, from the monitor it didn't look like he did any damage or anything, but I thought I'd better make sure. I didn't know you were down here. Are you spending the night again?"

"Yes." Trevor hoped he could ease Keith's mind about the man he'd seen on the monitor. The last thing he wanted was for the security guard to scare his mystery man away. "Don't worry about my car. I saw a couple of people using the garage as a shortcut to get to The Varsity earlier. They looked harmless."

Keith stared out of the glass door. A covered drive connected the hotel to the garage, so it wasn't uncommon for passers-by to use the area as a cut-through. "I'll take a quick look just to make sure."

Trevor held his breath as Keith strolled towards the garage. He came within fifty feet or so of the invisible man, but didn't even slow. Evidently, Trevor's protector heard him coming and moved deeper into his nook. Keith disappeared into the garage and moments later came out with a piece of paper in his hand.

Trevor held his breath once more when Keith passed the shadowed crevice. "Anything?" he asked when Keith stepped back into the hotel.

"This was under your wiper." Keith handed Trevor a tattered and stained envelope.

"Thanks." Trevor made no move to open the envelope while Keith stood over him. "I'll let you know if I see anyone else nosing around," he told the guard.

"Have a good night," Keith said as he stepped onto the escalator.

The only light in the room came from outside the building, so Trevor moved closer to the window. He opened the envelope and peered inside. Money? He pulled out a five and five one-dollar bills. Had the mystery man tried to pay him back for the food? For some reason, it didn't sit well with Trevor. He'd given the man dinner as a way to thank him for coming to his rescue with Danny, not to be paid back.

Before he could think too much about it, Trevor went out of the back door. "I don't want your money."

"And I don't need your charity," a deep voice replied from the shadows.

"It wasn't charity. It was a thank you." Trevor tried to calm his racing heart. After a week spent thinking and fantasising about his invisible man, he was finally speaking to him. "I appreciate the help you gave me. I thought I'd do something nice in return."

The mysterious stranger said nothing for several moments. "Thank you for the food, but you can keep the money."

Trevor sat on a cement security pylon. "Will you at least tell me your name? I'm Trevor."

Another moment of silence before he heard the deep voice again. "Jonah."

Jonah. Trevor mentally connected the name to the voice. He had so many questions he wanted to ask, but he knew he couldn't push. "It's nice to finally talk to you, Jonah."

"Why?" Jonah asked.

Why? What kind of question was that? Trevor cleared his throat. "You have a nice voice, and I've been thinking a lot about you this week. So, I guess I'm happy to meet you even though it doesn't seem like you're going to come out here and do it in person."

"You don't want to meet me that way. I've seen you watching me through the window because I've been keeping an eye on you, too."

"I've been watching you, hoping to get a glimpse of you in the light." Trevor knew that wasn't the whole truth. "And because I feel better knowing you're out here."

"Is that guy who attacked you coming back?" Jonah asked.

"I don't know. I doubt it, but Danny's unpredictable." Chilled, Trevor rubbed his shirtsleeves. He should've put his suit jacket on before coming out. "Are you warm enough? I can probably find you a blanket."

"I have one."

"Is there anything you don't have that you need?" Trevor had always been generous to a fault, but he couldn't help himself. He hated the thought of Jonah living on the streets.

"This. Someone to talk to is nice."

Trevor felt his chest tighten. "Yeah, I can understand that. I'm the GM here, so I try not to make friends with the other employees. It blurs the lines for a lot of people, including me. Since I work all the time, it doesn't really leave time for friends."

"Can I ask you something?"

"Sure." Trevor leant forward to rest his forearms on his knees.

"Was that guy who attacked you your boyfriend?" Jonah asked.

Shit. Did Jonah have a problem with gay people? Trevor hated to lose the new friendship that had popped up between them, but he couldn't deny who he was. "Ex. We broke up a couple of months ago, but when Danny drinks and can't find anyone to take home from the bar, he starts harassing me again."

When Jonah didn't say anything, Trevor narrowed his eyes. "You have a problem with me being gay?" Trevor asked.

"No. It makes things harder, that's all."

The door behind Trevor opened, scaring the shit out of him. He jumped to his feet and spun around to find Keith standing in the doorway. "I saw you sitting out here on the monitor and thought maybe you'd come out for fresh air and had gotten yourself locked out."

Trevor didn't like the idea of Keith watching him. It could potentially expose Jonah. "I've got my keycard, but thanks for worrying about me. The chilly night hasn't quite driven me back inside yet."

"No offence, sir, but this isn't the best place to be alone after dark. If you want some fresh air, you should step out front where the lighting's better and the valets are around," Keith offered.

"Thanks, but I'm safe here. The door's ten feet away if I get spooked." Trevor waited, hoping Keith would go the fuck inside and leave him and Jonah alone to talk.

"If it's all the same, I think I'll wait with you if you don't mind."

Trevor ground his teeth. He knew Keith was just doing his job, but he didn't need a fucking babysitter. "You don't have to do that. I'm ready." He followed Keith inside, after glancing once more towards the dark nook. "Sleep well," he silently whispered to Jonah.

* * * *

Jonah Mayberry tucked himself tighter against the cold cement wall when he heard the hotel door open. He listened quietly while Trevor talked to the security guard who had made rounds earlier. It was obvious to him that Trevor was trying to get rid of the guard, but had finally given up and had agreed to go back inside.

Jonah relaxed and stretched his legs out in front of him. He'd enjoyed talking to Trevor. It had been the first real conversation he'd had since the fight with the superintendent of his old apartment building more than a month earlier. Of course, that conversation had gone much differently because it had been in broad daylight and the old sour puss hadn't been able to take his eyes off the burn scars that covered half of Jonah's face.

Involuntarily, Jonah started to reach for the scars but stopped himself. It had been six months since the supply truck explosion. He'd spent the majority of his recovery in a military hospital in Germany before finally being transferred back to the United States. The skin grafts he'd prayed would make the scars less noticeable had helped in the healing process but not in the vanity department. As Trevor's ex had so eloquently announced, Jonah looked like a freak.

Jonah closed his eyes and rested his head against the wall. He hadn't mentioned it to Trevor, but he'd been watching the thin, yet incredibly stylish black man for almost two weeks. It hadn't been fate that he'd been around to keep the ex-boyfriend from strong-arming Trevor. Watching Trevor come and go from the hotel without the barrier of a window between them had become the highlight of his day. Fuck. He needed to get over it.

Although Trevor was kind and willing to talk to him, Jonah knew one look at his face would put an end to the romantic musings he dreamt of at night. Still, he would love nothing more than to continue their conversations through the veil of darkness.

Jonah pulled the blanket up around his exposed neck. It was only October, but obviously Mother Nature had decided to fuck with them by pushing a cold front through. He probably should've taken Trevor up on the offer of another blanket, but he had nowhere to put it during the daylight hours. As it was, everything he owned fit into his military-issued backpack, which was perfect for clearing out of a place in a hurry when he needed to.

* * * *

Trevor handed Barbara a twenty and waited for his change. "Did you remember to order soy milk for that big GRL group coming in next week?"

Barbara pushed Trevor's order across the counter towards him. "I put it on the list."

"Thanks." Trevor shoved the change into his pocket before tucking the sack under his arm and picking up the two cups of coffee. He nodded to Christopher, the

Meliá's concierge, on his way to the escalator that would lead him downstairs. "Morning."

"Good morning," Christopher returned.

Before going to his office, he went outside. He set one of the coffees on the ground just outside of Jonah's hiding place, along with the sack. "Brought you coffee and a bagel for breakfast," he said.

Jonah coughed several times. "You didn't need to do that."

"I know. It's just me buying a friend a cup of coffee. No big deal," Trevor explained.

Jonah coughed again. "Thanks."

Trevor winced at the wet-sounding cough. "That cold's getting worse. I don't suppose you'd let me take you to the doctor?"

"No. No doctors. I'll be fine." Jonah reached out, wrapped a large strong hand around the cup and pulled it back into the shadows. "Thanks again for the coffee."

It was killing Trevor that he still hadn't seen Jonah's face, but he tried to respect the mystery man's privacy, so he never pushed. "I'll go home at lunch and see if I have any leftover antibiotics."

"Not necessary," Jonah said around a cough.

"Yeah, sounds like you're healthy as a horse." Trevor took a sip of his coffee. "I have a dinner meeting after work, but I'll be back after that."

"You don't have to. You're allowed to have a life outside this place," Jonah said.

Trevor glanced around. "I am outside." He grinned to himself. "Besides, you're infinitely more interesting than anyone else I deal with." He tapped the sack with the toe of his shoe. "Eat your bagel and stay warm. I'll talk to you later."

* * * *

Trevor swung by the pharmacy on the way back to the hotel. He hadn't found antibiotics at his place, so he'd called in a favour from a friend who had begrudgingly phoned in a prescription for him. He pulled into his usual spot and prayed the security team would assume he was burning the midnight oil again. "I brought you some medicine."

When Trevor didn't receive a reply, he took a step closer. "Jonah?"

A deep moan and weak-sounding cough was Jonah's only answer.

"Shit." Trevor put aside Jonah's need for privacy and rounded the ridge of the nook. Jonah was curled into a ball, shivering with a thin blanket wrapped tightly around him. "Jonah!"

The seconds ticked by as he tried to figure out what to do. Even with his adrenaline pumping, there was no way he could carry someone of Jonah's size. Kneeling next to Jonah, it was still too dark to make out his features. "I'll take care of you," he whispered.

Decision made, he pulled out his phone and called the one man he knew could keep his secret.

"Hello?"

"Esteban, I need your help," Trevor said.

"Mr Sharp?" the front desk manager questioned.

"Yeah. I need a favour, a big one." Trevor reached out and touched Jonah's broad shoulder. "I need a room and your help."

Chapter Two

Trevor set Jonah's boots in the closet. He'd have to do some explaining to Esteban later, but his first concern was Jonah. Unfortunately, he'd never been in the position to nurse someone back to health. He stood at the foot of the bed and tried to figure out what to do next. *Water.* He filled a glass and dug the pills out of the pocket of his suit jacket.

Jonah had protested between coughing fits when they'd practically carried him to the elevator.

Trevor sat on the edge of the king-sized bed and held out one of the pills. "I need you to take this."

Jonah coughed as he struggled to lean up on his elbow, keeping the blanket pressed to the side of his head. "You shouldn't have brought me inside."

Trevor cupped the back of Jonah's neck as he took a sip of water to swallow the medicine. "I had two options, calling an ambulance or bringing you here." He wanted to pull the ratty thin blanket away from Jonah's face but suppressed the urge.

After Esteban had helped him bring Jonah up the elevator and into bed, Trevor had gone back to retrieve Jonah's backpack. Definitely National Guard-issued. "How long have you been back in the States?"

Jonah collapsed and buried his head in the pillow. "I was officially discharged about five weeks ago."

"I know you're trying to hide your face from me, but you don't have to." The burn scars ran from temple to clavicle in a two-inch-wide strip, but, at least in Trevor's eyes, they didn't diminish Jonah's appeal in any way. He rested his hand on Jonah's side. "I've seen them, and they don't change the way I feel about you."

Jonah closed his eyes. "A few years ago, I would've asked you out."

Jonah was gay. *Thank you, Jesus!* Trevor brushed Jonah's shaggy dark blond hair away from his face. "I would've said yes then, and I'd definitely say yes now."

Another coughing fit assaulted Jonah's poor body. Trevor did what he could to help the man sit up. He patted Jonah's back, hoping to loosen the congestion in his lungs. The moment the cough seemed to diminish, Trevor reached for the glass of water and held it to Jonah's lips.

Jonah took several sips before nodding. "That's good."

Trevor set the glass on the table before easing Jonah back onto the mattress. "I'm going to run downstairs and get you some cold medicine. Do you want something to eat? Soup, maybe?"

"My mom used to make me drink hot tea when I had a cold." Jonah rolled to his back but tucked one side of the pillow up between his head and arm to cover the side of his face.

Trevor was in awe at Jonah's muscular physique. "Do you think you're strong enough to soak in a warm tub if I fill it for you?" The bath was to make Jonah feel better, but the thought of seeing more of Jonah's incredible body was too much to pass up.

"Are you saying I stink?" Jonah asked.

"No. You smell like a man. Lucky for you, I like men." Trevor leant down and kissed Jonah's forehead. "Let's get you into the bath, and you can soak while I get you a few things from downstairs."

Jonah stared up at Trevor for several moments before answering. "I'm probably the worst person in the entire Atlanta area for you to get involved with."

"That's definitely not the case," Trevor argued. "You're down on your luck, so what? You think I haven't had my share of hard times? Would you rather I was still with someone like Danny? Because that's the kind of man I usually attract." He moved his lips to hover above Jonah's. "I want to kiss you."

Jonah surprised Trevor by turning his head. "I can't."

Trevor felt crushed at the rebuff. He sat up straight. "I understand."

Jonah grinned. It was the first time Trevor had ever seen the lighter side of his invisible man and it melted him on the spot.

"I don't want you to get sick," Jonah replied. "Wait a few days."

Relieved, Trevor got to his feet. "I'll start a bath." He made sure the water was warm, but not hot before plugging the tub. He set out two fluffy white towels and a washcloth before unwrapping a bar of soap and putting it on the edge.

When Trevor returned to the bedroom, Jonah was sitting on the edge of the bed. He'd managed to get his shirt off, but hadn't made a move to remove his pants.

"Need help?" Trevor asked, staring at Jonah's pale, but incredibly constructed eight-pack. Holy fuck. How'd Jonah manage to stay in such terrific shape?

"I can get myself into the tub. You can do your errands without worrying that I'll drown myself," Jonah said, his head turned away from Trevor.

Trevor sat on the mattress next to Jonah. He wasn't allowed to kiss Jonah until the antibiotics started doing their job, but that didn't mean he couldn't touch him. Taking a huge gamble, he pressed his palm against the soft skin of Jonah's back and started to rub circles into the fevered flesh. "I know you don't trust me yet, but I hope one day you will."

Jonah moved his hand to rest on Trevor's thigh. "No one's touched me like that since…"

Trevor smiled. "I'd like to do more than touch you."

"Why? I have nothing. I'm dirty, sick, and I look like a freak," Jonah said, removing his hand.

Trevor stood. He'd naively fallen in love with the invisible man, but it wasn't until he'd lured Jonah out that he realised the darkness in the man had nothing to do with the shadows he chose to live in. "Your scars won't drive me away, but your lack of faith in me might."

* * * *

Jonah heard the click as the hotel room door shut. He squeezed his eyes shut as he tried to push the hurt in Trevor's voice from his mind. How was he supposed to trust someone with his heart again when it had cost him everything the first time?

Coughing, he stood and unzipped his dirty jeans. It had been weeks since he'd used more than a restroom sink to clean the stink from his body.

When he'd first found himself homeless, Jonah had rented a shabby hotel room, but he found he could only afford to stay a day or two at a time. Mentally, it had been hard for him to go back and forth, so he'd decided to save his money and live on the streets. He couldn't complain too much because he knew he had it better than some. His old landlady might have been mercenary when it came to selling off his belongings and renting his apartment to someone else, but at least she'd agreed he could continue to have his small cheques delivered to his address on record.

Taking his dirty clothes with him, Jonah used the wall and furniture to support him as he made his way into the bathroom. "Shit." He dropped the clothes and sat on the edge of the tub to turn off the water. If he'd wasted any more time, he'd have flooded the bathroom and probably cost Trevor his job.

He let some of the water out of the tub before easing in. He groaned as the warm water surrounded his cock. The first thing he did was to bite off a sliver of the soap. He gagged as he did his best to wash out his mouth. It was gross, beyond gross, but he didn't have much choice if he had any hope of actually kissing Trevor.

It was wrong to want something so much, especially from someone as kind as Trevor. He rinsed his mouth out before leaning forward to dunk his head under the water. He opened his eyes and wondered if it was possible to drown himself. It wasn't a real desire to die that prompted the question. Since waking in the hospital after the explosion, he'd played the death game.

Figuring out different ways to kill himself had helped pass the time while the nurses had scrubbed and cleaned his burned flesh. He had a small notebook in his backpack that held the detailed list he continued to add to each time he needed to escape the real world around him.

Jonah sat up and wiped the water from his eyes. He grabbed the soap and started to rub it into his hair until he noticed the tiny bottles of shampoo and conditioner that Trevor had so thoughtfully put out for him. He coughed as he twisted the cap and poured the entire amount into his hand.

"I got you some chicken broth from Steve, in the kitchen," Trevor announced as he came back into the hotel room.

Jonah had never liked chicken broth, but he loved the gesture. "Thanks." He heard Trevor sit on the bed. "It's been a while since I've had a bath." His chuckle ended in a series of deep, wet coughs. "But I guess you figured that out," he said once he could breathe again.

"I told you it didn't bother me, and I meant it," Trevor replied.

They were back to talking without being able to see each other, and while it was comforting to Jonah, he knew it hurt Trevor. He touched the scar with his soapy hand. *Trust.* "Would you mind coming in here? I'm too big to lie down, so I need help rinsing my hair."

Jonah heard Trevor moving around in the other room before he appeared in the doorway. He'd taken off his suit jacket and held up a glass. "This should help."

Trevor set the glass on the edge of the tub. He knelt and started to roll up his sleeves. "You know it's not going to be easy for me to be this close without touching you."

"It's okay." Jonah leant forward and allowed Trevor to rinse his hair. The touch of Trevor's long fingers against his scalp reminded Jonah of better times. Shane, greeting him at the door of their apartment with candles and champagne, eager to make love in the large bathtub. The secret touches from friend and fellow soldier Evan Brahms moments before the blast. Jonah sucked in a deep breath, prompting another coughing fit.

Trevor pounded Jonah on the back. "You okay?"

Jonah felt lightheaded. "I think I'm gonna pass out."

Trevor eased Jonah back. "Just relax. You're probably dehydrated." He got to his feet and left the bathroom.

Jonah closed his eyes and rested his head against the tiled wall. It was the memories, not the need for water that made him lightheaded. He heard Trevor's return, and knew he owed his new friend an explanation. "I was living over on St Charles Avenue Northwest with my partner Shane, when I got the word that my unit was being deployed." He opened his eyes and stared up at Trevor. "I wasn't a very good boyfriend. Well, I guess I was when I was here, but once I landed overseas I cheated."

Trevor toed off his shoes as he unbuttoned his shirt. "Do you know where Shane is now?"

Jonah shook his head. "When I was first deployed, I'd send him my half of the bills every month. After I cheated for the first time, I couldn't not tell him."

Trevor soaped the washcloth before pressing it against Jonah's chest. "Is that when he left?"

"If only it had been that easy." Jonah bit his lip when Trevor began to wash his chest and stomach. God, it felt so good.

"So what happened?" Trevor went to work on Jonah's arms.

"Shane said he forgave me, and we'd work it out once I got home. So, like an idiot, I continued to send him my money every month." Jonah closed his eyes as Trevor began to scrub his face. When Trevor got to the scarred skin, he dropped the washcloth and used the soft pads of his fingers to apply the soap. "What I didn't know was that Shane was keeping my money without paying my bills. I got home to nothing, no Shane, no car, no apartment, and with a face like this, no job."

"Were you a model or something?"

"Fitness instructor," Jonah corrected. He glanced down at his body. Although he'd lost some of his muscle mass due to lack of regular protein in his diet, he still tried to keep in shape by exercising in his own little corner of the world.

Trevor gently rinsed the soap from Jonah's face, making sure to get the suds out of Jonah's rough beard. "Your body's incredible. Mine's too skinny, but I do look good in an expensive suit."

"Yours is perfect, and mine used to be better." Jonah appreciated Trevor's trim waist and tiny dark brown nipples. "How long before those pills kick in? Because I'm feeling better."

"That's because part of your problem was that you were chilled to the bone. You'll probably feel even better once you eat something." Trevor soaped up the washcloth again and handed it to Jonah. "I'm going to let you take care of your cock and ass." He smiled. "I don't trust myself."

Jonah felt his cock begin to harden. Hell, it took a special man to get a rise out of him, as shitty as he felt. He lifted his hips off the bottom of the tub and his cock made an appearance above the waterline. Grinning, he handed the washcloth back. "You told me earlier I needed to learn to trust you."

Trevor dropped the washcloth and picked up the soap. He lathered both hands. "So this is your way of testing me?"

Jonah groaned when Trevor's hand encircled his cock. He gripped the side of the tub as Trevor thoroughly cleansed every inch. "Should I continue?" Trevor asked with one perfectly shaped brow arched.

Jonah ground his teeth. It had been too long since he'd felt someone else's touch on his cock, let alone someone as good at giving pleasure as Trevor. "I'll come if you go any further," he warned.

"Is that a problem?" Trevor asked, bending over the side of the tub to lick the crown of Jonah's cock.

"Hang on. Let me get some fresh water in here." Jonah used his toe to push the lever on the drain. The dirty water was a constant reminder of where he'd been and how he'd been living.

The moment the water was low enough to expose Jonah's ass, Trevor soaped his hands once again. "Give me a second before you turn on the faucet."

Jonah spread his legs and closed his eyes. He loved the way the soapy fingers felt sliding between the cheeks of his ass. Bottom had never been his favourite position, but Trevor moved with such skill that Jonah started to wonder if he, too, preferred to be a top. Just when he thought he'd died and gone to heaven, he started to cough again. *Fuck.* The rattle in his chest didn't sound good at all.

"Damn." Trevor used what little water was left in the bottom of the tub to rinse the soap from Jonah's skin. "Let's get you dried off and back into bed."

Still coughing, Jonah leaned on Trevor as he got to his feet. Trevor reached to the rack and wrapped a couple of towels around Jonah. "I'm going to call downstairs for a pot of hot tea and some more broth. No doubt what I brought earlier is stone cold."

"No broth," Jonah said. "Tea will be enough."

"You need to eat something," Trevor argued, helping Jonah out of the tub and into the bedroom.

Jonah fell into bed. He hadn't realised how weak he was while Trevor's hands were roaming his body. Now that he was out of the warm water, the days of little rest and illness were catching up with him. "Drink?"

Trevor was already buttoning his shirt. He moved around the bed to the table and retrieved the water. "I also got some cough syrup." He poured the vile-tasting green liquid into the tiny plastic cup and handed it to Jonah.

Jonah winced when he gulped the shit down. "I hate that taste."

"Yeah, you and every other person on the planet, but it does the job." Trevor carried the plastic cup into the bathroom.

Jonah heard the water turn on for a moment before shutting off. "I think I'll just worry about the tea and food after I get some sleep."

"Oh, okay." Trevor shifted from foot to foot. "I guess I'll go then and see you in the morning."

Jonah shook his head. "Get undressed and climb in here with me."

Trevor's face lit up. "You sure?"

Jonah ran a hand through his beard. He'd need to ask Trevor for a razor if he planned to do much kissing, but he was several days away from that anyway. "I'm sure." He watched Trevor closely as the designer clothes slowly came off and were neatly hung in the closet. Wow. He hadn't expected the muscular definition on display. Trevor might be naturally thin, but his body was a true work of art.

Trevor turned out the lights in the bathroom and entry before joining Jonah. He slid under the sheets but stayed on his side of the bed.

"I didn't ask you to join me because I had extra mattress space available," Jonah grumbled. He lay on his side and reached for Trevor. It had been a long time since he'd felt the warmth of another man while he slept. "Spoon with me."

Trevor rolled to his side and scooted back against Jonah.

Jonah sighed. Trevor felt so right in his arms. "Thank you," he whispered.

Trevor shook his head. "No, thank *you* for trusting me."

Jonah realised he hadn't tried to cover his scar since he'd eased into the bathtub. It hadn't been a conscious decision, making it all the more beautiful. He settled down, exhaustion and illness stealing the last of his energy. He might not understand why Trevor had befriended him, but he would grab the few moments of happiness while they were offered.

* * * *

After a quick trip home to shower and change, Trevor stopped by the front desk. "Morning."

"How's your guest?" Esteban asked.

"Sleeping. I think his fever's down, but he's not out of the woods yet." Trevor leaned against the counter. "I'd like to go ahead and book the room for the next week if we have it available."

Esteban keyed the request into the computer. "The room he's in is booked starting Wednesday with that big reader convention coming in, but I can move him up to twenty-four at no extra charge if you want me to?"

"I'd appreciate it." Trevor glanced at his watch. "See you upstairs in an hour?"

Esteban nodded. "I'll be there."

Trevor stopped at the bar and ordered two large coffees. "To-go cups, please," he told Gib.

"You got it."

Trevor grabbed a menu. "Would you have room service bring two orders of chicken strips up to fourteen-twenty-six?"

"Sure thing, boss." Gib set the coffee on the bar in front of Trevor. "Anything else?"

Tearing open two packets of sugar, Trevor poured them into his cup. "I heard you mention something to Esteban about a part-time job you're working. I don't suppose they're hiring?"

Gib coughed and shook his head. "Not that I know of. You looking for another job?"

"Not me, but I've got a friend who needs something." Trevor fit the lid on his cup.

"You might talk to housekeeping or maintenance. I think there might be something open in one of those departments."

Trevor nodded. He wasn't sure if Jonah was interested in getting a job, but it wouldn't hurt to ask. "Thanks."

"I'll have them send the food right up. Fourteen-twenty-six, right?"

"Yep." Trevor carried the coffee to the elevator. He wasn't sure he liked the idea of Jonah getting a job in the hotel, but maybe a safe place to work was just what the man needed to take that first step.

After a short ride up in the elevator, Trevor stepped off on the fourteenth floor. He rounded the corner and noticed a cleaning cart outside Jonah's room. "Shit." He hurried down the hall.

Quinn, one of the housekeepers was in the process of changing the sheets on the bed. Trevor didn't want to startle the ex-war vet, so he set one of the cups on the cart and knocked on the open door.

"Yeah." Quinn glanced up and dropped the sheets to the floor. "Excuse me, Mr Sharp."

"Where's the man who had this room?" Trevor asked.

Quinn shrugged. "There wasn't anyone here when I knocked." He gestured to the TV stand. "Room key was sitting right there."

Trevor did a quick tour of the room. He noticed the empty bedside table where Jonah's medicines had been.

"Did I do something wrong?" Quinn asked.

Trevor shook his head. "No." He shouldn't have left that morning without waking Jonah. Hell, he'd even put the *Do Not Disturb* sign on the door, so no one would bother Jonah. "Thanks," he told Quinn before walking out of the room.

* * * *

Jonah moved his backpack in an effort to try and get comfortable. He should have known one night in a warm bed would weaken his ability to adapt to the realities of his life. He wouldn't trade the hours spent with Trevor in his arms for anything, but his fucked-up situation wasn't Trevor's problem to solve.

"I thought I'd find you here." Dressed in another of his expensive suits, Trevor squatted beside Jonah. "Coffee?"

Jonah held his pounding head as he sat up. He took the cup from Trevor. "I didn't get you into trouble, did I?"

Trevor chuckled. "I may be the general manager, but I'm also a guest. I rented that room for the next week."

"Why?" Jonah had no idea how much the nightly rate was in the hotel, but it couldn't be cheap.

Trevor stood and held out his hand. "Can we talk about this upstairs?"

Jonah wondered how he would cope with the cold after spending an entire week inside. "As much as I want to, I don't think I can. I'm having a hard time acclimating to the cold, and I was only out of it for one night."

"Then I guess we need to use this week to find you a job and place to live so you don't have to live like this anymore." Trevor continued to hold his hand out.

Jonah's pride kept him from agreeing immediately, but he was smart enough to realise he might never get another chance like the one Trevor was so graciously offering. He put his coffee cup in Trevor's outstretched hand. "You carry that, I'll get my stuff."

Trevor stepped back out of Jonah's way. "No argument?"

Jonah unzipped his pack and tucked his thin blanket inside. He stood and slipped the hood of his sweatshirt into place, shielding his scars from anyone they might meet on the way to the room. "No, no argument." He took his cup back from Trevor before kissing him on the forehead.

"Do that again," Trevor ordered.

Jonah did as asked. He wished he could kiss Trevor like he wanted to, but although he was feeling better, he didn't know whether or not he was contagious. He refused to take the chance of getting the man, who was saving his life, sick.

Still holding the cup, Trevor used the back of his hand to touch Jonah's forehead. "You don't feel as warm as you did last night."

"I think the fever's pretty much gone." Jonah took his coffee. "Another day or two and I'll be able to thank you properly."

Chapter Three

On Wednesday, Trevor had helped Jonah move upstairs to the twenty-fourth floor. He pointed out 'The Level' when they got off the elevator. "If you need anything to drink or a piece of fruit or something, you can get that in there. It's only for guests on this floor, so it's usually fairly empty."

"I'll be fine." Jonah wiped the sweat from his forehead.

"You okay?" Trevor asked, concerned.

"Guess I'm weaker than I thought I was." Jonah reached out and steadied himself against the wall.

"Lean on me." Trevor wrapped his arm around Jonah's waist. The antibiotics weren't helping much, and Jonah still refused to go to the doctor. Jonah's trip back outside a few days earlier hadn't help his condition either.

"I'm sorry," Jonah mumbled.

"Don't be. I've already talked to Esteban. He gave me a great deal on an extended stay, so you just concentrate on getting better."

Trevor dug the keycard out of his suit pocket and opened the door. The room was a little bigger, but overall the same as the one Jonah had used downstairs. He helped Jonah to the bed before kneeling to take off his shoes.

"Will you let me pay some of the room?" Jonah unzipped his pants, and Trevor helped take them off. "I can't pay all of it at once, but I'll get another cheque next month."

Trevor wanted to turn down the offer, but he knew Jonah's pride wouldn't let him stay otherwise. "Sure, but it's really not too bad. I got a good deal because I work here, so it won't be as much as you think."

Jonah nodded as he lay back on the bed.

Trevor couldn't help but notice the thick flaccid cock that rested against Jonah's thigh. He wasn't sure if Jonah was too weak to care about exposing himself or if he'd grown accustomed to being naked around Trevor. Either way, the beautiful sight was too much temptation for Trevor to ignore. He decided to take a chance, and reached up to brush the length with his palm.

Jonah closed his eyes without issuing a protest.

Praying he wouldn't go to hell for taking advantage of a sick man, Trevor continued. He wrapped his long fingers around the thickening girth of Jonah's cock and rubbed the sensitive area under the head with his thumb. "Is this okay?"

"Better than," Jonah replied. He held out his hand. "Do you have time to get undressed and join me?"

Trevor glanced at the bedside clock and silently cursed. "Not really, but I have to do this."

Still wearing his clothes, Trevor climbed onto the bed. He swiped the head of Jonah's dick with his tongue and was rewarded with a soft moan and a generous dollop of pre-cum. Jonah's reaction spurred Trevor on. He enveloped the crown of Jonah's growing erection with his mouth and sucked.

Jonah moaned again before reaching for the fly of Trevor's dress pants. "Let me feel you."

Without taking his mouth off Jonah's cock, Trevor unbuckled his belt and slid the catch free of the fabric. In no time, Jonah managed to push Trevor's pants and underwear down far enough to free his cock.

Trevor sighed as he swallowed as much of Jonah's dick as he could. He pulled back and repeated the action several times.

Jonah's grip on Trevor's cock was firm but not painful as he began his own rhythm up and down.

Shit. It was their first real sexual encounter, and Trevor knew he wouldn't last long. He thrust his hips against Jonah's hold and released the cock in his mouth long enough to cry out. "Close."

"Yeah, me, too," Jonah groaned.

Refusing to miss a drop of cum, Trevor swallowed Jonah's dick once again and began to fondle his heavy sac. He wanted everything Jonah was willing to give him, and the longer he knew the man, the more he realised his desires didn't stop at sex.

The first stream of Jonah's seed hit the back of Trevor's throat, and Trevor knew he couldn't fight his own climax any longer. He came hard and fast as he continued to swallow the thick cum that shot from Jonah's cock. The pleasure he felt was so intense that Trevor began to wonder whether he even wanted to return to work. By the time they'd both drained their balls, he could barely summon enough energy to reposition himself to lie beside Jonah.

Jonah rolled to his side to face Trevor. "Thank you."

Trevor chuckled. "No need for that. I got as much out of it as you did." He stared into Jonah's eyes. "I want to kiss you."

"I don't want you to get sick," Jonah countered.

"And I don't want to go another second without the feel of your tongue in my mouth." Trevor closed the distance and pressed his lips against Jonah's.

With a deep groan, Jonah placed his hand at the base of Trevor's skull and gave Trevor what he'd asked for. *Yes*, Trevor inwardly sighed as he gave himself over to Jonah's skilful tongue. He couldn't remember a kiss ever making him feel so cherished and desired at the same time. Jonah was an expert at mixing soft and sweet with rough and passionate. Hell, Trevor no longer cared whether he caught the bug that had knocked Jonah on his ass. All he wanted was more kisses and lots of them.

* * * *

"Did you get the carpets cleaned in twenty-five?" Trevor asked.

Bruce, the maintenance manager, glanced up from his clipboard. "Yep, they did it yesterday."

"And those damn louvered bathroom doors? How many of those did we get changed out this week?"

"Seventeen, but that's all the doors we have right now."

Trevor silently cursed. "You have more on order?"

Bruce shook his head. "I put the request in, but I haven't heard back from corporate with an okay yet."

As frustrating as it was, there was no need to take it out on Bruce. "Okay, well, I guess they can wait." He crossed his arms over his chest. "Are you still looking for help in your department?"

"Yeah, why, you looking for another job?" Bruce asked, a wide grin on his face.

"You're a funny guy. I've got a friend who's looking." Trevor went on to tell Bruce the basics of Jonah's situation.

Bruce nodded. "We can put him on paint duty. Why don't you have him give me a call?"

"Actually, he's staying in the hotel." It was day ten in nursing Jonah back to health, and Trevor couldn't believe the progress Jonah had made.

"Even better. Have him stop by my office at lunchtime, and I'll talk to him while I eat," Bruce offered.

"Thank you." Trevor left Bruce and headed to the elevator. He and Jonah had spent the last five days touching and sucking each other, but they'd yet to take things to the next level. With a job prospect lined up for Jonah, Trevor hoped they could celebrate.

On the way, Trevor made a quick call to his secretary. "Hey, Sarah, I'm taking an early lunch today."

"Will you have your phone with you?" she asked.

"Yes, but the ringer will be turned off. I'll check messages though." Trevor studied his reflection in the elevator's mirror. Did he look as horny as he felt? Sleeping in Jonah's arms had been heaven, but merely sucking the erection that occasionally prodded against his ass at night instead of feeling it inside him had been pure hell.

Trevor knocked on the door before using his key to let himself inside. "Wow, glad I came back when I did."

With nothing but a white towel around his waist, Jonah paused in the process of shaving the beard from his face. He met Trevor's gaze in the mirror. "I figured you were tired of sleeping with a mountain man."

Trevor wasn't, but the transformation was unbelievable. He moved to stand next to the sink and ran his palm down the side of Jonah's handsome face, grinning when his finger found a deep dimple. "As much as I love it, I'm worried that you're too handsome for me now."

Jonah rinsed the razor in the sink. "You're kidding, right?" He turned his head and stared at the reflection of his scar. "I'm the one who doesn't deserve someone like you."

Trevor's chest tightened. Despite everything they'd shared, how could Jonah still be concerned with his scars when they were together? He manoeuvred himself between Jonah and the sink and stared up at the gorgeous man. "I don't see you as a scarred man, I see you as a man with a scar. We all have them." He unzipped his pants and let them drop to his ankles. Pointing to a six-inch scar on his leg, he tried to prove his point. "I was in a wreck in college. It took two screws, but it works just fine."

"Are you really comparing that to mine?" Jonah asked.

Trevor unbuttoned his shirt and took it off. Next, he toed off his loafers before kicking his pants to the side. Standing in nothing but his underwear and socks, he held out his arms. "Do you notice the scar?"

Jonah licked his lips and pushed Trevor's underwear down. He knelt and within seconds had Trevor's cock in his mouth.

Trevor ran his fingers through Jonah's hair. Jonah might not have answered his question, but just then he didn't care. They could discuss scars later. Jonah wrapped his hand around the base of Trevor's erection and concentrated his particular talents on the crown of Trevor's cock. Much later.

When Jonah pulled away unexpectedly, Trevor frowned.

Grinning, Jonah stood and released the towel at his waist. "We still haven't used the supplies you brought last week."

"No we haven't." Trevor stepped back towards the bed. He glanced at his watch and sighed. "Unfortunately, we only have forty-seven minutes left of my lunch hour."

Jonah chuckled. "You've got a lot of faith in me. It's been a while since I've cared enough about someone…" He broke off as his expression clouded.

Trevor considered himself a thoughtful person, but he wasn't keen to share their first fuck with a ghost from the past. He fell back onto the bed and spread his legs.

Jonah went to the nightstand drawer and removed a condom and the lube. "You've given me so much."

"And I'd like to give you more if you'd stop talking." Trevor softened the statement with a smile. "I've been a very patient man."

Jonah used his superior strength to push Trevor farther up the bed. "Yes, you have." He knelt between Trevor's spread thighs and opened the lube. With a gentle touch, Jonah circled the pucker of Trevor's hole with his thumb. "Relax."

"Yeah, sure. How relaxed are you right now?"

Jonah smiled again, flashing those twin dimples. "Yeah, I guess that is a pretty stupid thing to say."

Trevor moaned when Jonah pushed his thumb inside. He stared up at Jonah, knowing he'd already fallen in love. Fear that Jonah would pull away and return to his life on the streets assaulted him. "Stay with me," he blurted out.

Jonah pulled his thumb from Trevor's ass and reached for the condom. "Believe me, I'm not going anywhere with you spread out in front of me like this."

"I mean stay with me for good."

Jonah paused in the process of rolling the condom down his length. "Excuse me?"

Shit. Trevor knew he'd fucked up. Just like he always had, he'd pushed too hard, too soon. "Nothing, I just meant I want to play hooky for the rest of the day and stay here with you."

"So do it." Jonah moved to lie over Trevor. He braced himself on his forearms. "I hate it when you leave in the morning to go to work. I'm not gonna argue if you want to take the rest of the day off."

Jonah's statement made Trevor feel better about the slip. He opened his mouth to Jonah's kiss. The brief taste he'd had of Jonah's kisses earlier that morning had been nothing compared to the full-on assault they were currently locked into.

Jonah insinuated himself between Trevor's legs. He reached between them and guided the head of his cock to Trevor's hole. It wasn't until he began to ease his way inside that he broke the kiss. "Been thinking about this for weeks. Since the night I first saw you working in your office."

Trevor wrapped his legs around Jonah's waist as his body stretched to accommodate the long, thick cock. He bit his bottom lip to keep himself from talking. His past lovers had always accused him of ruining the moment with idle chatter. He'd never considered it chatter. Walls lowered when people were getting what they wanted, and he'd always found it the perfect time to get to know the real man he'd gone to bed with. *Not with Jonah*, he urged himself.

Buried to the hilt, Jonah groaned. "Worth the wait," he mumbled.

Trevor nodded in agreement, still afraid to speak.

Jonah's eyebrows drew together. "Is something wrong?"

Trevor shook his head and wiggled his ass.

Jonah leaned up on his forearms and narrowed his gaze. "What's going on, Trevor?"

"Nothing. I'm just trying to stay quiet."

"Why?"

"Because I tend to ask questions and talk a lot during sex. It turns most men off," Trevor confessed.

Jonah leant down until they were nose to nose. "Pretend I'm unlike any man you've ever known."

That wasn't hard. Jonah was nothing like the boyfriends he'd had in the past. "In that case, can you speed it up?"

Jonah laughed and the action completely transformed his cleanly shaved face. "Hang on."

Trevor stared, transfixed by the dancing sparkle in Jonah's hazel eyes. He felt himself fall deeper with each thrust of Jonah's hips. The words were on the tip of his tongue, but he refused to say them.

In the next instant, Trevor forgot about talking. Hell, he doubted he could even form a coherent thought as Jonah turned up the heat. Trevor raked his short nails down Jonah's back as he fought to hold on.

When Jonah changed positions and began to rub his stomach against Trevor's cock with each snap of his hips, Trevor lost the battle. He cried Jonah's name as he came.

"Yeah, that's it," Jonah encouraged as he continued to fuck Trevor. Several moments later, Jonah let out a loud grunt and drove his cock as deep as it would go. "Fuuuckkk."

Trevor was prepared to welcome Jonah's weight against him, but Jonah surprised him by rolling them both to their sides. "I could've held you. I may be thin, but I won't break."

Jonah rubbed Trevor's bottom lip with his thumb. "I didn't notice the scar on your leg earlier, and I don't think you're too thin to hold my weight. It's more like, why should you? I'm a big guy." He gave Trevor a deep kiss. "Don't move. I'll be right back."

Trevor watched as Jonah got out of bed and removed the condom before disappearing around the wall to the sink. "I talked to the manager of the maintenance department. He said he has an opening if you're interested."

Jonah turned off the water. "What kind of work is it?" he asked, coming back into the room. He used a warm wet washcloth to clean Trevor's stomach.

"Painting and changing lightbulbs, nothing too exciting, but it's a job and if you hire on fulltime, you'll be eligible for benefits," Trevor explained. "If you're not ready, I understand. The last thing I want is to push you."

Jonah tossed the washcloth to the floor. "I'll talk to him."

"You don't sound sure." Trevor held his breath.

"No, I am. It's just that I don't want you to put yourself out there for me in case I fuck something up."

Trevor couldn't stay quiet any longer. He sat up and tucked the blanket around his waist. "I think I'm in love with you. I know it's crazy, and we've only known each other for a few weeks, but it happened."

Jonah mimicked Trevor's position. "It's not crazy at all, but I think you're leading with your heart instead of your head."

"Why do you say that? Because I don't care that you're down on your luck?"

Jonah reached for Trevor's hand. "I've got more against me than just being jobless and homeless." He tapped his head. "There're a few things I haven't come to terms with, so I've been thinking a lot about checking out some of the counselling services at the VA."

The announcement surprised the hell out of Trevor. "Okay. Just let me know if you want a ride."

"I can take the bus."

"I know, but if you want a ride, let me know," Trevor reiterated. He squeezed Jonah's hand. "And if you want to move in with me or you need help getting an apartment, I'd love to do that as well."

"I'll think about it. Let me talk to that manager guy first. I don't have a lot of experience painting, but I have done it once or twice."

Trevor glanced at the clock. "Bruce said to have you come by his office at noon."

Jonah did a double-take when he looked at the clock. "That's only twelve minutes from now." He leaned over to give Trevor another kiss, but, predictably, one wasn't enough and soon they were making out like teenagers.

Trevor was the first to pull away. "You'd better jump in the shower."

Jonah started to get out of bed but stopped. "All I have to wear is my regular clothes."

"Those'll work." Trevor got out of bed and reached for his underwear. Although Jonah refused to let

Trevor buy him more clothes, he'd at least agreed to send what he had down to have them laundered.

"You sure?" Jonah questioned.

"I'm positive." He noticed the time. "And now you only have nine minutes before you're supposed to be downstairs."

"Shit. Screw the shower." Jonah retrieved the washcloth they'd used earlier. "Poor Bruce's gonna have to be happy with a spit bath."

"Yeah, well, poor Bruce better not get close enough to you to care," Trevor replied. He finished getting dressed as they continued to talk about the job. The fact that Jonah hadn't mentioned Trevor's offer of a place to live didn't bode well for the chances, but, again, he promised himself he wouldn't push.

✳ ✳ ✳ ✳

After his interview, Jonah went back up to the room and grabbed his sweatshirt and coat. When Bruce had offered him the job, Jonah had politely asked for a few hours to think about it. It wasn't the job itself he needed to think through, it was the situation.

Hood up, Jonah headed towards Peachtree Street and the area of shops and restaurants a few blocks from the hotel. He didn't have a specific destination in mind, so he shoved his hands in the pockets of his coat and took his time, keeping his head down.

Trevor had asked him to move in, and even though Jonah's initial reaction had been 'hell yeah', he'd stopped himself. He couldn't rebuild his entire life around Trevor. It wouldn't be fair to either of them. With the job offer on the table, he needed to figure out what he wanted more, to work with Trevor or to live with him—because having both was out of the question.

Waiting for the stoplight to change, Jonah noticed a boy on his bike staring at him. The kid couldn't have been more than eleven or twelve, not nearly old enough for Jonah to take offence, but it still bothered him. The light changed and he started across the street.

"Are you a soldier?" the boy asked, riding alongside Jonah.

"Was." Jonah kept walking.

"Thanks," the boy said.

Jonah made it to the opposite sidewalk and stopped. "For what?"

The boy shrugged. "Fightin' for us."

It wasn't the first time he'd been thanked for his time spent in Afghanistan, but he'd never had a kid approach him. Uncomfortable with the situation, Jonah lowered his hood, hoping to scare the boy away.

The kid's eyes rounded at his first look of Jonah's scar. "That happen over there?"

Jonah nodded. He couldn't figure out why the boy hadn't rode away screaming.

"Sorry." The kid dug into the pocket of his coat and pulled out a bag of M&Ms. "Take these."

"Thanks, but I don't want your candy."

"But that's all I have. My dad said we owe you guys everything, and I should remember that."

For the first time since the explosion, Jonah felt the sting of tears. It was an honest reminder of why he'd been over in that fucking hellhole in the first place. The genuine reaction to his scars also made him feel less like a freak. He did something completely out of character and reached over to pat the boy on the back. "Thanks, kid. Your dad would be proud of you."

The boy waved before taking off on his bike, leaving Jonah to stare after him.

Jonah walked to the nearest bench and sat down. He needed to think. The run-in with the young patriot had knocked him off kilter as much as coming home to find himself homeless had. Unless he found his footing again, he wouldn't be good for himself or Trevor.

Chapter Four

Trevor was passing time, talking to Esteban while he watched the front door for Jonah. According to Esteban, Jonah had left the hotel almost four hours earlier. At first, Trevor worried that the interview with Bruce hadn't gone well, but when he'd called downstairs, Bruce had told him he'd offered Jonah the job. *So why has he disappeared?*

"Are you sure you're not letting this guy take advantage of you?" Esteban asked.

Trevor thought of the way Jonah had tucked himself into the shadows for weeks. If Jonah hadn't come down with a fever, Trevor was certain they would still be having their nightly talks. It was a connection like he'd never had before. "No, I know he's not." He sighed. "If anything, I'm probably guilty of taking advantage of him."

"I don't know how you can say that. You've given him a place to live, a job, what has he given you?"

The answer came to Trevor in a heartbeat. "His trust. His friendship and his love."

Esteban sobered. "I'm happy for ya, boss."

"Thanks." An extremely handsome man walking into the lobby caught Trevor's attention. "Damn."

"I'll second that," Esteban mumbled.

Jonah spotted Trevor and veered towards the front desk. "Hey."

Trevor reached up and played with Jonah's shorter hair. "You got a haircut?"

Jonah nodded to Esteban before pulling Trevor away from the desk. "Can we grab something to eat and talk?"

Trevor's heart sank. Jonah's disappearance, his unexpected haircut and now his need to talk didn't bode well. "Sure."

Jonah led the way into the lobby bar and chose one of the tables by the large window. Although he'd come into the hotel in a fantastic mood, Trevor's expression was quickly bringing him down. "Are you upset that I left?"

Trevor shook his head. "I was worried, but I don't expect you to check in with me before you go out."

Jonah ran a hand through his hair. "Is it because I spent some money and got a haircut? Because I had it done at Super Cuts, so it wasn't expensive."

Trevor smiled. "No, your hair looks great."

Reaching over, Jonah covered Trevor's hand with his. "So what's wrong?"

"I have the feeling I'm about to get dumped," Trevor admitted.

Jonah sat back in his chair. It was the last thing he'd expected to hear. "Nothing could be further from the truth. I've been out all afternoon trying like hell to get my life back on track so I can feel like I deserve you."

Before Trevor could say something sweet and supportive, Jonah needed to prove he'd meant what he'd said. "I went by my old gym. Derrek, the manager, didn't know I was back in the States because I was too ashamed before to talk to him." Jonah shrugged. "Anyway, he said he was sorry about my injury, but it wouldn't keep clients away as long as I'm still as good as I used to be."

"Are you ready for that?" Trevor enquired.

Jonah had asked the question himself many times in the last few hours. "Honestly? I'm not sure, but something happened to me when I first went for a walk that shook me up. A kid actually thanked me when he found out I'd been in the military."

"Of course he did. This is Atlanta," Trevor said.

"I was stunned, and I came to the conclusion that it's who I am and what I do that's important. Not what I look like. My scars didn't keep that boy from talking to me. I'm still scared, but I know if I don't push myself to get out there, I'll end up back where I was before I got sick."

Trevor turned his hand over and threaded his fingers through Jonah's. "And us?"

Jonah took a deep breath. The only hitch in his plan that he wasn't sure about, but needed to discuss with Trevor, was where to live. "Derrek said there's a little room in the back of the gym that has a couch and a microwave. He said I could crash on the sofa until I get back on my feet."

When Trevor started to withdraw his hand, Jonah hung on. "I need to build this thing between us on an equal footing. Even if I end up spending the night at your place most of the time, I still need to know I can stand on my own if I need to."

Trevor stared at Jonah for several moments before speaking. "This isn't your polite way of telling me you're ready to move on, is it?"

"Absolutely not." Jonah leaned over and gave Trevor a quick kiss. He would have liked a longer one, but it wasn't the place. "I couldn't tell you this until I got a few things straight in my head, but I love you, too."

"And the counselling?"

"I still plan to go."

Trevor nodded. "Good, because I think it's important."

Gib walked over to their table. "Sorry, Mr Sharp, I'm shorthanded tonight. What can I get you?"

Trevor glanced at Jonah. "Nothing, thanks. We're going out to celebrate."

"Oh, well, congratulations on whatever it is," Gib replied, smiling.

Trevor stood. "There's a great Chinese place around the corner from my apartment. Why don't we grab something to go, and I'll show you where I hope you'll be spending most of your nights."

"Is that where the celebrating will happen?" Jonah asked.

"If I have my way, we'll celebrate all night long."

Jonah couldn't believe how far he'd come since Trevor had cared enough to speak to him for the first time. He might not be able to say it to Trevor yet, but he absolutely credited the sharp-dressed man with giving him a reason to live.

On their way to the parking garage, Jonah stopped Trevor. "Thank you."

"For what?" Trevor asked.

"Seeing me."

BLOWN AWAY

Amber Kell

Dedication

For Stacey, because she told me the glass artist needed his own story.

Chapter One

Christopher spun the blowpipe, slowly gathering up globs of molten glass from the bottom of the furnace. With practiced ease, he collected the proper amount of glowing material for the vase he visualised in his mind. The beginning of a piece always filled him with the tingle of anticipation, like meeting a sexy guy at a club and trying to calculate how quickly he could strip him down. When working with glass, his finished art never quite matched his initial idea. Sometimes the glass spoke to him and he had to follow where inspiration guided him. Humming happily, Chris watched the growing sphere at the end of his pipe. Now he was ready for the next step.

Despite the protective shield, the heat from the furnace set at around one thousand, one hundred and fifty degrees Celsius blasted across Chris' face. Sweat poured off his body, soaking into his shirt as he smoothly slid his pipe from the searing heat. Mindful of the sudden weight, he carefully lifted the rod off the stand and moved it to the next station.

He hoped his friend appreciated all the effort. With college tuition and fees for glass making Chris' pockets lighter by the second, he didn't have tons of money for gifts. However he knew Amanda loved his work and he wanted to make something just for her. He could've just grabbed one of his already finished pieces, but Amanda had helped him through a bad breakup a few months ago and he thought she deserved a special present.

Carrying his prize over to the metal table where he'd laid out the frit, Chris gently rolled his soft glob over the tiny pieces of coloured glass, embedding them into the material in one smooth motion. After covering all sides he smashed the bottom into the table to collect frit on the bottom. It looked a bit like a caramel apple rolled in sprinkles when he finished. Chris smiled at the analogy. He loved sweets.

Walking over to the glory hole, he settled the blowpipe in the metal support then opened the glory hole with one hand. Scooting back he pushed the quickly cooling glass into the hot oven and spun it around in a slow, steady rhythm, making sure to not leave it in one position for too long. If it overheated, the entire piece could melt off the pipe and end up a blob on the bottom of the unit. The shop owner hated it when that happened and Chris would prefer to avoid a lecture.

He kept a close eye on the glass until it glowed orange and became viscous again. Glancing behind him to make sure no one stood in his path, he slid the still spinning globe out of the glory hole. Walking fast, Chris propped the lower half of the rod on the edge of the steel table, making sure the glass cleared the surface and didn't touch. Keeping the pipe in motion, Chris gave a hard puff into his end of the pipe. The injection of air caused a bubble to form inside the glass and enlarged the globe. After a series of additional puffs, the solid mass of glass had inflated like a balloon. Chris stopped when it had reached the size he wanted.

He set it back into the furnace to warm it a bit more. If the glass cooled too rapidly it would go into shock and shatter. He really didn't have time to make another one before Amanda's birthday and it still needed several hours to anneal. After pulling it out of the fire again, Chris took it over to a steel bench and settled the pole on the metal arms at either side. Still keeping the rod in motion, he grabbed a pad made out of wet newspaper to round out the edges a bit more. The smell of hot paper and steam peppered the air, a scent that always filled Chris with a tingle of anticipation as he imagined the finished piece.

"Need any help, Chris?" Lena asked. Lena worked as a hot shop apprentice while she learnt the art. As part of her job, she hung around and helped the other artists manage punty transfers and taking things to the annealer. Occasionally Chris let her do some of the basic marvering or rolling out the glass so she could learn. However he didn't have time to give her any tips today. He needed to wrap it up and get his ass to work.

"Yes, hand me that torch and get me a punty. I'm ready for transfer. It's getting too cool," Chris said as he watched his piece lose its nice molten orange glow.

"I'm on it."

Seconds later, Lena lit the hand torch before giving it over to him. Chris warmed the piece slightly at the top while running a jack along the edge where glass met pipe. He wanted it to be a clean break. A poor transfer from pipe to punty could have the glass dropping off and shattering on the floor. Lena prepped the punty, a solid metal rod with a dollop of melted glass.

"Ready?" Chris asked. He warmed the bottom of the vase. He wanted it hot enough to accept the transfer, but not molten.

"Ready," Lena confirmed.

She pressed the solid rod to the bottom of the glass. Chris ran the jack over the end one more time until he had a deep groove.

"Now?" Lena asked.

"Yep."

Lena held steady until both sides cooled enough to stick together. Chris gave it a gentle tap with his metal jack.

Twin sighs of relief were audible when the vase broke off from Chris' pipe and stayed with Lena's rod. If it had failed the glass would've fallen and shattered.

"Nice job, Lena," Chris praised.

"Thanks, Chris. I always like helping you," she said sincerely.

Unsaid but implied was the truth that some of the guys in the shop were complete asses to the assistant and treated her like a slave instead of a fellow glass artist. She might not have had much experience, but she worked really hard to pick up all of the instructions sent her way.

Lena handed over the punty and Chris gave her the pipe to be cleaned for the next user. Chris reheated the entire piece in the glory hole before returning it to the bench to work it with his tools and pull out the little details.

Lena returned to roll it steadily while Chris used a hand held torch to keep it warm. He opened up the top of the vase and shaped the sides a bit until the piece had a nice curved appeal. Amanda could use it for the flowers her infatuated boyfriend always sent her.

Snatching up the puffer from the table, he smoothly added a clean edge to the inside of the opening. Once he was pleased with the shape he set down the tool and took over turning the vase while running a quick flame over the glass so it didn't get overly cool.

"It's pretty," Lena commented. "Are you going to do much more?"

Chris shook his head. "I want to keep it simple. She's not a real fancy kind of person." Amanda liked things with clean lines and elegance.

"I'll get suited up then?" Lena said. Her words ended in more of a question than a statement.

Chris gave her an absent nod of agreement as he worked on his final shaping. He didn't want to give his friend a lopsided vase. Concentrating on the perfectly smooth lip he almost jumped when Lena spoke beside him.

"I'm ready."

Chris blinked as he adjusted his vision without the burn of the flame. He set the torch on the stand beside him.

Lena stood a foot away wearing protective Kevlar gloves and facemask. Chris tilted the vase towards her and she accepted the glass between her hands. Chris made short work of breaking the glasswork off the punty. A quick polish of the bottom to smooth the rough edges and it was ready for the annealer. Letting the vase sit in the giant kiln for at least fourteen hours would help prevent it from cracking.

Chris rolled his shoulders as the suspense faded. He never knew which step in the process might go wrong and destroy hours of work.

"It's all set. It'll be ready tomorrow," Lena said. She returned the mask and gloves to their shelf then gave Chris a smile. Her red hair was frizzy and sticking out all over her head. Like her personality, her auburn locks were always chaotic. Chris really liked that about her.

"Thanks for the help, Lena."

"It's always a pleasure to help you, Chris. You make the most beautiful pieces."

Chris knew Amanda would like the vase. It was similar to one she'd admired in the gift shop a few months ago before it had sold.

After carefully putting all his tools away, Chris grabbed his backpack. Checking the clock, he was relieved to find he had enough time to run home and shower before his shift. He hated starting work with sweat from the hot shop still coating his skin.

* * * *

Chris rushed through the back entrance trying to resist the urge to knock people over in his rush to clock in. He'd zipped through his shower then rapidly dressed, but he still ended up running late when the bus hadn't come on time. One of these days he'd get a car, but he didn't need the added expense right now. Between paying for school and making enough money for extra hot shop fees, Christopher could barely afford groceries along with the rest of his bills. His tips kept him afloat. Not everyone tipped the concierge but the ones who did rewarded him well. He had two more months before he graduated and then...

Well, then he'd probably still be an artist working at a hotel but he didn't mind. He really enjoyed working there. It might not be his dream job but it paid the bills and he got to meet a lot of interesting people.

The manager of the hotel had begun to discuss putting some of Chris' work in the lobby. Management liked the idea of having the artwork of an employee on display. The blown glass ornaments and small vases he'd placed for commission sale in the gift shop at Christmas had sold well. He doubted he'd ever be the next Chihuly, but he enjoyed his art and savoured the chance to spend a chunk of his time nurturing his passion.

"Easy, Chris."

Chris screeched to a halt when Trevor stopped in front of him. "Sorry, sir," he replied, self-consciously sliding a hand through his hair. Trevor always made him nervous. No one should ever look that good all the time.

Trevor's chocolate brown eyes lit with laughter. "Running late?"

Chris grimaced. "I spent the morning at the hot shop then the bus was running behind schedule."

"It happens. I look forward to seeing your latest work, but try not to run over any of our guests in your rush to get to your station," Trevor advised.

"Yes, sir." Chris excused himself to head to the concierge desk. Trevor had recently been promoted to general manager and from all reports was doing an amazing job. They were willing to schedule him around special events like art shows and receptions.

Chris rounded the corner and stopped dead. A man sat in the lobby intent on his newspaper. Dark hair, glasses and a long sleek body Chris wanted to slide his hands across, caught his attention.

Yum.

If he could call in and special order a guy, the one right there would've been exactly what he'd select. He'd best make sure the hotel guest had everything he needed. It was his job, after all.

Leo stared at the paper in his hand but didn't see the text. Instead his mind drifted back to five years before when he'd visited the same hotel with his lover. Mel had loved Atlanta. Leo had had to move all the way to Seattle to escape memories of his dead beloved. Now, to support his cousin, he was back in town again at the Meliá Hotel.

His chest ached. He'd heard of people dying of a broken heart but he'd always thought it romantic bullshit. Now, he wouldn't mock those stories quite so much. When Mel had passed, he'd taken Leo's heart with him. He still hadn't found a way to move on.

He'd always hoped to wed Mel but only recently did Washington allow same sex marriage. Too late. Cancer had stolen his lover away and Leo doubted he'd ever find anyone to take Mel's place. Now in his early forties, starting over sounded like too much work. Leo was tired.

Barb, pregnant and marrying the love of her life, had wanted to share her moment with her favourite cousin. Leo hadn't thought watching her getting ready for her nuptials would be like an ice pick to his heart.

Mel had adored Leo's cousin and he would've loved the baby bump swathed in an apparently endless sea of silk and lace. When she'd tried on her gown for a fitting, Leo had had to discreetly turn the other way so she didn't see the tears in his eyes. She looked beautiful and extremely girly for a woman who'd sworn she'd never settle down and do the motherhood thing. Twins, she'd told Leo with a flush brightening her cheeks and a sparkle in her eyes. He knew she'd make a great mother. Despite her previous wild ways Barb was fiercely protective of her family. Barb had stepped in and handled all the details after Mel's death when Leo had fallen apart and couldn't be bothered to remember to eat much less write thank you cards to people who'd attended Mel's funeral.

Seeing his favourite relative try on her dress had cracked a chip off the shell encasing his heart since Mel had died. He'd almost broken down right there, but he'd held back. Now wasn't the time to focus on what he'd lost but on what Barb was gaining. This was her moment and he wouldn't ruin it for the world.

"Are you doing all right? Can I get you anything, sir?" a smooth tenor voice asked.

Leo looked up and met a pair of honey brown eyes. For a moment he was trapped in the stranger's gaze as electric attraction sizzled between them. He caught his breath as he scanned his mind to recall what the man had asked.

"I'm sorry?" He couldn't stop his gaze from sliding up and down the stranger's body. *Sexy*. The word spun in his mind with surprising vehemence. In the past few years only a couple of men had caught his attention and none of them this powerfully.

"I didn't mean to interrupt your thoughts. I'm Christopher Garland, a concierge here at the Meliá Hotel. You looked a bit upset so I was wondering if there was anything I could do to help?" The concern in the concierge's voice sounded sincere but the cynical part of Leo figured Christopher probably used that tone for everyone. It was the man's job to make sure people were happy with the hotel.

Leo couldn't stop the slightly hysterical laughter. There were so many things wrong in his life, looking lost was probably a step up. "I'm Leo Abbott and I'm pretty sure there's nothing you can help me with," Leo replied. At a different time in his life Leo would've whispered several filthy things he'd love to do with the sexy concierge. However, those adventurous days had passed and the sad, empty shell of that man was all that remained.

The concierge had beautiful cheekbones. Mel would've wanted to sculpt him. He could see it now, Mel tracing Christopher's cheeks with his delicate artistic hands. "Mel would've loved you," he blurted out.

He hadn't thought about Mel so much in months. Barb's wedding had turned into a nightmarish memory lane filled with a ghost of visits past. Leo didn't know how much more of his dead lover's shadowy haunting he could take.

The past few years had dulled his memory to a throbbing ache. Strange how coming for a wedding ripped off the bandage covering his buried wounds and now Leo felt like he was bleeding out. There wasn't enough gauze in the world to staunch the bleeding of this wound.

"Mel?"

Leo could feel the blush growing on his cheeks at Christopher's question. "Sorry, sometimes I say whatever is in my head. Mel was my partner but he died two years ago. He was a sculptor. He would've loved your face," Leo ended sadly.

Mel had found Leo's tendency to speak whatever ran through his head charming, but Leo knew from experience that Mel had been the exception rather than the rule. Most men didn't like being put in a possibly embarrassing situation because their companion had to say whatever came into his head.

"I'm sorry for your loss, sir. But I have to say, I like your honesty. If everyone said what they thought, there would be fewer miscommunications in the world," the concierge replied.

Leo smiled. "Yes that's true but there might be more fights. Sometimes people's thoughts aren't always polite to share." He couldn't count the number of times he'd said something completely rude to an important person at a gallery showing only to have Mel smooth things over. Leo didn't think he'd ever appreciated how much work Mel did to keep things going peaceful and happy for Leo. No one glossed over Leo's awkward social lapses anymore, which could be why he rarely went out.

"Hmm. Maybe there'd be more fighting and I might not keep my job if I said everything I thought whenever a customer is rude." Christopher's mischievous grin invited Leo to enjoy the humour of the situation.

Leo flushed as he realised he was flirting with a complete stranger and enjoying it. He stood up and made a show of refolding the paper carefully before tucking it under his arm. "I've got to go. Thanks for checking on me."

He needed to go find Barb. She'd gone upstairs for a nap and Leo had promised to make sure she woke up in time for a late lunch. They were supposed to go to a glass blowing demonstration at two and she'd kill him if she missed it. Her fiancé was going to meet them there after he picked up his tux.

Leo didn't know much about glass blowing, but he'd seen shows on PBS once or twice and the technique fascinated him. The creative process had always entranced Leo, maybe because he didn't have a drop of artistic ability in his body. People who were talented in some form of art had always intrigued him. His string of galleries attested to that fact. Mel had been one of the first artists Leo had sponsored at his gallery and one of the more successful ones.

Barb always teased him about being an artist junkie. She might have had a point. Before falling in love with Mel, Leo had fallen for a painter. The creative types did it for him. He found it interesting that a concierge would have the same effect when he didn't fall into Leo's usual type. He doubted being a hotel employee took much creativity past finding the perfect solution to a guest's problem. Still, there was something to be said about a man's beauty and the concierge had stunning brown eyes and a lush mouth that all but screamed for a kiss.

"Well, you have a good day, Mr Abbott. Let me know if there is anything I can do for you."

Leo didn't think he imagined the pointed look Chris gave him when he'd said 'anything' but maybe it was wishful thinking on his part. After all, he'd been alone for a while now and he hadn't had sex for years. With the chemo treatment Mel had been too sick to do anything sexually. Leo wondered if he'd even know what to do with a willing man. Sadly, men his age didn't fare well at nightclubs and Leo had been too much of a recluse to garner many friends. Most of their friends had been Mel's. They had faded into the woodwork after his lover's death, and truthfully, Leo didn't miss them enough to make the effort to keep in touch.

Leo admired Christopher's tight ass as he walked away. He appreciated beauty in all its forms and the concierge's ass was a piece of art all on its own. Mel would've approved, maybe even had it bronzed.

* * * *

Leo watched the glass artist spin a long metal rod with a glowing tip of molten glass.

"What do you think he's making?" Barb asked.

"I'm betting a lampshade," her fiancé Greg said, pointing to some of the lamps their guide had shown them before the demonstration. They were spun into a flattened oval and made in a multitude of striking colours. Being from Seattle, Leo had seen a lot of art glass and these were as good as any he'd seen in the Emerald City.

Leo didn't know if he liked Barb's fiancé yet. The man had a friendly smile and always appeared attentive, but Leo had seen Greg's eye wander more than once when a pretty girl walked by. Not an unusual occurrence for a red-blooded hetero male, but Greg's gaze had a piercing intensity as if he were judging the woman's qualities in bed and how fast he could discover them.

Maybe it was Leo's suspicious nature, but he couldn't help wondering how long Barb's marriage would last. Greg triggered enough warning bells to have Leo biting his lip to prevent saying anything to his cousin. He couldn't ruin Barb's future happiness or cloud her marriage day by being doom and gloom. Who wanted to hear from anyone on the best day of their life that they thought their marriage wouldn't last?

Leo couldn't say anything to Barb unless he actually witnessed Greg misbehaving—it was only a feeling, after all. Of course, if he always listened to his instincts he would've chased after Christopher to get the man's number.

Leo compared the current piece of glass to the ones lining the metal shelves. "It could be one of those bowls." He pointed to a row of wide rounded bowls on the top shelf.

There were some nods of agreement in the group. Leo wondered how many sales they had at the art glass studio. The workers certainly didn't push their art. In fact, they did little to showcase it other than point out where the glass was located to purchase. If it had been one of his companies they all would've received a firm talking to.

Leo turned his attention to the photos dotting the wall. One familiar face popped out at him as if fate was scolding him for missing his chance.

"What are you looking at?" Barb asked. Her pregnant stomach brushed against his arm as she looked over his shoulder. He resisted the urge to rub the baby bump. Her annoyed rant earlier about people touching her whenever they wanted had stuck in his head. She didn't need to tell him twice.

"That guy in the photo. I think that's the concierge at our hotel," he said, pointing. What kind of weird coincidence would that be?

Barb peered closely at the photo. "Yep, that's Christopher. He's super sweet. He created all the glass art in the hotel gift shop. I didn't realise this was his studio." She lowered her voice confidentially. "I think he's gay."

Leo laughed. He was pretty sure Christopher was, too, but he still asked because curiosity demanded he did, "Why do you say that?"

"Because I saw him talking to you and when he left I was shocked you still had all your clothes on. I thought his eyes were going to burn all that pesky cloth away. He looked really into you," Barb teased.

The memory of Christopher's hot gaze had Leo hardening. Good thing his pants were baggy. He'd lost a lot of weight over the past two years. Without Mel there to fix meals for Leo, he had little incentive to remember to eat.

"You think all gay men should be matched together. Just because we both like men doesn't mean we are a perfect match," Leo objected. "You wouldn't automatically assume a man and a woman were compatible."

"No, but I'd try to match them up if they shared the same interest like a love of art." Barb poked him in the side, not gently. "Don't you pull the bigot card with me, Leo. You know I'm not like that."

Leo ran his fingers through his hair. "Sorry. I'm attracted to Christopher. I just don't know what to do about it."

"Huh, I had no idea you've been a virgin this entire time. Maybe we can get you a book on the subject," Barb mused.

"Smart ass," Leo said fondly.

Barb laughed. "Seriously, it's time to move on. You know Mel would want you to."

Leo nodded. He did know that. Mel had the biggest heart and had loved Leo until his last breath. He'd said many times during his illness that he wanted Leo to move on after he'd passed. Still, guilt over betraying a dead man lingered like shadowy fingerprints on his soul.

Barb shook her head and squeezed his arm. "You need someone to share your life with. I don't know if Christopher is the answer, but I haven't seen that spark in your eyes in too long. For that alone I wanted to kiss him."

"Hey!" Leo and Greg said together.

Leo laughed. He didn't like the idea of anyone else's lips touching Chris. Stupid since they just met and he had absolutely no claim on the man.

"I said I wanted to. I didn't say I did." Barb smirked.

"He's too young." Leo estimated he probably had a good ten to fifteen years over Christopher. "I don't want a guy who sees me as a father figure or something."

"Nonsense. You'll be a good steadying influence. I know you. You love the artistic types and you like to be in control. Chris is a super cute guy with a creative streak. He's totally your kind of man," Barb insisted.

"What are you, the matchmaking mama?" Leo asked.

Barb laughed.

"Want me to buy you a piece of glass as a memento?" Greg asked Barb, interrupting their discussion. Greg flashed Leo a disapproving look Leo didn't understand. Was Greg upset for Leo for monopolising his future wife's attention?

Barb shook her head. "I'd rather we buy something at the hotel or get it from Leo's hottie directly. It means more if it's from someone you know."

Leo sighed. "You're about as subtle as a sledgehammer."

"I don't have to be subtle. I'm pregnant. Subtle vanished about the time my stomach eclipsed my toes," Barb replied.

"You weren't exactly subtle before that," Greg countered. The affectionate smile he flashed to his future bride made Leo smile. Maybe he'd been wrong about the guy. Greg could be the perfect groom for Barb. He smiled when Barb patted her stomach. Leo saw Greg cast a quick glance at his future bride, a frown crossing his face.

Unconventional in Atlanta

74

Why would he scowl at Barb? Leo shook his head. He was nit-picking now. He needed to be happy for his cousin. He wanted Barb to find the perfect guy, not just one who happened to knock her up. She deserved someone who loved her for her. Leo wondered if Greg was there because he loved Barb or because he'd knocked her up and wanted to do the right thing. After having met the in-laws, Leo bet they'd insisted on this wedding. A more uptight couple had probably never been born. They struck Leo as the type to shove a gay son into conversion therapy and hope he came back 'fixed'.

Leo shivered as he thought of his happy cousin trapped in that family. He vowed to take her aside and speak to her before the wedding, to make sure she was happy with her choices. He wouldn't let her be pressured into this marriage. Single motherhood didn't have the stigma it used to. He could help her get any kind of assistance she needed. Hell, he'd move her to Seattle if necessary. There were plenty of hospitals she could have her babies in. As far as he knew there weren't any complications with her pregnancy so she didn't need any specialists standing by.

Right now, watching the glassblowers, she grabbed her future husband's hand to point something out. Greg's fond expression soothed some of Leo's fears but the nagging in the back of his head wouldn't be subdued. It chipped away at the happiness he knew he should feel for his cousin.

Leo sighed. He'd turned into the critic of other people's dreams. If Barb had decided Greg was perfect for her, who was Leo to object? Whatever happened, he didn't want to be the one to say I told you so.

He'd once dreamt of having a family with Mel, but his lover hadn't been keen on the idea. Leo knew Mel would've given in eventually if Leo had insisted on children, but he refused to put a child in that position. Who wanted to be born knowing only one of their parents wanted them?

Leo had loved Mel, but he hadn't been blind to his flaws. Mel had needed the spotlight and Leo hadn't minded being the support structure for his more flamboyant partner. However, sometimes he did long to have a child to love. He'd have to settle for being an 'uncle' to his cousin's kids. Too bad Barb lived so far away.

He wondered if Chris wanted children one day. He blushed when he realised he was fantasising about a guy he'd met once and hadn't even kissed. He doubted a young vibrant artist would want to get together with an older man for diapers and formula.

Like the saying went, there was no fool like an old fool.

Before Leo's fascinated gaze, the glass blower added all the little details to his piece before handing it over to an assistant. The end result was pretty but unremarkable. Leo had seen nicer work at the hotel. An odd sense of pride over Chris' art went through Leo. Stupid…since he barely knew the man.

Leo wondered how much time Chris spent in the hot shop. Unlike Mel, Chris would have to do all his work outside the home. Leo had always liked wandering into Mel's studio and watching his lover work. A hot glass artist wouldn't have the same sort of accessibility.

"Leo, come on," Barb broke into Leo's thoughts. He snapped out of his musing to see their group had started to head out of the shop. "The demons in my stomach are demanding food."

"Then by all means let's feed them," Leo agreed.

Greg offered his arm and the three of them along with the other wedding guests piled out. They headed to the restaurant where they had reservations for the night.

Examining the high spirits of the group, Leo figured he'd be in for a long night.

Chapter Two

Chris wrapped up his workday a bit early. Deidre, another concierge, had been fighting with her boyfriend so she arrived half an hour before her shift officially began. Chris had agreed to take off so she could have the distraction of work. After a busy shift, Chris had been more than ready to end the night.

A conference of gay romance writers and readers had taken up most of the hotel. Who knew a bunch of writers were such kinksters? He'd had to tell four different guests that it was against hotel policy to provide male strippers and, no, he didn't have a spare set of handcuffs behind the desk.

Heading towards the employee staff room to retrieve his belongings, Chris spotted his new favourite guest walking across the lobby. Maybe staggering would be a better description.

Leo tripped over one guest's abandoned bag only to stumble over the leg of a lobby chair. It took Chris a moment to realise Leo must've had a bit more to drink than he could handle. Even inebriated, the man was fucking adorable.

Shaking his head, Chris changed his direction to intersect Leo's erratic path. He didn't want Leo to hurt himself or anyone else with his careening trajectory.

Leo caught sight of Chris and a wide smile crossed his face. Chris rushed to grab the taller man as Leo walked over to him and promptly tripped on absolutely nothing.

"Thanks." Leo smiled at Chris and wrapped a long arm around Chris' shoulders. "I could've fallen. If I'd hurt myself, Barb would be angry I'd ruined her wedding. I'm not sure she should get married."

His words had slurred together like one long garbled sentence. Smelling the whiff of alcohol on Leo's breath, Chris gave a quick prayer of thanks that Leo hadn't wandered near any open flames.

He tilted his head to get a better look at Leo. "And why shouldn't she get married?" he asked, curious about the drunk man's perception.

"I think her future hubby is a hound dog. I saw him checking out the bridesmaids' asses several times. He didn't even try to hide it."

"Did your cousin notice?" Chris frowned. He hated cheaters. He'd had one too many unfaithful boyfriends in his past to want that to happen to anyone.

Leo shook his head. "She's too happy getting ready for her wedding. She's usually pretty smart. I think the hormones are affecting her thinking."

"Possibly." Chris agreed. He didn't want to get into a guessing game about the thought processes of Leo's cousin. He'd only met her once. She seemed like a nice lady, but a lot of women would prefer to get married before giving birth. She would by no means be in the minority if she wed her guy for the kids' sake.

Chris tried to steer Leo towards the elevator, not an easy feat considering that Leo tried to get him to go in the opposite direction.

"What are you doing?" Chris asked when Leo once again tried to alter their path.

"I want to buy you a drink, Christopher," Leo said. His lower lip nudged just out from under his top one creating a subtle, kissable pout. Adorable.

Shaking his head, Chris resisted the power of the sulk. "Call me Chris and I think you've had enough alcohol, buddy. How about we go back to your room instead?"

"Can we fuck?" Leo asked brightly.

Chris almost tripped on the floor himself. "Um." He cleared his throat. "How about we just talk for now?"

"Then fuck? It's been a long time since I've had sex," Leo offered the information with a hopeful look in his eyes.

If it had been since his partner died, Chris figured it *had* been a while.

"Two years," Leo confirmed Chris' guess.

"How about we see if you're still interested after we chat for a bit," Chris demurred. He didn't want Leo to do anything drunk that he'd regret when sober. No way could Chris in good conscience have sex with an inebriated man, especially one who still mourned his dead lover. For some people two years would be long enough, but Chris could tell Leo still hadn't recovered. Chris wondered how long Leo had been with the man.

Once Leo decided to be amenable, Chris was able to manoeuvre them onto the elevator.

"What's your room number?" he asked. It would probably help this entire process if he knew where he was taking Leo.

"Three oh two," Leo muttered.

Chris released Leo to step forward and press the button for the third floor. Leo grabbed his ass. Chris jumped from the pinch.

"Sorry," Leo said. His expression didn't show he was sorry at all as a grin spread across his face.

"Uh-huh." Apparently alcohol reduced Leo's inhibitions to zero. Good to know.

As soon as he stepped back, Leo wrapped himself around Chris. When did Leo grow two more hands? The tipsy man had definitely turned grabby. "Do you want kids?" Leo unexpectedly asked.

Focused on the hands sliding all over his body, it took Chris a moment to register that Leo had asked a question.

"Kids?"

Leo nodded. "I always wanted kids, but Mel didn't really like them. How do you feel about children?"

"I like kids," Chris admitted. "I don't know if I want them tonight, but I'd like them sometime."

Good thing he couldn't get pregnant. He had a feeling if he were a woman Leo would've concentrated on trying for kids this very night.

"It's important that partners want the same thing," Leo said seriously.

Chris opened his mouth to answer, but Leo kissed him and sucked all the thoughts out of his head. Nothing else survived the onslaught but desire and hot, wet kisses. His cock urged him to forget caution and let the gorgeous man have his wicked way. However when his shirt buttons began to be slipped out of their holes, he called a halt to Leo's actions.

"What?" Leo asked, his expression pained.

"You aren't in any condition to seduce me. You've had too much to drink. You need to get some rest. If you're still interested tomorrow, come look me up. I go on shift at ten in the morning and get off at seven." He hoped Leo would remember their conversation. If Leo left before Chris got to see what was underneath those clothes, it would be a lost opportunity, one he'd regret for a long time to come.

Leo yanked Chris to him until their chests pressed together. Chris could feel not only the firm muscles of Leo's body but the hard erection rubbing against his own. The size of the cock confirmed his belief that he wouldn't be disappointed when he finally stripped Leo naked.

"Tomorrow is way too late," Leo purred. He slid his cheek against Chris' neck, sending jolts of desire down Chris' spine.

Chris bit back a moan. He had to resist.

Leo's words finally seeped into Chris' mind and his heart sank. "Why? Are you leaving soon?"

He realised he had no idea about Leo's schedule. For all Chris knew, Leo's cousin had already married and he'd been out drinking to celebrate.

"Nope. But my cock is impatient—it wants you now." Leo's lopsided drunken grin shouldn't have made Chris' cock stand up and take notice. He should've been appalled at being pawed by an obviously inebriated man. Instead he couldn't help thinking Leo's mussed hair and slightly clumsy movements were adorable. The urge to let Leo have his way tempted him like the apple tempted Adam in the Garden of Eden.

"Your cock will have to wait," Chris said, trying to stay firm. He almost talked himself into falling for Leo's persuasion. However, he didn't know Leo well enough to judge if he'd regret his actions the next day. Chris didn't need Leo going to his boss tomorrow to tell him Chris had taken advantage of a drunken man.

Chris' fingers twitched with the urge to pet and stroke Leo's erection.

"I don't want to wait. I want to fold you across the couch and fuck you until you forget your name," Leo insisted.

Chris' mouth opened and closed with no sound coming out. How could he argue against a man who had such amazing ideas?

He shook his head trying to dispel the delightful visions racing through his brain. "No! No. You can't change my mind. Give me your phone."

"My phone?" Leo frowned, but reached into his pants pocket and pulled out a smart phone. Obvious confusion crossed his face as Leo handed over the device.

Chris typed in his name and number in Leo's contacts and pressed save.

"When you wake up tomorrow, if you haven't changed your mind, give me a call. I can be here before my shift starts or we can meet somewhere afterwards for drinks."

Leo accepted his phone back. "What time do you get off?"

"Seven."

Leo stood silently for a long moment. "I'll call you in the morning if I remember this conversation." His wry expression made Chris laugh.

"I hope you will." Chris knew he'd be more than a little devastated if Leo forgot all about him overnight.

"Oh, I'm almost certain of it." Leo kissed Chris one more time as if verifying his taste. "If you plan on remaining unmolested, you'd best get going. I only have so much willpower."

Chris laughed. "Good to know. I was worried for a minute you might have nerves of steel."

Leo shook his head. "Nope, I'm just a man. However, other things feel like a steel rod in my pants. Wanna feel?" Leo wiggled his eyebrows playfully.

"Um...I'll take a rain check on that." Chris was in a special gay man's hell, where the object of his lust offered him everything on a platter only to make him turn it down.

"Do I get a goodnight kiss?" Leo asked.

"I'll even tuck you in bed," Chris offered. He wanted to make sure Leo made it to the mattress. If Leo fell asleep on the couch, his back might never untwist from its new pretzel configuration.

"I wish you were tucking yourself in with me." Leo offered a wistful look that held too much lechery to be believed.

"Uh-huh. Let's go, big boy." Chris wouldn't fall for it. He wouldn't. Damn, he wanted to. Tucking himself beside Leo in the big bed sounded like an amazing idea. However, he knew if he got that close to Leo it wouldn't stay platonic. He wanted to pounce on the man too much and he knew the mutual attraction between them wouldn't allow them to sleep together without a great deal of naked wrestling.

"I am big. Wanna see?" Leo persisted.

"I can see you need to stay away from the alcohol in the future. I should be recording this to blackmail you later," Chris muttered as Leo stumbled over to the king-sized bed that dominated the room.

Chris rushed to help Leo take off his shoes so he didn't get them on the bed. The maids had enough work to do without dealing with dirty soles on the sheets.

"Sure you don't want to join me?" Leo asked. His words were slurred now from the need to sleep instead of only from alcohol.

"I do want to join you but not when you're sloshed. Get back to me when you've consumed less booze."

He helped remove Leo's pants and shirt, but he refused to pull off Leo's underwear despite the temptation to strip him bare. He yanked the blankets up to cover Leo's body and hide the sexy half-naked man from sight. Chris set a glass of water on the side table beside the bed. He knew Leo would wake up dehydrated. Unfortunately, he would also wake up alone.

Chapter Three

Leo woke up with an entire team of construction workers drilling, hammering and banging inside his head. That was the only explanation for the incredible throbbing in his skull because surely he hadn't been stupidly drunk enough to invite an entire desert into his mouth.

Spotting the glass of water by his bed, he sighed gratefully as he grabbed at the cup. After draining the entire container he felt a tiny bit better. He hoped the headache medicine he had brought with him would take care of the residual pain.

Tumbling out of bed, he rooted through the compartments of his small suitcase until he found the bottle of pills. Leo had brought it figuring he'd need headache medicine because of the loud parties he'd be attending. He'd never thought he'd need it because he'd drunk too much.

After another glass of water he finally felt well enough to contemplate taking a shower and preparing for his day. A glance at the clock revealed it was ten in the morning.

"I wonder why Barb hasn't come for me yet," Leo muttered. He knew a brunch was scheduled for the morning and his cousin relished dragging him out of bed even after a late night. Since she was pregnant and not drinking, she was usually the only one left without a hangover.

Deciding his cousin could wait a bit longer, Leo grabbed a change of clothes and headed for the bathroom.

Twenty minutes later Leo was refreshed and almost feeling human.

After dressing, he noticed the flashing light on his phone indicating he had a voice mail.

It took him a few minutes to figure out how to retrieve his message but eventually his cousin's voice came across the line. "Hey, cuz, I hope you're having fun with the cutie concierge. Meet us in the lobby at noon for lunch. See you."

He hung up the phone and sat down on the bed. "Cutie concierge?"

After a moment, recollections of the night before began to filter into his brain. Chris. Flashes of Chris putting off Leo's advances and promising to see him later had Leo snatching up his phone.

Scrolling through the contacts, Leo laughed. Chris had put his phone number under 'hottie concierge'. Still chuckling, Leo pressed the button to dial Chris' number.

"Hello?" Chris answered.

"Hello, hottie concierge," Leo teased.

A rich laughter rolled across the phone line. "Hello, Leo. How are you feeling this morning?"

"I'm feeling better than I was. Did you put the water by my bed?"

"Guilty as charged. I'm sorry I didn't have any aspirin or anything."

"That's all right. I had some in my bag."

"Oh good." Chris' friendly tone made Leo smile. The concierge had a cheerful personality that warmed Leo in places he'd thought had frozen over after Mel's death.

Leo cleared his throat and picked at the bedspread with his fingers. "Listen, I was wondering if you'd be interested in having dinner with me later." His words all blended together in a rush as he hurried to get them out. He hadn't had a date in almost ten years. Eight years with Mel and two years of nobody after his death didn't lead to a lot of dating experience.

"I'd love to," Chris said after a long pause where Leo wondered if he'd messed the whole thing up. "I get off at seven. Where did you want to meet?"

"How about the hotel lobby? I don't really know a lot of places around here," Leo explained.

"Sounds good. You didn't forget you promised me hot sex, did you?" Chris teased.

Leo scoured his mind and winced. "I-I'd like to apologise for my behaviour, Chris. I really can't hold my liquor."

Chris' light laughter calmed his nerves. "You did a lot of things I liked, just nothing I wanted to do while you were drunk. I want to have sex with you, but I'd like you sober enough to remember it in the morning."

"I promise not to even accept a mimosa if it's offered to me," Leo vowed. Hell, he'd even turn down the wine.

He'd promise just about anything if it got the sexy artist into his bed.

"I'm sure one mimosa is fine, but I appreciate the thought. What are your exciting plans for the day?"

"They said something about a walking tour this afternoon," Leo offered.

"There are some good ones. Wear comfortable shoes," Chris advised.

"Will do." Leo cleared his throat. "I'm looking forward to seeing you again."

"Me too."

After exchanging goodbyes they hung up.

"What did I do?" Leo whispered. Running his hands through his hair, he wondered how he'd thought dating a younger man was a good idea. He took long, even breaths to stop his sudden panic.

A knock at the door yanked him from his thoughts.

Frowning, he wondered who it could be. Good thing he'd already showered and dressed.

Peeking through the peephole, he made out a distorted view of his cousin. After flipping back the lock, he opened the door with a quick yank.

"Barb, honey, what happened?"

Barb stood in the doorway, tears streaming down her face, her skin a mottled pink. The devastation in her eyes gripped Leo's heart. The lack of her fiancé's presence spoke to him louder than words that his concerns about Greg weren't entirely unfounded.

He stepped back to let her inside.

"I...I'm sorry if I woke you up," Barb said in a soft, broken voice.

"No, it's all right. Shit, tell me what happened." He waved her towards the couch.

"I'm not getting married," Barb announced. She sat down abruptly as if her legs had given out. He sat down beside her so she didn't have to hurt her neck by looking up all the time.

"O-okay..." Leo let the word draw out a bit as he contemplated this new announcement. "Any particular reason?"

"I found him making out with my bridesmaid," Barb sobbed. "He didn't know I'd laid down for a nap. He thought I was out shopping with his mother, but I'd cancelled because my stomach was queasy. It didn't improve when I saw his hand up her skirt."

"Oh, honey." Leo squeezed Barb's hand. "I'm so sorry."

Leo couldn't even imagine the level of betrayal, especially to a pregnant lady. Barb had been so happy to find a guy to love and now he'd proven to be a bastard. At least she'd learnt that before she married him.

"What are you going to do?"

"I called his parents and told them exactly why I couldn't marry their son," Barb said venomously. Her green eyes flashed with malice.

"Good girl." Leo felt a spurt of pride. The bastard didn't deserve the courtesy of discretion. "You still have to deal with him as the father of your children. You might regret doing that one day."

Barb shook her head. "I won't tell the kids why we didn't get married unless he tries to tell them lies. I won't use my children against him, but I have a feeling he's not exactly going to be the devoted father type. His parents were really nice about it. I didn't expect that. They offered to help pay the bills if I would allow them to visit their grandkids."

"What did you tell them?"

Barb shrugged. "They seem like really nice people. I told them I didn't need their help paying bills but as long as they didn't say bad things about me to my twins, I had no reason not to let them see their grandkids. They live close enough they can visit without being too intrusive."

"Can you get any of your money back for the wedding?" The thrifty part of Leo's soul hoped so.

Barb shook her head, dashing his optimistic hopes. "No. But Greg's parents said they'd make sure Greg paid me back for everything since he's the one who caused the breakup. I think I'm going to really like them better as non-in-laws than if I'd married into the family."

"What can I do to help?" Leo didn't think there was much assistance he could offer at this point, but he felt like he needed to do something.

Barb's warm smile eased his anxiety over her future. "You did so much just be being here for me. I can't tell you how much I appreciated you coming and staying to support me. With Mom and Dad gone, I didn't really have anyone else to ask. You've always been there for me, Leo. I wanted you to know how much I love you."

The crying started up again. Leo wrapped an arm around his cousin and gave her an awkward one-sided hug. "We'll get you through this. Did you want to come stay with me until the babies are born?"

Barb shook her head. "No. I wouldn't do that to you."

"Are you still working?" Leo eyed Barb's rounded stomach and tried to remember how much longer she had before the twins were born.

"No. Greg said he wanted me to take it easy during my pregnancy since I'm carrying twins." Barb rolled her eyes. "Now I wonder if he just wanted me out of the way. A new executive started at our company and she's really pretty."

If Barb hadn't just found her fiancé groping another woman, Leo would've said she was imagining things. Sadly, her hunch was probably right.

"Then there's no reason you can't come stay with me. I doubt you want to be around Greg. Or I can come and stay in Atlanta until the babies are born," Leo offered.

Relief crossed Barb's face. "Thank you, Leo." Tears filled her eyes. "I can't ever repay you for your help."

Leo squeezed her fingers. "You always stood by me, Barb, when some of our family turned away when I came out. This is the least I can do."

It might have been twenty years since Leo had come out at eighteen, but he remembered who had stood by him and who had conveniently forgotten he even existed. Invitations to family gatherings had dried up and his loving parents became cold strangers. When Mel had died, they hadn't even sent flowers to the funeral.

"Hey, people are assholes," Barb said as if reading his mind. "Speaking of assholes, did you get close to the concierge's last night?"

"Barb!" Leo's face burned with embarrassment. "I can't believe you said that."

Barb rubbed her stomach as pregnant women tended to do. "I need to live vicariously. I haven't seen any action since I lost sight of my toes."

"Greg isn't into pregnant women?"

She shook her head. "That should've been the first indication. He used to be all over me. That changed after I started to show." She indicated her advanced pregnancy with a grimace.

"And you're still beautiful," Leo said. Pregnancy added a new fullness to her thin face and a nice flush of pink to her cheeks. She had one of those rare physiques where she gained most of the baby weight in her stomach and little anywhere else. Leo knew she carefully watched her food intake so she wouldn't have a lot of post-pregnancy weight to lose. She looked gorgeous.

"When did you want to leave? I already kicked Greg out of my suite," Barb said, deftly avoiding discussion of her appearance.

Leo ran his fingers through his hair. "I was hoping to take Chris out tonight, but I can cancel if you need to leave. I'd completely understand."

A wide smile crossed Barb's face. "That's a great idea. I've had a rough morning. I wouldn't mind a long nap and bubble bath. We can head out tomorrow. After all, I'm paid through until then. I might as well enjoy it while I can. I'm going to watch sappy girlie movies and order room service for the rest of the day."

"Are you sure you don't need company?" He felt terrible leaving her all alone after her relationship tragedy.

Barb smiled. "I haven't seen you interested in a guy in a long time. Take advantage of this. Go have fun. We can straighten out my life tomorrow."

"If you're sure."

"I'm sure."

Leo scanned his cousin's face, but she really seemed sincere. "I'm not meeting him until seven. We can hang out until then."

Barb nodded. "Sounds like fun. Let's go have some breakfast. I'll buy. It's the least I can do since I chose such a loser to marry."

"Hey, everyone makes mistakes." Leo wouldn't let her beat herself up about stuff. "We can still go on the walking tour if you want."

Barb laughed. "The only reason I signed up for that thing was because Greg wanted to go. The thought of walking around watching my ankles swell was not my choice. I guess that should've been a good clue."

"Maybe. But sometimes you just want someone to love and you overlook those minor faults."

"Yeah, unfortunately I overlooked his wandering eye thinking that all men look. I didn't think all men touched, though." Barb's eyes began to fill with tears again. Leo squeezed her shoulder in reassurance.

"A real man wouldn't cheat on his pregnant fiancé on the eve of his wedding. Where were you going to honeymoon anyway?"

Barb sighed. "We were going to do something after the twins were born. I didn't want to be far away from our doctor in case there were complications."

"Good thinking. And now you don't have to worry about missing your trip."

"Yeah, at least something good came out of this farce of a relationship."

Leo's heart went out to his cousin, but he knew nothing he could say would heal her wounds. They were too fresh. Being there for her beat all the nonsense phrases he could think of saying.

He thought again about cancelling on Chris. He hadn't dated the guy and there was no reason his cousin couldn't be made comfortable away from her cheating fiancé, but Barb insisted they stay so he could have his date. She had been so excited he'd met someone he was willing to see romantically. He had a feeling she'd blame herself if he didn't go out with Chris.

* * * *

After a long afternoon trying to cheer up his cousin, Barb went to lie down and Leo headed to the lobby.

Chris stood by the check-in counter talking to a dark-haired girl with a pretty smile. The animated way they spoke to each other indicated they were friends.

Catching sight of Leo, Chris' expression lit up. "Hey."

"Hi." Yep, he was Mr Slick. He couldn't stop staring at Chris. Never had a pair of jeans looked so good. The younger man certainly knew how to fill them out. Leo bit his lip as he tried not to drool over the shiny tile.

"I need to stay close in case my cousin needs me. Maybe we could eat here?" Leo indicated the sign to the Lobby Bar. "Unless you eat there too much."

If Barb had a breakdown in the middle of the night, he needed to be around for her. He might not be the most touchy feely person but he had a strong shoulder to cry on if she needed one.

Chris shook his head. "They've got good food, but I don't usually stick around after my shift ends. It'll be fine. What's wrong with your cousin?"

"We can discuss it later. I don't want to ruin our evening together. Let me treat you." Leo smiled in anticipation. He really just wanted to drag Chris to his room and strip him naked, but he'd try the gentlemanly thing first and see how it went. They had electric chemistry between them but would they be able to have a conversation? Leo didn't mind a hook-up but he wanted to know the score before he began building a relationship in his mind around them.

* * * *

Dinner went far better than Leo had hoped. Chris talked about his passion for glass art and his dreams of continuing to be an artist in the future. Leo told Chris about Mel and he could see the sincere compassion in Chris' eyes. Leo laughed at Chris' jokes and learnt the artist had a sly sense of humour and a quirky personality that Leo enjoyed. Mel had been a serious person with deep passion and an intensity about him that had drawn Leo to his side. Chris was almost his opposite, with a lightness of spirit and a perpetual smile dancing across his lips.

When Chris picked up a French fry and gave it an expert blow job, Leo almost came in his pants.

"Sorry, was that too obvious?" Chris asked. His eyes didn't reflect the apology given by his lips.

"A bit. I'm too old to be coming in my pants," Leo said wryly.

"Oh, hon, you never get too old for that," Chris replied.

Looking at the few remains of their dinner, Leo asked, "Did you want to go back to my room? I'm only here until tomorrow."

Chris frowned. "And then you're gone forever?"

"I'll be staying in Atlanta for a few months helping Barb get ready for her babies," Leo confessed. "Then I'll be returning to Seattle."

A long silence met his statement before Chris nodded. "Let's go back to your room and I can show you how a good date is supposed to end."

Leo quickly paid the bill and rushed Chris to the elevator. "You won't get in trouble for coming upstairs with me?"

"They probably won't approve, but at least you're sober, and as long as they don't think I'm hustling, I'll be fine." Chris shrugged.

"You have a lot of problems with that?" Leo asked.

"Not really, but there is the occasional professional who thinks they can make a quick buck with visiting businessmen, and I have gotten some weird requests from time to time."

Leo wanted to ask about those strange requests, but Chris stepped closer and kissed him. Questions flew out of his head along with anything else he might want to think about. Soft, warm lips wiped away all thoughts and he doubted the neurons were even firing in his brain as all rational thought tumbled southward.

Leo yanked his lips away only to have Chris plunge his fingers into Leo's thick hair and hold him steady for another hot kiss.

It took all of Leo's willpower to stop from slamming Chris against the wall of the elevator car and mindlessly fucking him. Instead he grabbed Chris' slim hips and held him still while he rubbed his erection against him.

"So damn sexy," he growled then nipped Chris' throat, pleased when goosebumps shivered across his skin.

"I'm not the sexy one," Chris gasped.

The elevator dinged letting them know they had reached Leo's floor.

They stumbled down the hall to Leo's room where he shoved the key card into the reader and pushed the door open.

Chris tasted like a combination of the lemonade he'd had for dinner and sexy male. "Delicious," Leo rumbled. He felt needier than a college kid who had just figured out what to do with his cock.

Impatient to see bare skin, he pulled at Chris' shirt until it slid out from the waistband of his jeans.

Chris laughed good-naturedly. "Impatient, are we?"

"You have no fucking idea." Leo sighed when Chris stripped off his shirt and tossed it to the floor. He grabbed two handfuls of Chris' ass and yanked him closer. Kissing, licking, biting, he tried to consume Chris as the floodgates of desire broke open and he lost control of the passionate beast he'd kept reined in for too long.

"Whoa, wait!" Chris said.

Leo jerked back. "What? What's wrong?"

Chris' wide smile settled his anxiety over having done something wrong. "You're too dressed."

"Oh, sorry." Leo stripped off his shirt and tossed it to the floor. Before he could remove anything else, Chris dropped to his knees. With amazing dexterity, he had Leo unbuckled, unzipped and Leo's pants and underwear around his ankles. Before Leo could say anything or even form a thought, Chris swallowed him down.

Leo flailed to grab hold of something as his world spun around him. "Wow," he whispered. Mel had never been much for blow jobs. He'd done them but not with the amazing talent and cock worship of the man currently on his knees. Leo pushed thoughts of his dead lover away. It wouldn't be fair to Chris to compare him to another man, even favourably.

Chris' tight suction almost had Leo losing control. A warning tingle in his balls alerted him to the possibility of ruining the fun before it got started. He gripped Chris' hair and pulled him back. Chris reluctantly relinquished his prize.

"What? I know I was doing that right. I've got amazing lip control," Chris bragged.

Leo laughed. "I was about to blow and since I'm not twenty anymore and still want to fuck you, you need to stop that if you want me inside you."

Chris daringly lapped at Leo's cock once more with his tongue before allowing Leo to help him to his feet. "It's your own fault for tasting so good," he scolded.

"Um...sorry?" he offered.

"I'll let it slide this time but next time I get a full taste."

"Deal." Leo smiled as he helped Chris out of the rest of his clothing then stepped out of his own so he didn't trip with the mass around his ankles.

Chris crawled across the mattress and Leo's heart sped up at the sight of the sexy ass on display. The years slid away as the weight of sorrow he'd carried began to lighten. Maybe it was possible to move on after all.

"Hey, going to join me?" Chris asked. He'd turned around and now lay spreadeagle on the bed like a willing sacrifice.

"Absolutely," Leo confirmed. Chris' erection, long and thin, beckoned Leo closer. Unable to resist the invitation, Leo wrapped his hand around Chris' cock and gave it a friendly rub.

"Oh." Chris' eyes rolled back in his head as he arched into Leo's touch. "More."

Leo let go.

"Not until I'm in you. I don't want you to shoot until I'm pounding inside you."

Chris bit his lip as he watched Leo with wide eyes. Leo kissed Chris, plunging his tongue into Chris' mouth for another taste of Chris' particular flavour. "Delicious."

Leo hummed as he retrieved the new bottle of lube and a condom. It had been so ridiculously long since he'd needed either that he'd had to purchase them before their date.

He quickly popped open the lube and slicked up his fingers. It might have been a while, but he hadn't forgotten what to do. He slid one finger into Chris, who opened up to him easily, lifting his hips he pushed down into Leo's touch.

"More," Chris insisted in a tight voice.

"No rush," Leo countered as he slowly moved his finger in and out of Chris until the younger man jerked.

Found it.

Leo didn't even try to hide his grin.

"More, Leo—now!" Chris growled.

Leo pushed in a second finger and made sure Chris was well prepped before inserting a third.

"Need your cock!"

Leo couldn't help the rush of pleasure over this beautiful man. "It'll be easier if you turn over," Leo said.

Chris shook his head, a jerky motion Leo didn't know if it was meant to be a negative or uncontrollable muscle movement until Chris spoke. "I want to wrap my legs around you while you fuck me into the mattress."

Always the gentleman, Leo couldn't turn down such a reasonable request. He quickly slipped on the condom, lubed his cock then settled between Chris' legs. As promised, Chris locked his ankles behind Leo's back as he slid smoothly inside. Chris held him tighter than a vice, trapping him close.

"You're gonna have to release me, hon, if you want this to go any further," Leo said.

Chis clenched his ass and Leo damn near saw stars, planets and the universe exploding around him.

Chris' grip loosened enough for Leo to slide in and out with ease. Once certain he had the proper angle, he proceeded to pound Chris' prostate with each stroke.

Chris couldn't stop the gasps, groans or outright screams ripping from his throat. A wave of jealousy rushed through him at the lucky Mel who'd had this amazing lover until the day he died, while Chris only got Leo for a night or two. Leo definitely knew the way around a man's body.

A pinch at his right nipple sent an electric shock through Chris. His body was merely an instrument for Leo to play, and the man was a fucking virtuoso. Not a bit of him went untouched. Not the crease between his nipples, his ass or the little spot behind his left knee he'd damn well never known could make him almost come from a gentle stroke.

The slide of their bodies together rubbed heat and sweat against Chris' cock but not quite enough friction to get off. He reached down to help out with that problem only to find his wrists being encircled in a hard grip and pinned above his head. Without missing a stroke, Leo continued to fuck Chris while holding both Chris' hands still with only one of his own.

"Mine." Leo's blue eyes burned with possessiveness.

"Okay," Chris agreed, willing to give the dominant male whatever he wanted as long as he continued creating the delicious sensations pulsing through Chris' body. Chris clenched his ass to hurry his lover along. Leo shifted more of his body weight on his knees, moving slightly away from Chris.

It took all of his restraint not to try to pull Leo closer.

"Easy," Leo said as if reading Chris' mind. Leo wrapped his free hand around Chris' erection and all was forgiven.

Leo moved his fist up and down Chris' shaft with a knowing touch. In less than three strokes, Chris came all over Leo's stomach and chest. He couldn't stop the smile he knew spread across his face as he marked Leo as his.

Leo shook his head as if he could read Chris' thoughts, then, before Chris could ask anything, Leo leant back over and continued to pound into Chris, damn near causing his erection to harden again.

It took six more strokes—Chris counted—before Leo came with a roar and collapsed against Chris. After a minute or so, Leo carefully pulled out of Chris with more care than his previous lovers had ever shown. Leo disposed of the condom in the trash beside the bed before cuddling Chris close.

Chris snuggled in and rested his head in the crook of Leo's neck. "I'm going to miss you."

"I'll be around a few more months."

"But not downtown," Chris countered.

Leo tilted Chris' head up until he faced him. "I'd like to continue to see you. After Barb's babies are born, we can see where things are between us. I'm not making any promises, but Seattle has a pretty good art glass scene, I hear."

Chris laughed. "Yeah, I've heard that too."

Leo kissed Chris, a light affectionate touch of lips to lips. "Don't borrow trouble. I've learned life is too short for that. We'll take things slowly and see where things go."

"Okay."

Chris closed his eyes, letting the warmth of the man holding him close soothe him. He needed to finish up his degree anyway. Leo was right. They had some time to explore each other and whether or not they had a future together. Leo had already lost one person, but he appeared ready to try again. Chris had no doubt in his head about their compatibility and if Leo needed more persuasion before he was certain, well, Chris knew a thing or two about blowing. He was almost positive he could persuade Leo to see things his way.

Holding Leo tightly, Chris tumbled into sleep, confident everything would work out just fine.

HIS LAST CLIENT

T.A. Chase

Dedication

To Devon, Carol, Amber, Stephani and Jambrea —
thank you for asking me to join you on another
exciting ride.

Chapter One

No matter how many times Gib stared at the balance in his checking account, the numbers didn't change. He was going to be short for rent this month. Sighing, he rested his chin on his hand and frowned. He couldn't ask for more hours at the Meliá, the hotel in downtown Atlanta that he tended bar at. They were already giving him as many as they could. No, he was going to have to make up the difference in his usual way. After picking his phone up off the table, he dialled a familiar number.

"Gib, you haven't called in a while."

"I know. Do you have any work for me?"

His agent chuckled. "Funny you should call. One of your regulars called me. He has a friend coming into town, and wondered if you'd do him a solid. His friend is looking for a little fun for a night or two."

He chewed on his lips as he thought. After a bad encounter with a new client, Gib only went with men he knew. Silly that it took him almost five years of selling himself to figure out some people were assholes, and thought that just because they could pay him for sex, that gave them free rein to do whatever they wanted to him.

"Which client?"

Jake hemmed and hawed for a few moments, then said, "Mr Y."

For privacy reasons, Jake only used the client's last initial to identify them. Gib didn't care since he had no real interest in finding out who the men were.

After getting out of hospital, Gib had told Jake he would only work for certain men. He'd given his agent a list, and Jake had been good about sticking with it, even though Gib had been one of his most popular guys. So hearing it was one of his regulars made him consider doing the favour. Since Mr Y knew what had happened to Gib, he wouldn't try to hook him up with someone who'd hurt him.

"He'll pay double your usual rate." Jake dangled the carrot.

"Double?" Gib blinked. That was a helluva lot of money. He wouldn't have to worry about rent for a couple of months after that. As much as he didn't want to do it, he said, "Yes. I'll meet him."

"Good. Mr Y said you could give him a call, and he can give you some information on the guy. If you wanted reassurance, I guess." Jake hummed, and he was obviously waiting for Gib to say he didn't need to be reassured.

He couldn't say it, but he could pretend to ignore what Jake said. "No problem. You know the drill. Have him meet me at Ashley's."

"Yeah. I know what to do. What time do you get off shift tonight?"

Glancing over at his calendar, he checked the time. "I close tonight. So tell him to show up there around as close to two o'clock as he can. We can go once I'm done. You don't think he'll get mad that I have another job, do you?"

Jake snorted. "Dude, he's hiring a whore to spend the night with him. He doesn't have any room to complain about you having another job."

"I really appreciate you being so understanding about this whole thing, Jake."

And he really was. There were thousands of horror stories of pimps who beat the shit out of their whores, and forced them to do things they didn't want to do. Jake hadn't been like that to him, being rather nice about the whole situation.

Gib placed his fingers on his ribs that had been broken during that terrible beating. Those had not been good days while he recovered from his injuries. Jake never once told Gib he had to work off the hospital bills or anything like that. Maybe it was good Catholic guilt getting to Jake, since he'd been the one who had set up the appointment with the client who beat the shit out of Gib.

"There's nothing to understand. Now can we forget all this mushy shit and get this deal done?"

"Yes, sir. Thanks for letting me know about it." He hung up before Jake could say anything else.

After setting his phone on the kitchen table, he went to his bedroom to change into his work uniform. Black pants that were relatively tight, framing his ass perfectly, and a black T-shirt that fit his chest like a glove. Gib knew how to dress to showcase his body. If he hadn't been working at the hotel, he would dress a little more flamboyantly, but he couldn't advertise while he was bartending. But still, looking good helped him make more tips.

He went into the bathroom to fix his hair. Standing in front of the mirror, he turned to check out how his butt looked.

"Looking awesome per usual, Schultz." Gib grinned and winked at his reflection. He chuckled. "God, I'm an idiot."

Gib finished getting ready, then grabbed his overnight bag. The one he took with him when he went on appointments. It had a change of clothes, bathroom items, plus condoms and lube. He never counted on his client having supplies. Some of them believed that just because he was a rent boy, he'd be willing to go bareback.

Not on his life, and that was what he would be playing with. He might have left school at fifteen, then lived on the streets until he was eighteen, but that didn't make him stupid. *Well,* Gib thought, *it does make me stupid in one way, but I'm not dumb enough to risk my life just because some guy is paying me.*

He chose to ignore how silly that statement was. Gib wandered into his kitchen, then scoped up his phone, keys and wallet on his way out of his apartment. While he stood at the bus stop, he checked his phone, and found he'd got a text from Esteban, the front desk manager at the Meliá.

Need to talk to you asap. Stop by front desk before your shift.

What was so important Esteban needed to talk him asap? Gib shrugged, and got on the bus. He was going to have to get the key anyway, so he would've had to see his friend at some point. After scanning his metro pass, he took a seat halfway down the bus, then pulled out his headphones. Listening to music helped pass the time for him while he rode the bus.

He hoped whatever Esteban needed to see him about wasn't the room. For some reason, Esteban had taken it upon himself to ensure Gib always had a safe place to take his clients. Being the front desk manager, he had the opportunity to keep a certain room out of service indefinitely, and he did, allowing Gib to use it.

At first, Gib had insisted he didn't need to be taken care of like that. Just because he'd almost died from going with a client he'd known better than to go with didn't mean he was incompetent or anything like that. It just meant that on that night, his need for money had outweighed his common sense.

Gib never quite understood how he'd ended up telling Esteban about the whole situation, and why Esteban had taken it upon himself to give Gib some safety and control over his life. Yet he had, and Esteban did. Somehow along the way, they'd become friends, which freaked Gib out a little because he didn't do friends or any kind of long-term relationship. Nothing close to commitment, though he was getting tired of coming home to an empty apartment night after night.

Shaking his head, Gib tried to erase those thoughts. No sad or depressing emotions. Not today when he needed to be on to earn good tips, and make a client think he was the only man in Gib's world.

His stop came into sight, and Gib tucked his things in his bag. When the driver opened the doors, Gib stood before climbing off. He walked three blocks to the hotel, then went in the front entrance. Normally, he'd go in through the employee one, even though he worked in the lobby bar, but since Esteban had summoned him, he strolled into the lobby then glanced at the front desk.

They were swamped, and Gib remembered there was a convention starting in the next day or so. He tried to think of what it was for, something to do with gay romance writers and readers. He'd have to look at the schedule when he got to the employees' area. Esteban was standing behind the desk, but he must have been watching for Gib because he signalled him to wait.

Gib checked his watch, and this time his habit of being anywhere ten minutes early worked for him. After nodding and pointing to one of the sitting areas, Gib went to sit. He glanced around, absorbing the hectic hum of check-in time.

Trevor, the general manager, was chatting with Christopher, the concierge, and Gib slouched slightly in his seat. He'd never had much interaction with Trevor, and while he was sure the general manager was a good guy, he just didn't want to do anything that would bring him to Trevor's attention.

He waved at Reno as his friend rushed by, on his way to where the children's rooms were. Reno coordinated all the different kids' events the hotel held to help parents entertain their offspring. Gib didn't know how Reno did it. He wouldn't want to be trapped in a room with screaming kidlets for hours on end.

A trio standing just to the side of the check-in desk caught Gib's attention. Two handsome men and a beautiful African-American woman were holding a silent conversation with their hands. Gib didn't know any sign language, but he recognised it when he saw it. He wondered if they were all here for the convention. He thought it was cool that there was an actual gathering for gay romance books. He didn't read much, having struggled with it while still in high school, then after dropping out, he never had time to work on his skills.

But he admired people who could create such wonderful worlds with their words. Gib envied the people who got to read those stories, and who had a chance to live different lives from their mundane ones, if only for a moment.

"Gib, come with me."

He looked up to see Esteban standing at the end of the counter, gesturing for him to follow. After jumping to his feet and grabbing his bag, he went with Esteban back to his office. He'd always thought Esteban was one of the best-looking men he'd ever seen, but there had never been any physical attraction between them, just a friendship Gib had fought against at the beginning.

Well, really Esteban wouldn't take no for answer. He'd kept right on being nice to Gib, no matter how hard he tried pushing him away, until finally he had given in and accepted Esteban's stubborn friendship.

"Please sit." Esteban motioned to one of the chairs. "I have to talk to you about the room."

"Weird. I was just going to let you know I was going to use it tonight." Gib noticed the frown on Esteban's face. "What's wrong?"

"I'm...letting someone use the room for the weekend."

Gib was surprised, and he shot his friend a questioning look. "Okay, I guess I can find a different place to go, but can I ask who and why?"

Esteban wrinkled his nose, and on anyone else, that expression would look stupid, but somehow Esteban made it look good. "A young man came in for the convention, and he'd made his reservation for next month."

"You gave him the out of service room? How are you going to explain that?"

"That's my problem, though I need you to keep it quiet like usual." Esteban sighed. "I couldn't help but feel sorry for him. He seemed really naïve, but sweet."

"Oh my God, did you give him the room because he was cute?" Esteban started to protest, but Gib spoke over his words. "You totally did. Do you have a crush on him? I can't wait to see what he looks like. I bet he's hot. He'd have to be to catch your eye."

"Shut up, and I'm sorry about not having the room for you. Do you want me to look around at some of the other hotels to see if they have a free room?"

Gib shook his head. "Nah. It's not important. I'll figure something out. Hell, we might as well go to his hotel. He's meeting me at Ashley's around one-thirty since I work until two."

Esteban gave him a pointed look. "If you do go to his, text me where you are." Esteban stood. "All right. I work until two as well, so if you change your mind, you can text me and I'll try to find a place for you. Thanks for being so understanding. Now I need to get back out front, and you need to go clock in."

"No problem, man. I'm flexible, which makes me popular with the guys." Grinning, he winked at Esteban, who shot him a dirty look. "And I'll check in with you tomorrow."

That was another rule Esteban had established. He expected Gib to call him the next day after an appointment, checking in so that Esteban knew he was still alive and okay. He would never admit it to his friend, but he appreciated that Esteban cared so much to make the effort.

After leaving the office, Gib went across the lobby to the bar, then slid behind it to go to the break room for the bartenders and wait staff. He stuffed his bag in his locker before clocking in. He headed out to get filled in by Margie, the first shift bartender, about what had been going on.

"We haven't been that busy yet, but I think as the night goes along, you're going to get swamped. The convention people have been checking in all day, and from what I've heard, they like to hang out in the bar." She smiled at one of the men sitting at the bar as she handed him his drink. "Hopefully that means they like to drink, and you'll be making some good tips."

Gib chuckled. "I hope so. I can use some extra money right now."

"Couldn't we all?" Margie walked to the other end of the bar to wait on a new customer while he worked the opposite end.

As he worked, the night sped by, and he didn't think about his upcoming appointment, even though he should've been working out where to take the man. Being busy was a good thing. It didn't give him a chance to start panicking about not having a room. If he allowed himself to dwell on it, he'd be surprised at how much he'd come to count on having a safe place to take the men he met up with. Silly really, considering he rarely did that anymore.

Business started picking up around seven and remained hopping until around one-thirty when Gib's client was due to arrive.

"Are you Gib?"

Gib looked over his shoulder to see a distinguished-looking dark-haired man standing at the bar. After pouring the rest of the gin into the tonic he'd already put in the glass, he turned to face him.

"Yes."

Is this my client? If it is, I hit the fucking jackpot.

"Jake sent me." The guy's smile was confident, hitting Gib right in his groin.

After taking a deep breath, Gib flashed him a bright smile. "It's nice to meet you. I have to deliver this drink, then we can talk a little bit."

"All right."

Gib watched the man slide onto a bar stool before he picked up the glass to deliver it to the waitress waiting for it. When he got back to where his client sat, he held out his hand. "I am Gib. What would you like me to call you?"

"Edwin is fine." Edwin shook Gib's hand. "You might have seen me on TV, though I'm really only on when there's a crisis in the Middle East or Africa. My friend, Chen Yu, said I could trust you because you're discreet."

Wincing, Gib shook his head. "I don't know who you are in 'real' life, and I didn't know Mr Y's full name. A guy like me doesn't need to know that."

Edwin shrugged. "But you know my first name, and trust me, you have to know who I am. I'm pretty well-known, and pretty recognisable."

Just as Gib started to confess that he didn't watch much TV—especially news—a woman walked up to Edwin, squealing.

"Oh my God, you're Edwin Masters. I can't believe you're here. I think you're the best reporter ever." She threw herself into his arms and hugged him tight.

Edwin gave her a quick pat on the back before he eased her away. "Thanks. Would you like my friend to take a picture of us?"

"Oh my God, yes."

She handed Gib her phone, and he framed them up on the screen. The woman was obviously drunk, her smile bright and slightly crazy as she leaned against Edwin. He focused on Edwin, whose smile seemed rather intimate, but maybe Gib was seeing things he wanted to see in Edwin's face.

He had no idea why he'd want to see something like that. Shaking his head, he tapped the button to snap the picture. Once it was done, he handed the phone back to her.

"Thank you so much. I'm so glad you got out of that hostage situation in whatever country that was. I was so worried." She bounced, and Gib worried her large breasts would blacken her eyes.

"We were all worried, but things worked out okay." Edwin was gracious, but even Gib could tell he was getting annoyed with the woman. "How about I buy you and your friend a drink?"

Edwin gestured over where a guy sat, pouting in a corner booth. The woman looked over at the man like she'd totally forgotten he was there.

"Oh thanks. That would be awesome." She clapped her hands, and ordered drinks for them both.

Gib quickly poured them, then handed them to her. "I bet it was like your ultimate dream to meet Mr Masters, but he's probably trying to relax and everything, so maybe you should let him get back to his drink. I bet your boyfriend over there would like his own drink and to spend some time with a beautiful lady like you."

"Oh, I'm sorry, Mr Masters. I didn't even think about it. I was just excited and shocked to see you here." She patted Edwin's arm. "I'll let you get back to whatever you were doing."

Edwin and Gib watched her weave her way back to the guy, who greeted her with a scowl. Gib met Edwin's gaze, and shrugged.

"Sorry about that." Edwin grimaced. "I get that a lot, though usually only when I'm home. Anywhere else in the world, they're pretty good about giving me my privacy."

Gib bit his lip, then decided just to confess. "Man, I'm sorry, but I still don't have a clue who you are. I gather you're some kind of reporter. I don't watch TV that much, and hardly ever any news. All that shit's too depressing, I can't deal with it."

Edwin chuckled. "I sort of guessed you might not know me when you didn't react at all the first time you saw me. I'm the Middle East correspondent of one of the networks—a big deal to news junkies."

"Well, excuse me, Mr Hotshot. Then I guess there won't be a problem going back to your hotel tonight. I usually provide the room, but it's being used."

He assumed Jake would've mentioned the arrangement to Edwin. The man nodded.

"Yes, and going back to my room is fine, since it's right here in the Meliá."

"Really? How'd you get so lucky as to snag a room here? It's been full for weeks because of this convention we're having this weekend." He wandered away to fill a drink order, than wandered back to prop his hands on his side of the bar.

Edwin looked left, then right before he leaned closer to Gib. "A friend of mine got me a suite here because I didn't know I was coming to Atlanta until the very last minute. He has some pull in the city."

Gib could just guess what kind of pull Edwin's friend had. Edwin struck him as the kind of guy who knew powerful people in all walks of life. He studied

Edwin's face, finding the faint crows' feet around the corners of Edwin's bright hazel eyes attractive in a way he'd never found them on any other man before.

Edwin's dark hair was cut short, and gave him an air of distinguished elegance. The men Gib slept with were older than him, but none of them show any signs of aging. It was like they fought against getting old, and one way they got their 'youth' back was by fucking a younger man. Yet something told Gib it wasn't that way with Edwin.

"Why are you looking to hook up with me? You're handsome, famous and probably well-off because I don't come cheap." Gib snorted at his words. "Literally and figuratively."

"I just got in town after having spent most of the last year in the Middle East. I could find some company for a night or two, but it wasn't something I could advertise for. And for the last eight months I haven't had any release that involved another person." Edwin shrugged. "I'm looking for a little company for a night or two to remember what it feels like to have another person in a bed for a change."

Gib pursed his lips, and smiled inside at the way Edwin's gaze dropped to Gib's mouth. He stuck out his tongue to wet them. Edwin's eyes dilated with desire.

"Oh okay, I guess that makes sense." Gib glanced over at Isaac. "I have to get back to work. Can I have your room number?"

Chapter Two

Edwin blinked, slowly processing what Gib had said as the lust slowly faded from his mind enough for him to think. "Oh, I'm in the Sono Suite."

"Wow, you do know people." Gib winked as he tugged his phone out of his pocket. Edwin watched as he sent a text to someone. *Is he letting someone know where he's staying tonight? Good idea to have a safety net, even though he doesn't need one with me.*

It wasn't like Edwin didn't know some men were bastards from all his years covering war-torn countries ruled by dictators. Things like a young man getting beaten up weren't supposed to happen here at home, though Edwin wasn't naïve enough to believe they never did. Hell, Gib sold his body for money to make ends meet, and while he wasn't cheap, he still wasn't making nearly as much as Edwin did, and in many ways, he risked his life just as often.

"I'm glad you're telling someone, Gib."

Gib's head shot up. "What are you talking about?"

"I'm sure you're letting someone know where you'll be. Good idea to keep you safe. Hell, Chen knows about me meeting up with you." He saw Gib wince again. "Why don't you like hearing Chen's name?"

"Because I don't want to know his real name. That isn't how I work. It's easier for both my client and I if we stay as anonymous as possible." Gib shrugged, then left to pour out some drinks before wandering back. "To be honest, I'm not interested in knowing who they really are. For a couple of hours during our time together, they can be whoever they want to be, and not who the world sees them as."

Edwin took a sip of the drink he hadn't even remembered getting as he thought about what Gib had said. It was true in a way. He had hired Gib for the night so he could pretend he wasn't alone in the world, and while he knew that when he woke up tomorrow, he'd be just as alone, tonight he'd be happy.

"I guess you have a point. Here's for the drinks. Keep the rest for a tip. I'm going to wait out in the lobby for you. I know you have to shut everything down." He tossed a fifty-dollar bill on the bar before nodding at Gib.

He walked over to one of the sitting areas, then sat. It was almost two, but he knew it would take a little while longer because Gib had to clean up. He didn't begrudge the man his job because even though he was paying a lot of money to spend the night with Gib, Edwin knew it was expensive to live in the city. His phone beeped.

What do you think?

He frowned at the text he got from Chen.

What are you doing up so late?

Not so late when you're on the other side of the world.

Right. Sorry. He's cute.

He wasn't sure if he should've commented on Gib. Chen wouldn't let him live it down.

Ha. Thought you'd like him. Young and hot, but a good guy as well.

Does he have to be a good guy? Can't he be just a good fuck?

He sent the message, then looked up to see Gib shooing the last stragglers out of the bar. Gib caught him looking, and waved.

Good one, Masters. I would've sent you to a different guy if I thought you just wanted a fuck.

Was he that easy to read? He didn't like anonymous sex much anymore. Maybe it was because he was forty-one, and was feeling his age.

I'm not looking for anything serious, Chen.

Keep telling yourself that. Have a good time. Call you later in the week to see how you're doing.

He didn't get another text from Chen. They'd been friends since college, and they'd chased bed partners together, yet it was more than that. They'd both come from privileged backgrounds, but didn't want to follow in their fathers' footsteps. Chen had become one of the world's most sought-after neurosurgeons.

He'd made a fortune in his job, but he also travelled the world, performing pro-bono surgeries for charities and poverty-stricken countries. Chen's father had wanted him to be a corporate lawyer.

Edwin had turned his back on his father's well-thought-out plan for his only son's political career. He had no interest in following in his father's footsteps. No, Edwin wanted excitement and the pursuit of truth. He'd become a journalist to try and keep governments honest. It didn't always work, but he did his best while dodging bullets and being taken hostage. His father kept trying to get him involved in his campaigns, and other people Edwin Masters Senior supported. He'd managed to stay away from picking anyone. As a reporter, he had to remain neutral, much to his father's disappointment.

He didn't understand Chen's last text. Keep telling himself that he wasn't looking for anything serious? But he wasn't. He didn't want to leave someone behind who would hurt if he died.

And he didn't want his life restricted by having someone else dependent on him. Edwin enjoyed flying around the world, reporting from exotic places. He returned to the States to remind himself that there were modern conveniences out there, then he got a new assignment and headed out again.

Having a relationship would put a damper on those adventures, and Edwin didn't think he was ready to stop taking them.

"Are you ready?"

Glancing up, he saw Gib standing a few feet away, holding a bag. Edwin tucked his phone away, then stood.

"Yes, I am."

"Sorry about making you wait and all, but having an honest job sucks." The younger man laughed as he led the way to the elevator.

Edwin let his gaze drop to study Gib's ass, flexing under the tight fabric of his black pants. His hands itched to grab a handful of that bubble butt, but he kept himself under control. Being an adult, he could control himself until they got to his room.

Once they were alone in the elevator, Gib turned to look at him. Edwin watched as he stepped closer and closer until his chest pressed against Edwin's. He didn't think Gib was trying to intimidate him, and if he was, it wouldn't have worked. Some of the most powerful men in the world had tried to do that, and while Gib was drop-dead gorgeous, he really wasn't as scary as a crazy dictator with several armed bodyguards.

"Do you like to kiss?"

Gib's question caught him off guard. "Do I like to kiss?"

He nodded. "Some of my clients don't like to kiss. I'm okay with that, though I love to kiss."

Edwin didn't respond with words. He encircled Gib's waist with his arm, then pulled him as close as they could get with their clothes still on. After burying his hand in those curls, he tilted Gib's head for a better angle, then brought their lips together.

Gasping, Gib melted into Edwin's embrace, seemingly willing to give himself over to Edwin. He nibbled on Gib's bottom lip, trying to persuade him to open. He leant forward, bending Gib over his arm and forcing him to grab a hold of Edwin's shoulders to keep his balance.

When he moaned, Edwin swept his tongue in, tasting Gib for the first time. He must've had a drink at some point before he came to get Edwin, since he found a hint of hops in Gib's mouth as he duelled with and sucked on Gib's tongue.

He slid his hands down to grab Gib's ass, enjoying how firm his butt cheeks were under his fingers. Edwin tugged him until their groins brushed together. His entire body jerked when their erections rubbed against each other.

The ding of the elevator doors broke the spell, and he muttered as he moved away from Gib, who grinned at him.

"I guess you do like to kiss," Gib commented as he bent to pick up the bag he'd dropped when Edwin kissed him.

Edwin bumped their hips together. "There are lots of other things I like to do as well as kiss. Let's get to my suite, and I'll show you."

"Can't wait." Gib patted him on the ass before strolling down the hall towards Edwin's room.

Edwin caught up to him right in front of the door. After sliding his key card, he shoved the door open before gesturing for Gib to go in.

He followed his soon-to-be lover into the living area of the suite, then watched as Gib glanced around.

"I've never been in this suite," Gib told Edwin as he wandered over to the windows to look out over the city. "It's beautiful."

Joining him, Edwin studied the lights making up the cityscape. "It is, but I've seen a hundred beautiful cities like Atlanta. And I've seen a hundred cities that looked like it at one time before the bombs and wars destroyed them."

"Is it hard to see wonderful old places defaced by violence like that?" Gib leant back against Edwin's chest, forcing Edwin to encircle his waist with his arms.

Edwin rested his chin on Gib's shoulder as he thought about what Gib had asked. He grimaced as he realised something. "It used to bother me a great deal. When I first started out as a war correspondent, my network embedded me with an army unit during the invasion of Iraq in two thousand and three, and I'll admit I cried when I saw the city. Bombed-out shell of what was once one of the most magnificent cities in the Middle East. It broke my heart, but I cried in private. I had to be professional."

"And now?" Gib must have heard something in Edwin's voice.

"Now, I've seen so many war-torn places that I don't really notice them anymore. I'm there to report the news, to tell the world about what's happening in a place they might not have even heard of. There are so many spots in turmoil right now, yet we only hear about the ones that affect us." Edwin closed his eyes, and hugged Gib closer to him. "How do I make them see that every place is important? That every person who dies in a war, no matter how small or insufficient, is important to us as a part of the human race."

Silence settled around them as Edwin thought about all the reports he'd done, all the news shows where he tried to get across the desperation of the people caught between the fighting factions. Yet he never once felt like he'd done them justice.

Gib turned in his arms before wrapping his arms around Edwin's neck. "I'm not discounting what you're saying or feeling, but you're supposed to be on vacation. Let's see if we can't get you to think about something else for a little while. Maybe something fun."

Edwin let Gib kiss him, while pushing all the depressing thoughts to the back of his mind. As much as he went over the issues he had with the world at large, he'd never been able to come up with a solution, and he wouldn't in the next several hours, so he should enjoy the time he had with Gib.

This time their kiss held passion and a tiny hint of friendship, or so Edwin thought. God, he really was a sap if he believed Gib saw him as anything other than a client for the night. Yet Edwin couldn't help feeling there was a different kind of connection between them. Something beyond escort and client.

Gib ran his fingers through the hair at the nape of Edwin's neck. Edwin shuddered at his gentle touch. *Christ! It's been a long time since I've been touched like I matter.* He took the kiss deeper while slowly moving backwards. Gib stayed with him, not letting go, but allowing Edwin to lead him wherever he wanted to go.

When Gib swept his tongue into Edwin's mouth to tease his own tongue, Edwin lost track of where they were in the room, and ran into the couch. He managed not to close his mouth and cause Gib irreparable damage.

Laughing, Edwin eased away. "Maybe we should get to the bedroom before we do any more. I don't want to break anything and ruin the night."

"Sounds like a plan to me." Gib snatched up his bag before heading towards the bedroom.

"Do you always pack a bag?" Edwin didn't know what the protocol for an escort was. He didn't know if Gib planned on spending the night or not.

"Sure. You have me for the night, Edwin. Plus I bring my own supplies." Gib frowned.

"I made sure to pick some up earlier." Edwin wasn't going to sleep with any man without protection. He'd been to Africa and seen the ravages of HIV and AIDS on the populace there. And while the causes of those cases were different than his would be, if he could prevent it by simply using a condom, he would do it. It didn't take that much time to put one on.

"I'm glad to hear that, but I've run across a few clients who thought that because they were paying me, that meant they could go bareback." Gib shook his head. "Got hit a couple times for refusing."

"Hit? Men hit you?" Edwin clenched his hands. "That's not right. Just because you're taking money from them doesn't give them the right to abuse you" — he paused for a second — "unless that's what they're paying you for."

Gib chuckled. "I don't mind it rough once in a while, but I'm not into the lifestyle or anything like that. Jake has a few guys who are, and they command a good fee from what I hear."

Edwin nodded. "I've never seen the pleasure in receiving or giving pain, but hey whatever makes others find a measure of peace or happiness is fine with me."

"True." Gib set his bag on a chair, then unzipped it. He pulled out a bottle and a strip of condoms. After tossing them to Edwin, he grinned. "How about we get the night started?"

"Do you want to take a shower or something? I know you've been working all night, and I have to admit I feel kind of bad making you work some more."

Gib stared at him, and Edwin wondered if he'd said something strange or even spoken in a foreign language because Gib was looking at him like he didn't understand a word Edwin had said.

"Did I say something wrong?"

"No." Gib frowned. "Why did you ask that?"

"You were staring at me like you didn't understand what I said. I was wondering if I said something wrong." Edwin shrugged.

Gib shook his head. "You didn't. I just wasn't expecting you to offer to wait for sex."

Edwin sat on the edge of the mattress, bracing his hands on his knees as he looked at Gib. "As amazingly hot as you are, Gib, I've gone without sex for several months now. I think I can control myself long enough to let you take a shower and relax a little bit before we get busy."

He didn't move as Gib walked over to him before straddling his thighs. He gripped Gib's hips, helping him keep his balance. Gib framed his face with his hands, then kissed him. It was gentle and easy like they'd been kissing each other forever. There was no awkward bumping of noses or wondering where to place their hands. It was a simple acceptance of what the other was offering.

When the kiss ended, Gib slid off his lap. "Thank you for treating me like a date, and not a sex toy."

Edwin brushed his fingers over Gib's cheek. "Honey, thank you for making me feel like I was the man you chose to spend the night with, and not some desperate fool who paid for your company."

Gib stretched, drawing Edwin's gaze to the tanned skin revealed by the lifting of his shirt. Edwin couldn't resist reaching out to stroke Gib's stomach. Gib shivered, and Edwin smiled.

"If you want to take a shower, you should probably go do that now, or you're never going to." Edwin poked Gib in the side, then nudged him towards the bathroom. "Go. Would you like something from room service?"

"No," Gib said as he walked away. "I'm good."

"Yeah, I bet you are," Edwin muttered as the bathroom door shut behind Gib.

Edwin flopped back on his bed and stared up at the ceiling. He was truly a complete ninny. Really, he let Gib go take a shower to relax instead of just having crazy monkey sex with the guy as soon as they got into the room. He thumped his forehead with his fist.

Obviously he was more pathetic than he thought. Edwin heard the shower turn on, and he rolled over on his side. He could check his emails and see what had become of his reports. Edwin jumped to his feet, then stripped out of his clothes. There wasn't any point in staying dressed when they were just going to get naked when Gib got out of the shower.

After grabbing his laptop, Edwin climbed into bed, then turned it on. Signing on to his email, he scrolled through it and read certain ones from friends and fellow reporters. There didn't seem to be anything new happening in the world, giving him a moment of peace. He knew that when his two weeks were over, he'd be sent somewhere else where people were dying and bombs were falling.

He glanced up as the bathroom door opened. Gib sauntered out, wearing nothing but a smile. Swallowing, Edwin let his gaze trail down from Gib's bright grin over his well-muscled chest down to where Gib's cock stood out proudly from a nest of dark blond curls.

"You like what you see?" Gib asked as he strolled closer.

"Oh yes, I do like." Edwin shut his computer before setting it on the floor next to the bed. He caught Gib's hand, then yanked him on to the blankets.

Gib tried to wiggle away, but Edwin wasn't willing to let him go at that moment. He twisted and turned with Gib, somehow managing to get the blankets out of the way. Their gasps mingled together when they touched chest-to-chest for the first time.

Edwin hummed as he rolled Gib over onto his back, then bent to lick one of Gib's nipples. "You're so smooth," he commented as he moved to repeat the motion with the other nipple.

"I've found that most men like me not to be hairy." Gib ran his hand over Edwin's chest. "But I like a guy with a little chest hair. I don't want a bear or anything, but a bit to tug on is always good."

"Fuck," Edwin cursed when Gib did as he said, and pulled on a few hairs. "You be good, boy."

"Or what? You'll spank me?" Gib bit his bottom lip while peering up at Edwin through his lashes. "Oh please, sir, don't spank me. I promise I'll be good from now on."

Edwin snorted, then laughed. "Do a little roleplaying, do you?"

Gib shrugged. "Once in a while. Why? Don't you like a little fantasy with your sex?"

"You know, I've never really thought about it. The last couple of years I've been in the middle of war zones, where having sex is dangerous enough as it is. Because, some places, being caught having anal sex could get me killed." Edwin pursed his lips. "I've just been busy trying to stay alive."

He didn't want to talk about it anymore, so he leant forward to take Gib's nipple into his mouth, sucking on it. Gasping, Gib arched his back, silently begging for Edwin to continue what he was doing. There was no forethought in Edwin's plan. He continued to tease and play with Gib until his nipples were red and probably aching.

"Please..." Gib begged.

Edwin wasn't sure what Gib was asking for, but he had an idea it probably had something to do with the hard length of flesh pressed against Edwin's stomach. He slipped down until he wedged his shoulders between Gib's thighs. He wrapped his lips around Gib's cock, then swallowed it.

Not stopping until it hit the back of his throat, Edwin impressed himself with his ability to do so without gagging. He didn't often give blow jobs. It was more often the man he was messing with who pleasured him, and didn't that make him sound a horribly selfish lover. He pushed that thought out of the way. There wasn't anything he could do about what was in the past, but he could try to do better in the future.

Gib gripped the sides of Edwin's head, not doing anything except holding on. Edwin appreciated Gib's restraint. Being relatively new at the whole oral part, Edwin didn't want to do anything that would hurt Gib by accident. He slowly let Gib's erection slide out until only the tip of it was still in his mouth, then he pressed the tip of his tongue into Gib's slit.

"Holy fuck!" Gib shouted, thrusting his hips up to drive his cock further into Edwin's mouth.

This time Edwin let Gib do as he pleased, not caring how fast or far Gib went. He braced one of his hands on the bed next to Gib's hip. Edwin took two of his fingers into his mouth, alongside Gib's shaft, to get them good and wet. When he thought they were covered enough, he removed them, then pressed them against Gib's hole.

"Do it," Gib ordered him. "Don't be careful or gentle. Just shove them in there. I've been aching for something in my ass since you sat at my bar tonight. Your fingers are just the start."

Edwin gave a mental snort, but did as Gib told him. He shoved one finger into Gib, then on the next stroke in, he inserted both of them. Gib groaned, but didn't try to get away. Soon they'd established a marvellous rhythm of him fucking Gib with his fingers, and Gib took his mouth with his cock.

Gib was undulated and shifting with every thrust, and Edwin couldn't stop from rubbing his own hard-on against the mattress under him. He knew Gib was getting close, and he wanted to make sure the man came because somehow he got the feeling that not every client of Gib's was considerate enough to make sure he enjoyed the sex they paid him for.

Edwin didn't want to be selfish like that. He wanted to be different and stand out in Gib's mind. And didn't those wants make him sound stupid again.

"Edwin, I'm going to come," Gib warned him.

He let Gib's cock slip out of his mouth, but wrapped his free hand around the slick flesh, then started pumping. He kept drilling Gib with his fingers, not wanting to let up on that either.

Gib let his head drop to the pillow beneath him and he cried out as hot cum spilled from his cock. It coated Edwin's hand, and some even landed on Gib's stomach. Edwin kept jerking Gib off until Gib wilted back onto the mattress with a sigh. All the tremors and shudders drained from both of them, and Edwin buried his face against Gib's hip.

"Oh wow," Gib said in a breathless voice. "I wasn't expecting that."

"Neither was I, but I think it was a pleasant surprise." Edwin trailed a soft kiss over the bump of Gib's hip before he somehow managed to push himself up, so he could find the condoms and lube. "Where did the supplies go?"

"Here." Gib held up a foil package. "You get that open and on. I'll finish getting myself ready."

Edwin caught the square packet, then used his trembling hands to tear it open. He rolled it over his erection with a light touch, knowing if he used any harder a grip, he'd come, and he wanted to be inside Gib when he did.

Gib's grunt caught his attention, bringing his gaze to where Gib had his fingers buried in his ass.

"God, you're beautiful," Edwin murmured as he watched Gib stretch his hole.

"Thank you." Gib flashed him a stunning smile. "Why don't you get some slick on? Then come here."

Edwin did as Gib suggested, then positioned his cock at Gib's opening. He met Gib's gaze, and Gib nodded, letting him know it was all right. He lifted Gib's legs over his arms, then slowly began to sink into that tight ass.

Gib bit his lip while inhaling deeply, and Edwin stopped for a moment to make sure Gib was okay.

"Don't worry, darling. I'm fine. You're just a little bigger than I'm used to."

Edwin couldn't help but beam a little with pride. "Well, thanks."

"Just get on with it." Gib chuckled, then moaned as Edwin pushed all the way in.

He paused, taking a moment to adjust to the way Gib seemed to fit him like a glove. Then he began to move, thrusting in and out with hard strokes, driving grunts from Gib. Soon Edwin was driving into Gib, losing himself to the rhythms and sounds of sex, something he hadn't seen or felt in months.

"That's it. Just let go. I'll catch you." Gib entwined his fingers with Edwin's, anchoring him to the present.

"Gib." It was the only thing he could say as his climax crashed through him, swamping him with emotions and sensations he wasn't sure how to deal with.

He trembled and jerked as he flooded the condom until he thought every atom of his soul had been drained from him. Edwin collapsed, barely managing to catch himself before he flattened Gib. He groaned and Gib flinched as his softened cock slid from Gib. Edwin lay there, getting his breathing under control. When he finally thought he could make his body do what he wanted, he climbed out of bed.

"I'll get something to clean us up with."

Gib flapped his hand at him in a vague shooing motion. "Go ahead. I'm going to lie here and try to figure out if you managed to fuck my brain out of my head. I never thought that was possible, but I think you came close."

Edwin chuckled, but continued on his way. He washed off, then brushed his teeth before grabbing a cloth to wet. After wandering back to the bed, Edwin cleaned Gib off before tossing the cloth towards the bathroom.

"Do you want to move to the other bed? Less of a mess."

Gib nodded. "You're right. We totally need to move. Once I've recovered the ability to walk, we can do that."

"You don't have to walk." Edwin swept Gib over his shoulder, then carried him to the other bed, tossing him on it when they got there.

"Shit. You're strong," Gib pointed out after he stopped bouncing.

Edwin got them situated under the blankets before he replied, "My news crew and I were held hostage for three weeks in Darfur several months ago. They didn't beat us or anything like that. Just threatened to kill or torture us, but never did. I did a lot of push-ups and other exercises to keep my strength up, and I kept up with the regimen since then."

"You were held hostage? Weren't you terrified?" Gib snuggled close to Edwin, lying his head on Edwin's shoulder.

"Sure, I was terrified. Anyone in their right mind would be scared to death, but letting my fear get the best of me wasn't going to help me survive. I've always known that being taken prisoner could happen in any one of the places I've gone to. It's just the roll of the dice or the turn of the wheel. However you look at it, my time was up."

"You sound so blasé about it." Gib traced circles on Edwin's chest. "I think I'd be a basket case if that happened to me."

"No, you wouldn't." Edwin ran his hand up and down Gib's arm. "You made a comment to me about having a rough appointment once, and while I don't have any details, I have a pretty good idea of what probably happened to you. I've seen the end results of beatings before in the brothels in India."

Gib's sharply inhaled breath warned Edwin he was about to say something, so Edwin rushed on with his explanation.

"I've seen the aftermaths, and don't tell me it was any different because you're a guy. A beating is a beating and it doesn't matter the sex of the one being abused. You were helpless and at the mercy of a stranger. And that stranger believed he had the right to do as he pleased with you, simply because he gave you some money."

Edwin remembered how much rage filled his heart while he listened to the stories of the women forced into the slum brothels and all they endured. Gib hadn't been that badly off, but still Edwin had a feeling what happened to Gib wasn't far away from what happened to the women.

"Yet you survived the beating. You went on to find a way to do your job while keeping yourself safe. You're never going to be put into that kind of position again. That's having strength, Gib, and you would've survived being held hostage as well as, if not better, than me."

Chapter Three

Gib snorted, not sure he believed what Edwin had said about him. He didn't think he'd been strong when he survived the attack from his client. Hell, if he had been, he would've brought the man up on charges like Jake had wanted, but he'd been afraid that because there had been money exchanged, the cops wouldn't have taken his claims seriously.

"I know you think I'm talking shit, but I'm serious, Gib. Maybe you think because I just met you, I don't really know you. And you're right, but I'm a good judge of character. Comes from meeting strangers in life and death situations, and having to make snap judgements that could cost me my life." Edwin traced the dips and curves of Gib's spine with his finger.

Trembling, Gib curled closer to Edwin. He didn't want to think about what Edwin had said. He started to fake a yawn, but it turned into a real one.

Edwin nuzzled Gib's temple. "I haven't slept well since I was released by my captors. Maybe having you here in bed with me will help."

Gib blinked, still trying to adjust to the fact that bad guys at some point had held Edwin prisoner in the past. He didn't know of anyone who had lived through something like that.

"All right." He wasn't entirely sure Edwin had got all that he had paid for. "But I'm willing to go again if you want to."

"I wanted someone to share their body with me, and you did that. I needed to know I wasn't alone in the world, and the only time I've ever had that was when I was in bed with someone." Edwin kissed Gib's forehead. "You gave me that."

Not convinced, Gib thought about it for a moment. "I work tomorrow, but I get off at eight. We could grab some dinner, then come back here."

He wasn't sure why he'd suggested they get together again. Normally, he only hung out with the client long enough to fuck, then he headed back home.

"I'd love to have dinner with you. I have a meeting in the morning, so I have to get up early, but you're welcome to stay as long as you want." Edwin shifted slightly until he must have found the right position. "Thank you, Gib."

"You're welcome," Gib said, then let silence fall between them. They would have some more fun tomorrow night, and Gib would make sure Edwin got his money's worth. There was a reason why Gib demanded a large payment.

As he absorbed the warmth emanating from Edwin's body, Gib let his eyes drift shut. There wasn't any point in worrying about Edwin being disappointed right then.

* * * *

Knocking woke Gib the next morning. Stretching, he rolled over on his back and blinked up at the ceiling. *Okay, that's not my ceiling, and it doesn't look like the ceiling in the room I usually use.*

"Gib, room service is here. I took the liberty of ordering breakfast for you. If you don't like anything, don't eat it, and order something you do like." Edwin peered into the bedroom from the living room area of the suite for a moment, then disappeared.

"All right. I'm getting up." He sat up in the bed and scrubbed his hands over his face, still trying to piece together what had happened. He wasn't a morning person, and he hated waking up in a strange place. It wasn't like he didn't remember Edwin or the fact that they'd done some stuff the night before, it was just his brain still needed to wake up some more before he could really function.

"You don't have to. I can bring yours in to you." Edwin appeared again. This time he carried a tray with a plate, glasses, and mugs on it.

Gib grinned at Edwin. "I've never had anyone bring me breakfast in bed before."

Edwin frowned. "I think that's one of the saddest things I've ever heard. Everyone should have breakfast in bed at least once in their life."

"Yeah well, when you run away from home at fifteen, there aren't a lot of opportunities to lie in bed all day and shit like that." Gib took a piece of toast, then stuffed it in his mouth. *Christ! Stop talking, idiot. Edwin's going to think you're a complete basket case or at least not worth wasting all this time on.*

He stopped chewing at that thought. Did he really want Edwin to spend time with him? It wasn't something Gib did. He didn't have breakfast with his clients or spend time outside of bed with them. All those actions seemed too much like having a relationship, and Gib didn't do relationships. He'd convinced himself that for the most part, but every once in a while, a tiny bit of his soul wished for something more than his clients and a random hook-up or two.

"You don't like the toast?" Edwin looked worried.

No one worried about him. Well, no one except for Esteban, and Gib only let him because it was easier to do that than to keep arguing with the man. He swallowed the lump of bread, then washed it down with a gulp of orange juice.

"No, the toast is fine. All of it's fine." He checked Edwin out. "You look good."

Edwin glanced down at the suit he wore. It was black with faint grey pinstripes. He wore a matching vest, dark blue shirt, and bright red tie. "Thanks. I don't normally dress up, but I'm meeting with the head of the network today. I'm not completely sure why he wants to talk to me, but I know I should look better than I usually do."

With his silver, short-cut hair and bright blue eyes, Edwin cut a striking figure, and Gib noticed it. His cock stiffened under the sheets that covered him to his waist.

"How do you not spend all of your time beating people off of you?" He shook his head. "Damn, dude. You're fucking hot, and I love that suit on you. So distinguished. You look like a Wall Street banker or a lawyer."

Edwin grimaced. "Don't say that."

"Why not?" Gib took a bite of his eggs.

"That's what my dad wanted me to be, and when I told him I wanted to be a reporter instead, he cut me off." Edwin sighed. "Christ, that sounds more dramatic than it is. My aunt ended up paying for my last year of college, so it's not like I had to work my way through."

"Have you two reconciled?" Gib hoped they had since he wasn't going to be getting in touch with his parents any time soon.

"Yes. Once he realised all those political plans he had for me weren't ever going to come true, and once I became a famous international war correspondent that he can brag about to his associates." Edwin rolled his eyes, and Gib laughed. "We tolerate each other. I'm closer to my mom and brother than my dad."

Gib fidgeted with his silverware, pushing them around the tray. "I haven't talked to my parents in ten years, ever since I left home."

Edwin sat on the edge of the bed, resting his hand on Gib's knee. "Did you ever try to contact them? Maybe call them or something."

He shook his head. "No. My father was very clear that he wanted nothing to do with me. I came out to them, thinking that since they were my parents, they'd love me no matter what. And it wasn't like I was a serial killer or anything like that, but you would've thought I'd eaten a baby right in front of them."

Edwin laughed. "That's a terrible image, but I know what you mean."

"My mom sat there crying and my dad yelled at me until I thought the vein throbbing in his forehead was going to burst. I couldn't take it anymore, so I grabbed a bag of my stuff and left. I had enough money to get me to Atlanta, and feed myself for a while."

"How long were you here before you started selling yourself?"

Gib studied Edwin, not seeing any signs of judgement or condemnation. "I was here for two years before I didn't have a choice any more. So I started hustling, and I found I could make good money doing it. Then I ran into Jake, and he convinced me to take him on as my 'agent'. He started getting me better clients, and more money."

Edwin nodded, but didn't say anything, so Gib kept talking.

"He was the one who suggested I go get my GED. Jake told me my looks weren't going to last forever and I should have something to fall back on. I turned eighteen and got it, then I started working at restaurants and places like that. After I turned twenty-one, I started working here and that was four years ago." Gib took a sip of coffee this time. "I don't take many appointments any more. Just when money's tight, and I can't make my rent. That doesn't happen often, but every once in a while I have an emergency expenditure, and it takes up my savings."

"Sounds like you took a bad situation and made it work for you." Edwin squeezed his knee. "Trust me, Gib, I think you did a marvellous job surviving on the streets without becoming addicted or getting yourself killed or worse. And, as a reporter, I have seen things that are worse than death."

As odd as it might have sounded to anyone else, Gib did know how lucky he was. Things could have gone horribly wrong if any other pimp besides Jake had found him. He could've become a statistic instead of a mostly well-adjusted person.

"Thanks." Gib held up his forkful of eggs. "Do you want to try some of this?"

Edwin shook his head. "No thanks. I had a cup of coffee, and that'll do me until I can grab lunch." He hesitated for a second, then continued, "Are you doing anything today? What time do you have to go in?"

"I have to be there at twelve. We have a big convention starting today, and I'm working the back bar. Guess this group likes to hang out in the bars." Gib grinned. "Might mean more tips for me. Definitely means more hours. I don't usually work today."

"Okay. Then where would you like to go for dinner? You said you got off at eight, right? Do you have to go home for different clothes?"

Gib thought for a second. "I'm going to head home in a few. I'll grab a set of clean clothes and stuff while I'm there. That way I don't have to wear my work clothes to dinner."

"Sounds good to me." Edwin held out a card. "Here's the key to the suite. You can just drop your stuff off here when you come back to work. About that restaurant?"

"Oh, that would be Escorpion. I love their food." He took the key from Edwin. "Are you sure you trust me to have a key to your room? I mean we just met and I'm a prostitute. I could rob you blind."

Edwin leaned over to give Gib a quick kiss before standing. "Are you going to rob me?"

"No, but..."

Edwin shook his head. "I trust you, Gib. Remember, I'm a very good judge of character. I'll make a reservation at Escorpion for us around nine. Will that give you enough time to change your clothes?"

"Sure." Gib watched Edwin stroll across the room.

"Good. I'll see you here at eight or shortly thereafter." Edwin flashed him a grin before disappearing into the living room.

Gib heard the door open, then close. He settled back to finish his breakfast. There was no point in letting it go to waste. Edwin had told him not to rush, and he had more than enough time to get back to his apartment, grab clean clothes, then get back to the hotel for his shift later that day.

After he cleaned his plate, he set the tray outside the door. He got dressed, hoping to get out of the hotel without talking to anyone. It wasn't that he didn't want to see any of the guys who he considered friends. It was simply that he didn't want to chat. He was still working things out in his mind about Edwin.

Something about the man had thrown Gib for a loop, and he was off-kilter because of it. Somehow, the whole experience felt different from any of the other clients Gib had ever dealt with. He was afraid he was going to develop feelings for Edwin, which would be so stupid because he couldn't fall in love with a client. And Edwin would never be caught dead having a serious relationship with a prostitute, even an occasional one like Gib.

Gib managed to get out of the hotel without anyone seeing him. When he saw the front desk, he remembered to text Esteban, letting him know that Gib was still alive and well.

Alive and heading home. Have to work in back bar at noon.

A beep told him Esteban had sent a message back.

Edwin Masters is your client!?! The man won a Pulitzer for his reporting on the genocide in the Sudan.

Gib rolled his eyes as he climbed on the bus. Maybe he should watch more TV because it was beginning to feel like he was the only one who hadn't heard of Edwin Masters.

You shouldn't have looked him up on the computer. Keep your mouth shut.

Oh, he knew he didn't have to tell Esteban that. His friend would never say a word about Gib's personal life or side job. Gib trusted Esteban in a way he trusted very few people.

My lips are sealed like always. I can't wait to hear if he's as good a lover as he looks.

Like Gib ever told Esteban anything about his clients. The man had to get a life if he was starting to ask Gib about his business.

I don't kiss and tell, man. I'll see you later today when I get back to the hotel.

He didn't wait to see Esteban's reply before he plugged in his earphones and turned the music up. For many people, riding the bus was an exercise in stress and annoyance, but Gib kind of liked riding it. He enjoyed watching all the other people who shared the vehicle with him. Gib made up stories about them in his mind, giving them outlandish jobs or unusual lives. It was how he passed the time as he went back and forth between his apartment and the hotel.

Gib got off at his stop, then headed to his apartment. He took a shower, got dressed in his usual work uniform before packing another bag. He'd left his lube and rubbers in Edwin's room. He was determined for them to use at least two of them in the strip before the night was over with.

He did a load of laundry, needing to get some more of his uniforms clean. Gib puttered around his apartment while the washer ran, then he threw the clothes in the dryer. He sat down at his laptop to type Edwin's name in his search engine.

He wasn't entirely sure about what he was doing. Gib didn't research his clients, but then again he rarely knew their real names, so there'd never been any reason to go looking them up. Yet he was struck by a restless kind of curiosity about Edwin. He found he wanted to know all he could about the man, and what he'd gone through all those months ago when he was kidnapped.

Gib slowly scrolled through the links on the screen, clicking on one after the other. He stared at the pictures of a hollow-cheeked Edwin standing with three other men who looked as rough as he did. It had been taken just an hour or so after Edwin had been released.

As hard as he could, Gib couldn't find any articles on how Edwin ended up being returned to the American embassy in the next country over from Dafur. Who had talked the kidnappers into letting him go? Or had money been exchanged to facilitate their release?

Smiling, Gib knew he wouldn't ever find out the truth. It wasn't like Edwin was going to spill all the facts about the whole experience. Heck, Gib was surprised the man had told him as much as he had. Though being a paid companion had its advantages. Men tended to spill their secrets to people they didn't think they'd ever see again. So he had, over the years, come into some private information that could've brought him a lot of money if he was into blackmail.

He checked his watch. It was time to head back to the hotel, and excitement raced through him at the thought of seeing Edwin again later that night. He'd never felt that way before, and he wasn't sure if he liked feeling it.

When he got back to the hotel, he dropped his bag off in Edwin's suite, then headed down to the bar to clock in. He nodded to Quinn, one of the housekeepers, as the burly man stepped out of one of the rooms. Quinn wasn't much of a talker, which was why Gib had been surprised when the man had stopped at the bar for a drink to talk to him about Kasey. Now Gib had only met Kasey once at Escorpion, where Kasey was a waiter, so he wasn't sure he was the right guy for Quinn to ask for advice from. Yet he'd found that was also one of the hazards of being a bartender. At some point, everyone spilled their guts to him.

Gib got to the bar and clocked in with a few minutes to spare. He grinned at Tabitha, the waitress who was working with him on that shift. He wasn't sure who was scheduled to come in a little later, but for now, the two of them could handle the crowd.

As the day progressed, the crowd in the bar got bigger, and Gib had to work faster to keep up. Most of the people were wearing lanyards, so he had a feeling they belonged to the convention taking up the hotel that week. While the different groups were a little loud, they weren't obnoxious. Their noise came from laughter and simply talking, which was better than yelling and getting into fights.

He delivered a Kahlúa and cream, and a vodka and tonic with extra limes to two ladies at the end of the bar. Their brightly coloured hair and gorgeous tattoos had caught his eye when they had arrived, and he'd chatted with them while he mixed some drinks. By the time he'd finished serving them, he was convinced to go and try some of their books. The bull-riding series by one of the ladies really intrigued him.

The clock closed in on eight, and Gib glanced around the bar. He spotted Edwin in one of the corner booths, talking on his phone and frowning. That didn't look good, but Gib tried not to let it worry him. Edwin was just a client, and while Gib rarely had an appointment with the same guy twice in a row, he'd been willing to break that rule because he didn't think Edwin got his money's worth last night.

A small voice in the back of his mind told him he was crazy. Gib was seeing Edwin again because he wanted to, not because he owed the man anything. He had to admit that there was something special about Edwin—even though they'd just met, he had the sneaky suspicion that Edwin could come to mean more to him, then any of his other clients.

He snorted softly. Even if that was true, what man in his right mind would want a prostitute as his boyfriend? It might be the world's oldest profession, but that didn't make it respectable. Gib would give it and the money up for a man who loved him, sordid past and all.

Trying not to think about it, he went off shift. Gib waved to Isaac, who'd come in to work the rest of the night. He wound his way through the tables and people to where Edwin sat. He tried to ignore how his heart skipped a beat when Edwin smiled at him.

Why was he fighting how he felt? It wasn't like Edwin was going to be sticking around. He'd told Gib he'd be here for two weeks, then be sent off on another assignment. Gib had always been the kind of guy who grabbed his happiness where he could find it, and for some reason Edwin made him happy. He wasn't going to overthink the whole experience.

"Are you ready to head up so you can change? I got us nine o'clock reservations at Escorpion." After standing, Edwin bent slightly to kiss Gib's cheek. Gib inhaled sharply, and Edwin shot him a glance. "Was I not supposed to do that? Do you not like public displays of affection?"

Gib grinned. "Dude, I practically climbed you in the elevator. I don't think public displays are anything you have to worry about."

"Then why did you react that way?" Edwin placed his hand on the small of Gib's back, seeming to stake his claim again.

"I've just never had anyone greet me that way, like I was important to them and not a dirty secret they had to hide." Gib shrugged. Well, that had come out sounding needy and silly.

Edwin pulled him to a stop, out of the way of the wandering crowds. They were tucked in a quiet spot in the lobby where no one was likely to see them. He placed his knuckles under Gib's chin, lifting it until their eyes met. Gib wasn't sure he could trust what he saw in Edwin's gaze. Respect was there, along with something that Gib wanted to call caring, but he could just be imagining that.

"Honey, you deserve to be treated like the treasure you are, and if none of the men you've gone out with realise that, then it's their loss." Edwin kissed him again, and Gib brought his hands up to hold onto Edwin's shoulders.

Only after Edwin had kissed him breathless did they break apart, and Edwin smiled down at him. "I know we haven't even known each other for twenty-four hours yet, but I want to tell you this, and please don't panic."

"I hate that," Gib groused. "You tell me not to panic, and the first thing I want to do is freak out because I'm sure you're going to tell me something awful."

Edwin grinned, and again Gib's heart skipped a beat as it became obvious that Edwin did seem to care for him in some way deeper than just a quick fuck.

"Take a deep breath. This isn't awful, or at least I hope you don't think it's awful. I like you, Gib, and I mean I really like you. Maybe someday it could even be love, if you're willing to stick through being left alone for long periods of time while I'm out reporting in dangerous places." Edwin wrinkled his nose, and Gib couldn't help but laugh. "That wasn't a selling point, was it?"

Gib slid his hand around the nape of Edwin's neck, bringing the man closer to him. He waited until their lips almost touched before he whispered, "I'm sold. You're the first man to ever look at me like you see the person behind the escort. Sure, it's probably insanely early in our relationship to even consider making it serious, but what the hell. We're both the type of guys who grab what we want the moment we realise we want it."

He brought their mouths together, kissing Edwin with everything in him, hoping that Edwin understood all the words he couldn't say just yet. There was a promise of more when the time was right.

"Hey, you two, none of that here in the lobby and in front of the kiddos."

Gib broke away, licking his lips to savour the taste of Edwin on them. He turned to see Reno standing there, hands on his hips and a smirk on his face.

"I don't see any kids," Edwin pointed out.

Reno shrugged. "Maybe I meant myself."

Gib chuckled. "That's true. You are pretty young."

"Jackass, I'm only five years younger than you." Reno punched him in the arm.

"Yeah, well, I guarantee I've lived a lot more than you have in those five years." Gib winked, and Reno nodded.

"Somehow, I think you have." Reno glanced over to where Bruce stood a few feet away. "I have to go."

"See you later. Glad things are working out for you, Reno."

"One of your friends?" Edwin asked as they made their way over to the elevators.

Gib nodded. "Yeah. Reno's a good guy. Does all the different kids' events we have here at the hotel. Not sure how he does it. Spending time with all those children would drive me crazy."

"Do you not want children?"

Gib thought about it while they waited for the elevator to come to the lobby. "I guess I never really considered the possibility of kids in my life. I mean, I'm still young, and really what man would want to have a family with a prostitute? Though I'd be a former prostitute at that point. No way would I be able to sell myself if I was in love with a guy."

"That's good to know," Edwin murmured as they stepped into the car.

They had the elevator to themselves, so Gib stepped back to press his ass against Edwin's groin. Edwin wrapped his arm around Gib's waist, holding him in place. He rocked his hips, grinding into Edwin. He smirked at the smothered groan issued close to his ear. Then Edwin brushed his lips over Gib's nape, causing Gib to shiver.

"A little payback," Edwin whispered before he slid his hand down to cup Gib's fabric-covered cock, then squeezed.

"Fuck me," he ground out, and Edwin snickered.

"That will be later," Edwin promised.

Gib couldn't believe how his body was reacting to Edwin. Somehow, Edwin had become more than a client, because he normally didn't have the urge to spend any extra time with his appointments. He'd sleep with them, then leave when they were done. Not with Edwin. Gib found he wanted to spend as much time as possible with the man.

They got out on Edwin's floor, and Gib laughed as Edwin dragged him to the room. Once they were inside, Edwin started to drop to his knees in front of Gib, but he stopped him.

"I think it's my turn." Gib pushed Edwin back against the door, then sank to the floor.

He licked his lips at the thought of having Edwin's cock in his mouth. His hands trembled as he unzipped Edwin's jeans. He barely noticed that Edwin had changed out of his suit into jeans and a Henley.

After parting the fabric, he slipped his hand inside Edwin's pants to gently shove them down. Gib wanted to get at Edwin's erection. It was one of the things he'd thought about all day at work.

Edwin ran his hand over Gib's hair before trailing his fingers along Gib's jaw. Gib met Edwin's gaze, and blurted out, "You aren't a client anymore. I won't take your money. This isn't an appointment. It's just you and me being together. Two guys who want each other."

"I'm good with that, Gib. To be honest, last night wasn't just a quick roll in the hay with some stranger for me. You touched a part of my heart I hadn't wanted to acknowledge."

Gib swallowed, happy to know he wasn't alone in feeling like this was the start of something more than a client-escort relationship.

He made a rash decision.

"I won't do this anymore, not with anyone except you," he promised before he bent to take Edwin's length into his mouth.

Being a professional, he took Edwin in until the man's head hit the back of his throat. He swallowed around Edwin's shaft, and Edwin groaned. A thud sounded, causing Gib to shoot a quick glance up. He smiled around the flesh in his mouth when he saw that Edwin had let his head drop back to hit the door.

After those declarations, Gib wanted to focus on the important part, getting Edwin off. But a slight tug at his hair had him looking up again. Edwin held out a condom. Where he'd got it from, Gib didn't know, but he didn't take the time to ask.

"Just until I can prove to you I'm negative. I don't want you to take me just on my word."

Gib let Edwin slide out of his mouth before he shook his head. "I trust you, man. Besides, I want to taste you."

"Jesus!" Edwin jerked, causing his cock to smack Gib in the face. "I can't believe you'd trust me like that."

He shrugged, not sure why he did, but he just knew it would be okay. "It's my call, and I don't want to use a condom for this."

"Fine with me." Edwin tapped his cheek. "Now I want your wonderful mouth."

"You got it."

He wrapped his lips back around Edwin, taking him in as far as he could again. Gib started slow and easy, doing his best to drive Edwin out of his mind and over the edge. While he fondled Edwin's balls, he sped up and scraped his teeth on the vein running along the underside of the length of Edwin's cock.

Edwin shuddered, and Gib got serious, working Edwin with all his skill. He didn't stop him from thrusting into his mouth as much as he wanted. Gib braced his hands on Edwin's hips, and relaxed his throat. He made the conscious decision to allow Edwin to come in his mouth.

"Oh my God, Gib!" Edwin shouted as he climaxed.

Gib drank down every drop he massaged from Edwin, enjoying the salty bitterness coating his tongue. It had been years since he'd allowed any man to come in his mouth. When he'd first started hustling, he hadn't known any better, but once Jake took him under his wing, he'd learned to use condoms while doing anything.

When he was sure Edwin was done, he licked him clean, then let the softened cock slide from his mouth. He rested his head against Edwin's stomach while he caught his breath. Afterwards, he tucked Edwin back in his underwear, then let Edwin lift him up to his feet.

Gib wrapped his arms around Edwin's waist, pressing his face against Edwin's chest. They stood there for several minutes, simply holding each other and listening to their heartbeats fall into rhythm.

"Thank you," Edwin whispered as Gib stepped back.

"You're welcome." Gib checked his watch. "I have enough time to change before we head to the restaurant."

He kissed Edwin quickly before stripping, then changing into his clean clothes. When he came out of the bedroom, Edwin was sitting on the couch, staring at the floor.

"Did you mean it?"

Gib frowned. "Mean what?"

"That you weren't doing the escort thing anymore?" Edwin looked at him, and Gib could read the hope in his eyes.

Gib thought about it, and nodded. "I can always get a second job, but yeah, if you're serious about trying for a serious relationship, then I'm serious about leaving the business. In truth, I haven't been happy about doing it for a while now. Just never had a reason to stop."

Edwin stood before walking over to Gib. He cradled Gib's face in his hands. "I'm glad I'm your reason for stopping."

They kissed, so many promises and answers found in that embrace. Gib eased a few inches away, then rested his forehead against Edwin's.

"Are we going to be able to do this? You're here for two weeks, then you'll be leaving again for however long they want you to go." Gib took a deep breath. "I'm willing to try if you are."

"Maybe while I'm here, we could go looking for a house. I'll buy it, and you can live there with me. I want you to move in with me. It'll be our place, even when I'm not there. I won't stay away as long as I have been." Edwin shrugged. "I never really had a reason to come home before. Now I do."

Gib laughed. "It's crazy and wild, but I think it's a great idea. Let's find a house."

Edwin swept him up in his arms, then kissed him. Gib couldn't believe he'd agreed to move in with a man he'd just met, but everything in his heart said it was the right thing to do.

He was going to take a chance on love this time, and hope that his last client ended up being the man he loved forever.

WHERE TOMORROW SHINES

Jambrea Jo Jones

Dedication

To the individuals who made GRL possible. The organisers who work so hard to make our time at the retreat awesome! J.P. Bowie, Heidi Cullinan, Ethan Day, Teresa Emil, Carol Lynne, Damon Suede and the late William Neale.

To my two GRL roommates Rhonda and Ive. There is one scene in this book that I would totally be happy to walk in on, and you will too—just wait.

Danny Juris, I'll miss you this year!

And Joy!

Chapter One

Quinn Nelson finished making the bed, making sure the corners were tight. Being a maid wasn't all bad. At least it wasn't shooting insurgents and dodging bullets. Sure, there were some real skanky people out there who left the room in a way he wouldn't even see in his worst nightmare, but he was happy with his job. It was something mindless that paid the bills. When he went home, he didn't have to worry about explosions or how close to the enemy line he was. He had a beer or two and relaxed before bed only to start it all over again.

It was nice to be back in Atlanta. It had been years, but it was still home. The Meliá Hotel was a nice place and they treated their employees right. All he had to do was be on time and do his job. He could handle that in his sleep.

So what if he was a bit lonely? That was life. He'd spent the last thirty years with no significant other — he could last the rest of his life. Maybe he'd go out to eat at his favourite restaurant, Escorpion, after work.

The tequila was great and so was the food. Mexican was his favourite.

Kasey Adams.

Just the name made Quinn hard. *Fuck.* Nope, no matter how much he wanted a goat taco it wasn't going to happen. Kasey worked as a waiter at Escorpion. They'd met there one night and had really hit it off, but Kase was just too happy and shiny. Quinn was trying to avoid Kasey, not invite him back to his place for a fuck. Because if he saw Kasey, that invitation would be out of his mouth before he could think twice. Kasey was a sexy bastard and if Quinn laid eyes on him he wouldn't hesitate to ask him over.

Kasey still thought he could fix the world. He'd once told Quinn that 'everything is a path that leads us to where we need to go'. If that wasn't glass half full, Quinn didn't know what was. He was too old, too tired and the shine had worn off him at nineteen when he'd shot his first person in Afghanistan. He still had nightmares. They would be with him forever. He didn't need to bring that baggage to a relationship, so he was walking off the path and wasn't where Kase needed to be. Quinn would stick to one night stands. He was good at those.

After a month or so of dating, Quinn had to stop all communication. Kase deserved a younger guy who would be able to keep up. Someone who wanted to change the world with him, not a man with a busted leg who woke up screaming on a good night.

Quinn wasn't that guy, no matter how Kase's long, lean body looked in his bed. How his brown hair would stick up all over the place when he woke up. Or how his green eyes sparkled when he looked at Quinn. He'd done the right thing. He wasn't meant for relationships and that was that.

Maybe he'd go down to the hotel bar instead. See if Gib was working. For some reason he couldn't explain, he needed the company. His house was too silent. He wasn't sure if the TV would fill the space, and he knew Gib would be good to talk to. He wasn't into relationships either, from what Quinn could tell.

He wouldn't think about the fact that he'd avoided his place as much as possible since he'd stopped talking to Kase. Quinn didn't want to be there if the guy showed up. It had been two weeks since he'd declared radio silence without telling Kase why. It might make him an asshole, but a clean break was the best. Quinn rubbed his hand over his heart, trying to ignore the ache.

Quinn would keep telling himself that until he began to believe it.

He took a quick look around the room to make sure he'd cleaned everything and had all of his supplies picked up and out of the room. He checked the towels and the trash cans, checking off his mental list. They were getting ready for a conference and had a lot of rooms to get ready for the guests. He still had about ten more to do before he could break. He grabbed the dirty towels by the door and limped out to his cart, throwing them in with the others. The next room waited and he needed to keep a move on so he could get out of work on time.

* * * *

The repetition was good for him, most days. But not today. As he worked through his remaining rooms, his mind wandered to the day he'd met Kase.

Quinn walked into the place. It was nice and just starting to fill up. He was going to sit at the bar and watch whatever sports they had on, but for some reason he asked for a table – outside, away from the noise. It was warm enough that he could enjoy the evening air. Sports were on anytime at home. It would be better to get lost in the people walking around town.

His waiter showed up. "Hello, I'm Kasey and I'll be your waiter this evening. Can I start you off with something to drink?"

Quinn had been staring down at the menu and didn't look up right away. When he did – he couldn't breathe or speak. That didn't happen very often, but the guy in front of him pushed all his lust buttons. He was slim with spiky brown hair and brilliant green eyes – not to mention a smile that lit up the night. He was being sappy – it had been a long day. He was tired and hungry. He shook himself out of his stupor.

"Beer – whatever's on tap," Quinn managed to get out.

The cheeky waiter winked at him and turned from him.

Yes, Quinn watched Kasey's ass as he walked away.

Enough was enough. He needed a beer or three.

Quinn clocked out, changed into his street clothes and headed for the bar where there was a stool with his name on it. He walked over and sat down. It wasn't busy yet, but would pick up in a few hours.

Gib moved over to him and winked while wiping down the bar. "Well, hello, solider boy."

Quinn couldn't help but grin. Gib was cute with his curly blond hair, hazel eyes and tight little body. Quinn just wished the guy would stop with his second job before he got hurt, but he wasn't one to judge. He'd protect Gib the only way he knew how – by being there if he needed it and helping make sure he had a safe place to take his tricks.

"Hey, Gib. I need a beer."

"Sounding a bit desperate there, bro."

"Just…give me a beer." Quinn rubbed a hand down his face.

"Testy, solider boy. You need to get laid." Gib popped the top on a beer and slid it towards Quinn.

"Ah…no, I don't. I need a beer. And if I was desperate I'd go right for the whisky, but the night is young." Quinn took a deep pull.

Gib shook his head and went to help another customer. Quinn took another drink and looked around. Maybe he should get laid. There was a conference coming in called GayRomLit—there had to be someone he could have a one off with. But the thought of anyone but Kase made him ill. Fuck, he had it bad.

"You're an idiot." Gib had his elbows on the bar and cradled his face in his hands.

"Excuse me?" Quinn raised an eyebrow.

"Here you are moping and we both know it's your fault."

"You're a bartender—not a shrink." Quinn tipped the beer bottle towards Gib before drinking.

"And you need to loosen up." Gib straightened up.

"He's young—he needs someone not so beaten up by life."

They both knew they were talking about Kase. Gib was too easy to talk to.

Gib snorted. "He's not that young."

"He's a baby and so are you."

"Oh, no you don't. You're not turning this around on me." Gib pointed at him.

Quinn finished his beer and wiggled the bottle. "I need another."

"And I'm cutting you off."

"I've only had one. Come on, Gib."

"Go home. Call him."

"Why don't you call him?"

"He's not my type. And I don't think he'll pay. Also, something tells me you're his papa bear. Now, stop bringing down the mood and get out of here." Gib threw the bar towel at Quinn.

Quinn caught it easily and tossed it back. He put some money on the bar with a nice tip, not that it would keep Gib from turning tricks, but every bit helped. Shit, when did he become the protector of all? He was getting old.

"See you around, Gib. Stay safe. Call if you need me."

"I won't need you." Gib winked and turned away.

"I'm serious."

Gib nodded at him and went back to work. Quinn went out of the front door and waved to Esteban Parks, the Front Desk Manager. He was happy Esteban was working tonight—he'd keep an eye out for Gib. Quinn wondered what was up with Esteban and that conference attendee, Jayden, but it really wasn't any of his business. Esteban was good people. He was good to Gib—Quinn kind of wished the two would get together, but he wasn't up to playing matchmaker any more than he was to being in love with an untarnished hero. So, now Quinn would go home to his empty house. Maybe tonight he wouldn't dream of things better left alone.

Chapter Two

Kasey looked down at his watch before getting out of his car. Quinn should be on shift and Kasey's plan was to corner the big bastard. Kasey had skipped class that morning and even called in to take the night off work because this was serious, at least to him. Kasey was tired of the evasion techniques. He'd tried Quinn's house last night and he either hadn't been there or he'd been ignoring Kasey. Quinn also hadn't answered his phone or returned the hundreds of messages he'd left. Kasey knew what Quinn was doing and he wasn't going to let him get away with it.

For some reason the big lug thought Kasey deserved better. He'd grumbled about it a couple of times and Kasey ignored it because it was the most asinine thing he had ever heard. Quinn might be older than Kasey, but Kasey'd had his own life experiences. He wasn't a kid and he'd do whatever it took to prove that to Quinn. He was in love with Quinn and he wasn't going to stop loving him just because of some noble notion that Quinn was damaged goods.

Screw that.

He aspired to be as good a man as Quinn. Hell that was what his life goal was—to help other people so that what happened to his brother didn't happen to other kids. And Quinn—he was a bona fide hero. He'd served his country for many years, had even got injured in the line of duty. And he was so strong and his big hands...

None of that. He couldn't think of sex right now. Kasey did a quick adjustment of his cock because anytime he thought of Quinn he got horny. Today was about getting Quinn back. Moving the relationship along and staying together. Quinn wasn't forgettable in any way, shape or form.

Kasey was lucky enough to find a parking spot not too far away. The walk to the hotel helped him clear his mind. He would have to be on his game or Quinn would shoot him down with the whole '*I'm older and have seen too much*' line. He wiped his palms on his pants. He was getting a bit nervous. This was his life here and he had to convince a hard-headed former solider that they were right for each other.

The revolving doors were right ahead and beyond them lay his future. He smoothed out his shirt and took a deep breath. He'd need to talk to someone inside to find out what room Quinn was in. Maybe Gib? Or Quinn had talked about a guy named Esteban. He could be working.

Kasey walked up to the counter. "Excuse me, but is Esteban working today?"

"Yes, I am Esteban. How may I help you today?" Esteban smiled at him.

Kasey didn't know what he'd expected, but it wasn't the gorgeous man in front of him. It took a moment for him to find his words.

"I'm sorry to bother you. I'm looking for Quinn."

The smile disappeared. He wondered why.

"And you are?" Esteban cocked an eyebrow.

"I'm Kasey Adams and... I've heard Quinn talk about you. I really need to see him."

Kasey fidgeted while Esteban stared at him. This might have been a very bad idea, but he was running out of options.

Esteban sighed and moved to the computer. God, Kasey hoped he wasn't about to get booted out of the hotel by security. He was just about to let Esteban know he wasn't going to make a scene when his panic was alleviated.

"Don't make me regret this." Esteban clicked a few buttons on the keyboard. "He's on the fifth floor."

"Thank you. Thank you!" Kasey waved and hurried to the elevator before Esteban changed his mind and sent security after all.

It was the longest ride up—ever. The door opened on the fifth floor and he had no idea where to start. He should have got a room number, but maybe they didn't have that in the system. He didn't know much about what went on behind the scenes at a hotel. He just knew that after dating Quinn he would never leave a hotel room a mess like he had back in his younger years.

There was a cart by one of the rooms. Kasey hoped it was Quinn's. He should really find out how the assignments were given out. Did Quinn have the whole floor? And why did it really matter? The nonsense going on in his head right now was his coping technique. He needed to man up and get into that room.

He peeked around the door and sure enough—there was Quinn with his back to him. God, he was so striking. It was the way he held himself—one of the first things Kasey had noticed about him. He had a regal bearing. He must have made a noise because Quinn turned around. *Shit.* Kasey had startled him — probably not the best way to start a talk.

Quinn smiled at first then frowned. "What — ?"

"No. You don't get to talk right now. You have to listen." Kasey walked into the room and firmly closed the door.

"Kase —" Quinn took a step back.

"I believe I said I was going to talk. I love you. Yes, you heard that right. I know it's fast and unexpected, but that doesn't make it any less true. I'm not going to stand for you giving me the silent treatment. We belong together and I'm going to prove it."

"You need to leave." Quinn crossed his arms over his chest.

Kasey knew it was meant to be intimidating, but it only worked at turning him on — despite the words coming out of Quinn's mouth.

"I tell you I love you and that's your response?" Kasey laughed.

It was just like Quinn. But his man wasn't going to run from this. He'd been running too long. Kasey moved right in front of Quinn and pushed him down on the bed and turned to close the curtains.

"I'm working, this really isn't the best time." Quinn moved like he was going to get off the bed, but Kasey just pointed at him.

"When would be a good time? I'd call you, but you seem not to answer. And I could totally stop by your house, but guess what? You don't answer the fucking door, Quinn."

"Look, I know you're upset. I get it, but it's over, kid."

"No, you don't get to do this. I'm not some kid. I know you, Quinn, and I see what you're doing. This isn't protecting me. I'm not the one running from this."

Kasey knelt on the ground between Quinn's thighs and gripped his legs.

"It's just sex, Kasey. That's all it was every supposed to be. You got too serious and — "

"Bullshit. You're trying to be noble and you don't need to be. Why can't you understand that?"

He made the mistake of looking down at Quinn's crotch. Kasey gulped. Quinn was hard. This was it. He had to do this. Quinn thought it was just about sex? He'd show him what 'just sex' was like between the two of them. Maybe then he'd see the difference between getting off and the real connection they shared.

"Kasey — what... You can't — Shit — "

Kasey unbuckled and unzipped Quinn's pants. Before he lost his nerve, he took Quinn's cock into his hands. He was as hard as steel. Kasey licked the tip of Quinn's dick before sucking the head into his mouth. He ran his tongue under the edge — focusing on just that bit of skin. He scooted closer and used his hands to pump the shaft a couple of times before letting go. He knew what would get Quinn off the fastest. He gripped Quinn's thighs, took Quinn's shaft to the back of his throat and swallowed. Quinn squeezed Kasey's shoulders, but Kasey wasn't going to look up. This was about getting off as quick as possible. Quinn was close, which was a good thing because, for all of Kasey's focus, he heard voices coming down the hallway. He really hoped they weren't coming into this room, but with the way his luck had been, he wasn't going to chance it.

Kasey sped up and he started to use his hands again, bobbing up and down. The voices were getting closer. He needed to finish Quinn off.

"I really wish DC Juris had come. I wanted to see him again."

"I know. Maybe next year. Hey—what are you wearing tonight?"

Hurry, hurry, hurry.

The voices stopped at the door. Quinn shot down his throat as the door clicked. Fuck, they were using the card and would be in the room any second. His face exploded in pain. Quinn had jumped up so fast, he'd kneed Kasey in the face. He shook it off and stood. Quinn was getting himself together when the door swung open to the stunned faces of two women. He really didn't want to get Quinn fired. He tore the sheets off the bed Quinn had been sitting on and turned to face his lover.

"That right there, Quinn—that was just sex," he whispered and marched out of the room, brushing past the woman to throw the dirty sheets into Quinn's cart.

He really hoped he hadn't just fucked up his whole relationship because he'd had to prove a point.

Chapter Three

Fuck. Quinn had no idea how much the girls in the doorway had seen. He finished adjusting his pants. Talk about awkward. Quinn wasn't an exhibitionist and liked to keep his sex private. His face had to be red—he'd almost got caught with his pants down.

"Sorry 'bout that. I'll be done in just a minute."

The girls looked between each other and smiled.

"That's fine. I'm Ive. You? And who was the hottie that just left? He didn't look like housekeeping—boyfriend?"

"Ive!" the other girl all but shouted.

"Rhonda!" Ive teased back.

"Ahh...Quinn?" This was a new one for him and he was off his game.

"Ahh-Quinn, good to meet you. And the other hottie?" The one called Ive winked at him. She was bold.

"Kasey."

"Kasey and Quinn—you guys going to hang around this weekend? Come to some parties?"

"We're not... I—" He hadn't been this flustered since he'd stepped off the bus at boot camp.

"Yeah, your chemistry is off the charts and something tells me we should have gotten to the room a bit sooner for a show." If it was possible, Ive's grin got bigger. It didn't seem as if anything would shock her. The other girl—Rhonda?—she was quieter. She'd gone to sit in the chair out of the way.

"Let me just get your sheets."

Thank God he was about done with the room. He needed to get out of there. He hurried to the cart to get what he needed and finished the bed. He thanked all above that he'd got off before that door had opened. A few seconds earlier and the girls would have walked in on him getting the most unemotional blow job he'd ever received. He nodded to the girls and left the room to the sound of giggling.

He shut the door and pushed the cart to the next room. He felt empty and sick to his stomach and it was his own damn fault. If Kasey had wanted to prove a point, he'd done it. He'd been lying his ass off anyway. *God.*

It's just sex, Kasey.

He should have never uttered those words. They'd left a bad taste in his mouth the second they'd come out and the hurt look on Kasey's face would haunt him.

Quinn still thought it was for the best, but he couldn't leave things this way. Kasey had said he loved him. How could he know? Was the ache in his chest...love?

There wasn't anything he could do about it right then. He had to finish his job. The day was still young so he'd have to stew in this bad feeling for the rest of the day. He needed a beer.

And he needed to stop thinking about Kasey's eyes—the hurt in them and how they'd started to tear up. Quinn had done that. It was his fault things had got to the point where Kasey'd had to track Quinn down at work just so he could talk to him. How did Quinn repay Kasey? By telling him they had nothing but sex.

With a heavy sigh, he started cleaning the next room. He went to the bathroom first to scrub it down, hoping the work would take his mind off his issues, but just like yesterday it wasn't working.

He was going to have to sit down and talk to Kasey. Stop running off like the kid he kept accusing Kasey of being. He had no idea what he was going to say, but he needed him to understand that Quinn wasn't the guy for him.

How had Kasey known where to find him anyway? A knock on the door took him out of his thoughts.

"Quinn? You okay?"

Esteban. He should have known. The man liked to know what was going on in the hotel at all times and he'd probably talked to Gib. They all seemed to talk to the bartender. *Nosy bastard.* He went back to cleaning out the tub.

"Just a little afternoon delight, you know." Quinn shrugged.

"I'm sorry. I shouldn't have sent him up, but—"

"No worries, man. Once I'm finished here I'll head up and clean the out of service room."

"That isn't why I'm here." Esteban huffed.

"I'm good. You should get on out of here and let me finish up. Really, it's fine."

"All right, but if you need anything…"

"I'll give you a call. But like I said—we're all good."

The door clicked shut and he didn't bother to turn around. He couldn't, because if he had, Esteban wouldn't have left. Quinn hadn't cried in a long time, but it looked like he was going to start now. He was all over the place. Just once—maybe he should be selfish. Kasey made him feel… Feel, period. When he'd got home from the Army he'd been broken. Just a shell of his former self. Knowing Kasey was the one bright thing he had. Now he was on the verge of giving up and Kasey might really listen to him and move on. Then where would he be? Right back where he'd left off. Alone.

He *was* an idiot. Quinn hated that Gib was right. But what could he do now? It was his fault they were in this mess. He'd panicked and it would serve him right if Kasey did move on. Just seeing Kasey again after not talking to him made him dizzy. He'd never felt that way about another man. Did that really make it love? He didn't know how to deal with love. And who could he go to for advice? He didn't have any close friends. He had a buddy from his Army days, but he was over in Afghanistan. No way was he going to bother him with his petty bullshit. Gib would just call him an idiot again or worse if he talked to him. Quinn was on his own with this. That didn't bode well for anyone. Why was it easier to shoot someone than to fall in love with them?

It was going to be a long ass day with just him, the cleaning and his feelings. He had no idea if Kasey was working that night, but his first stop would be the restaurant after his shift. Someone there had to know where Kasey was if he wasn't working.

He walked into the next room and shook his head. The stuff the conference people left out in their room was enough to make most blush. This room had safe sex kits by the hundreds sitting on the table. There were some books around too. He picked one up and put it down really fast. It had two almost naked men wrapped around each other.

Quinn didn't need to see that because now all he could picture was him and Kasey in that position. He didn't realise until then how much it really bugged him to have had the blow job with no cuddle time after. Usually he would get to hold Kasey and they'd go to sleep or watch some television. But that was when they'd been together.

What happened back in that room was just sex. That was the fact he kept coming back to. Kasey wasn't a back alley fling. They did have more. *Damn it*. He needed to get his ass in gear and finish his rooms so maybe he could get off early and go hunt Kasey down before things got worse. It was all his fucking fault and he needed to fix it. Asap.

Chapter Four

Kasey put his head down on the table. He had no idea why he went to the restaurant. He should have picked a bar and drowned his sorrows there. Or gone home to be alone. That would have been his best bet, but he needed his friends and most of them worked here. So here he was—having a pity party for one.

"Kase, why're you here? I thought you were sick." He felt a hand on his shoulder.

"I am," he mumbled into the table.

"So?"

"I'm heart sick. I did something *really* stupid today." Kasey sighed and lifted his head. His friend Kelli was there—at least it was her and not Amber. Amber would just cry with him and tell him everything would be okay. He needed more than that tonight and Kelli was the person to help.

"What did you do, honey? Shit! What happened to your face?" Kelli brushed her finger over his eye.

Kasey flinched away. It wasn't too bad, but it did hurt.

"I went after Quinn. He wouldn't talk to me and—"

"Keep going. He didn't do this to you, did he? I'll hunt him down."

That wasn't how the conversation was supposed to go, but he should be used to that by now. Nothing should surprise him… "And I went to the hotel and gave him a blow job."

Not even what came out of his own mouth. He sounded so stupid.

"What?" Kelli laughed.

If he looked back, it was a bit funny — the part where he actually went to his boyfriend's work for a quickie. But…Quinn wasn't his boyfriend. He put his head back down.

"He told me it was just sex so…I showed him what just sex was like. It was awful — kind of. I mean, afterward it was. And then these woman walked in, he scrambled to get up and kneed my face and —"

Kelli laughed harder. "Hold on. I'm going to take my break."

Kasey moved his head so he could watch Kelli walk off. His life was a mess. College was a bitch, but he could handle that. There was a lot he could handle and he didn't want to just *handle* Quinn. He wanted them to hold each other up. Kasey wanted to be what Quinn needed, but maybe he wasn't that man.

He saw Kelli hurrying back with ice and drinks in her hand. Ahh — liquid courage. He could use a drink or five.

"Thanks." He took the shot she handed him and threw it back. Then she gave him the ice wrapped in a towel and he put it against his eye.

"Anytime. Now start at the beginning."

He nodded and closed his eyes. He was such a fool.

"Okay, Quinn stopped talking to me. Like — one day he wouldn't answer my calls and he sure as hell didn't call me. I thought everything was going great, I mean—this was after weeks of dating."

"Fucking you mean."

"Shut it, bitch," he said affectionately and gave a weak smile. "It was more than that. We were with each other in all of our spare time and we—I don't know—clicked. Then nothing. I got tired of waiting so I went to the Meliá and found out what floor he was on. He was all stoic when I got there, and I got pissed."

"So, when you get angry, you give out blow jobs?" Kelli chuckled.

"Stop." He laughed. "He said we were all about sex, but I know it was more than that. I *know* it. So I thought I'd show him the difference. Just as he was about to come—the occupants of the room showed up. I have no idea how much they saw and I really don't want to know. Then I said something mean and left. I don't know what I'm going to do."

"You aren't going to do anything."

"How can you say that? I might have ruined it." He couldn't believe the advice she was giving him. Shouldn't she be telling him to storm the castle, so to speak? To go get his man?

"No, if anyone ruined it, it was Quinn," Kelli insisted.

"No—it was totally me. He was trying to be noble and I wasn't going to let him."

"I think the ball is in his court now. He either loves you or he doesn't, but you can't keep chasing after him or you're going to let him break your heart even more. Give it some time."

Kelli was right. He'd done everything he could. Quinn knew he...loved...him...

"Oh. My. God. I told him I loved him," Kasey wailed and slammed his head back onto the table.

Ouch.

Good thing they weren't busy—he was making an ass out of himself. He really should have gone home.

"Breathe. Do you need another drink?" Kelli stroked a hand down his back.

It was soothing, but not the touch he wanted—the one he craved.

"No, I should just go home."

"And wallow? No. Amber gets off in about a half hour. You two can go out and dance or something. Get your mind off things for a while. I close, but I'll meet you there when I'm done."

"I'm not going to a bar for hours and getting drunk."

It wasn't like he drank a lot normally. If he went to a bar and started pounding back the liquor, feeling the way he did right now, he might never stop. It really wasn't the best idea and he was already behind in his school work. The classes kept getting harder as he went along, but it was his calling—something he loved—and he didn't want to fail. Working on top of going to college was tough, but he'd got into a nice pattern. The only thing missing was Quinn. And that brought him right back to thoughts of drinking away his sorrows.

"Why not?"

"Why don't I want to get my drunk on? I have makeup stuff from class to do tomorrow and a test to study for."

"Then don't get drunk. Just go have a bit of fun. Let off some steam. But—eat first. I'll bring you something out."

Kasey just nodded. There was no way Kelli would listen to him when she was in bossy mom mode. He'd just have to go out with Amber and see what trouble they could get into. Because, really? What more could he do to convince Quinn they were right for each other? If there was a next time, he'd need to keep it to talking and not sex. Lord knows that the sex between them was always off the hook, but it shouldn't be used as a weapon. It was the quiet times curled on the couch watching a football game or some lame ass chick flick that Quinn seemed to like—*that* was the 'more' he wanted and playing dirty wasn't going to get him there.

Or when Quinn woke up screaming and Kasey was there to talk him down and let him know it was okay—he was there. Quinn never talked much about his time in the military, but Kasey didn't blame him. He knew it would come in time—if they had more time. Oh, please God, let there be more time.

It didn't take long for his food to come. Amber came out to join him before he'd finished. One thing he could say for Escorpion, the food was really great and so was the atmosphere. It was one of the reasons he started working there. That was before his brother had died. Shit, he hated when he got sad because it always brought back memories of his brother and how he hadn't been able to save him from bullies. His brother had been a hero too. Trent, his brother, had seen a smaller kid being picked on by a group of kids and had gone to help. It had been in his nature to be the protector. He'd got shot for his efforts.

Man, he really did need that drink now. Good thing Amber was so happy and bubbly tonight. He wouldn't tell her about Quinn to make sure she stayed that way and maybe it would eventually put him in a better mood.

Chapter Five

Quinn was later than he'd expected, but he was off work now and it was time to get to the restaurant and fix things. He hoped Kasey was working. If not, he'd go by his house. He had to believe Kasey was more grown up about things and would answer the door. His last resort was a phone call, but he knew how easy those were to dodge. He was ashamed of himself and it had been a *long* time since he'd felt that emotion.

One of the things he'd always said to himself was he needed to be true to who he was. He might not have been out to all of the guys in his platoon, but he had been to the ones who mattered. His family knew and he didn't give a flying fuck about anyone else. Now, here he was, running from something good because he was scared.

He walked to the front door and saw that Kelli was working. Good. She was one of Kasey's best friends. She would know where he was.

"Kelli, is Kasey working tonight?"

She glared at him. That wasn't good.

"Why do you care?"

Shit. Yep, Kasey must have talked to her already.

"I need to talk to him." He tried to give her his best puppy dog eyes, but it wasn't working.

"I think you've done enough damage, don't you?" She crossed her arms over her chest. She was almost as big as he was—but not as muscled. She could hold her own in a fight. Her long dark hair was in braids and her bright green eyes seemed to look right through him.

"I've been an idiot. I know that and you know that, but I need to tell Kasey."

"You think he doesn't know you're a jackass? You didn't see his face, man." Kelli shook her head.

"Yes, I did. Please." He would beg if he had to. He wasn't above grovelling.

"He isn't here." Kelli dropped her arms to her side.

"Do you know where he's at?"

"Maybe." She wasn't giving an inch.

"Are you going to tell me?"

The please was implied that time. He wasn't playing hardball. He needed her help.

"I don't know if I should." Kelli shook her head.

"Just give me another chance." He clasped his hands together and closed his eyes.

"Don't hurt him because if you do I will hunt you down and you'll think you had your worst nightmare revisit from overseas. Got it?" Kelli poked him in the chest.

"Yes, ma'am." Quinn nodded.

He knew Kelli meant business. She was a bad ass former Marine. Men didn't mess with those chicks. The ones he'd met were all crazy—Kelli included—but he wouldn't want anyone else at his back. He was very happy Kasey had her as a friend.

"Amber took him to Mary's. I was going to head over there, but if you're going I won't. Have him call me."

"Thank you!" Quinn pulled Kelli to him and kissed her cheek before running to the door.

"Don't hurt him!" Kelli yelled after him.

Not this time. He had no intention of letting Kasey go again. He was done being stupid.

Traffic was hell on a Friday night and it didn't help that he was in a hurry. He should have taken a cab, but he wasn't in his right mind. He just wanted to get to the bar and see Kasey. To tell him he was sorry, and if Kasey wanted to, they could make it work.

He wanted to be the one in the stands when Kasey graduated with his Bachelor's degree. It should be him standing beside him when Kasey had a bad day. And there would be bad days. Kasey was going to work with troubled kids and there was no way he could save them all, no matter how he tried. Quinn wanted to be the one there to help him through those days.

It took him about half an hour to get to Mary's. It wasn't too busy yet. That would change around eleven. He was lucky to find a nice spot to park.

Kasey wasn't that hard to find. He was with Amber on the small dance floor. It was just the two of them jumping around. They looked like they were in their own little world. Quinn looked around. There weren't many people in the place. Granted, it was still early, but he'd expected more. Or—he'd thought it would be harder to get to Kasey. It didn't seem like such a grand display with only a handful of people about.

"Kasey."

Kasey stumbled and turned. Quinn reached out to steady him.

"What the fuck happened to your face?"

"You." Kasey pointed to him and giggled, but never once stopped dancing.

"What?" Quinn couldn't have heard right. He would never lay a hand on Kasey. Never.

"When you got up from the bed — kneed me in the face." Kasey gestured towards his eye. He was still unsteady.

Amber danced around them and waved to Quinn. He waved back and looked down at Kasey.

"Shit. I am *so* sorry." Quinn ran a hand down Kasey's cheek.

"No problem. That happens when you're just sexin' it up, dude." Kasey held a hand to his face and giggled again.

"How much have you had to drink?"

"Um...don't know. Why ya wanna know? None of your business, Mr Not Boyfriend." Kasey pushed Quinn away, skipped to Amber and twirled her around.

They were both drunk off their asses. He should have asked Kelli how long they'd been there. He made his way up to the bar.

"Hey, how much have they had?" He used his thumb to point behind him.

The bartender shrugged. He was no Gib, that was for sure. "Coupla shots, few pitchers of beer."

"Thanks." Quinn gave the guy a nod and went back to the dance floor. There was no way he was going to get his talk in with Kasey tonight. Somehow he had to convince Kasey to go home with him. It wasn't going to be easy.

"Kasey, let's go home."

"Don't wanna. Havin' fun."

"We need to talk."

"Tried that — denied."

"I didn't—"

"Oh yes, you did. Now"—Kasey held out his hand to Quinn's face—"good night."

"Please."

"Why? Huh? Why now? Was the blow job that good?" Kasey was almost shouting now.

"Fuck. Let's talk about this when you're sober."

"Let's not. It's more fun this way!"

"No. Okay. It sucked—"

Kasey laughed. It took a second for Quinn to figure out why. He rolled his eyes.

"Kasey, I was an ass. I know this. There is a difference between just sex and what we have."

"You couldn't have picked up the phone once?" Kasey held a finger in front of Quinn's face.

Quinn took a hold of it and drew Kasey closer. A slow song had come on and thankfully Amber left the dance floor. He rocked them back and forth, loving the press of Kasey's body against his. Kasey had melted into him and hugged him tight. He hoped that was a good sign. He had to make it right. They weren't over, they couldn't be.

Chapter Six

Kasey's head pounded. He groaned and pressed his hands against his temples, but it wasn't making the ache go away. He shouldn't have had so much to drink. And he couldn't remember—had Kelli ever showed up? Amber had driven them to Mary's. They'd had a couple of shots, some beer and... *Oh shit...*

He shot up in bed and winced. Slower would have been better. He opened his eyes. Kasey wasn't at home. This was Quinn's house. So Quinn *had* come to the bar. He remembered dancing...maybe some yelling. Only moving his eyes, he used his peripheral vision to see if Quinn was in bed with him. Nope, it was just him. He lifted the covers and—yep—he was naked. Kasey took stock of his body. He didn't ache in any odd places—just his head from all the booze.

There was a glass of water on the table and a pill. He gulped down the water and took the medicine. He needed more water. His mouth was very dry, but his stomach wasn't as queasy as he'd thought it would be—it was only his head bothering him and the ache was becoming a dull roar.

"Oh, you're awake. Sorry." Quinn paused at the entrance to the bedroom.

"No." He had to clear his throat. "That's fine. Ahh... Did we—um... You...?"

"We danced and I brought you home after we dropped off Amber. Nothing happened other than you throwing up all over yourself before I could get you to the bathroom. I made you take a pain reliever and drink a glass of water before you passed out. Your clothes are in the dryer."

Quinn looked so good standing there holding a tray in his hands in nothing but a pair of boxer briefs. All those muscles he wanted to touch and nibble and...

Oh, God. Wait. Not yet.

"We should talk," Kasey managed to get out before he made a fool of himself and started to drool.

"Yes, we need to. That's why I went to the restaurant last night."

"You did?" Quinn had come looking for him? Kasey's heart fluttered.

Or was that butterflies in his stomach? It could be the hangover.

"Yep. I was looking for you. Kelli was kind enough to tell me where you were."

Kasey managed to lift an eyebrow without too much pain. Quinn squirmed a bit in the doorway.

"Okay, I begged and she finally told me. I called her to let her know you'd be here and you'd get with her later today."

"Thank you." Kasey looked down at the comforter and plucked at it. It shouldn't be awkward, but it was, just a little. Quinn had never seen him drunk. At least not like he'd been last night. He wondered if he seemed even more immature to Quinn now. He didn't like this feeling at all.

"No need for that. I have to say, I'm sorry. Really, really sorry and I could understand if you never wanted to see me again. I was stupid. Can you forgive me?"

Kasey slowly moved his head so he could look at Quinn. It felt heavy on his shoulders and he wanted to lay back down, but not yet.

"Forgive you?"

He waited to see what Quinn would say. They both needed to apologise for how out of control the situation had got.

"Yes. For telling you we only had sex. I knew that was wrong before I even said it and then when you— Yeah, I understood even more than you can even imagine." Quinn wiped his hand over his face. "That was one of the emptiest experiences I've ever had. That includes back alley hook-ups."

"God, Quinn..." Now he felt like a shit and he should. What he'd done was out of line.

He'd taken the low road instead of sticking to his guns and talking. Communication was important. He'd learnt that from his parents after his brother had died.

"No, let me finish because I deserved what happened. I should have talked to you. I know that— but you're so...bright." Quinn waved his arm around and held onto the tray with one hand.

"That makes no sense."

Was he still drunk? What did being bright have to do with anything?

"I mean—shiny..."

Or maybe Quinn had been drinking. Something wasn't working right.

"Still not getting it." If this was talking, it was making his head hurt even more. He was so confused.

Quinn put the tray on the nightstand and sat down next to Kasey. His body was so warm and Kasey wanted to hug Quinn—and maybe lick him or something—but first they had to talk or they wouldn't make it. And he so desperately wanted to be with Quinn for the long haul.

"You have such a big heart and you want to make the world a better place. I get that. But I gave all I could when I served. I can't—"

"And I'm not asking you. Yes, I want to do my part, just like you did, but the military isn't my path. Helping kids *is*. I just want you to be there for me."

"That I can do. But you should have someone stand there with you—"

"I will have that. With you. Don't you get that? We don't have to be the same person. We can have different wants that mesh. I don't want someone like me—that might get annoying."

"Hey!" Quinn laughed.

"It's true. You ground me. I don't think you get that. When I get all gung ho, you bring me down to the real world. I love that about you. I..." Kasey was going to say it a second time before Quinn said it even once, but he could do this. "I love you, Quinn Nelson."

"I love you too, Kasey Adams," Quinn whispered before crawling up the bed to lay down beside Kasey.

"Say it again."

Quinn moved so he was hovering over Kasey, using his arms to hold him up. Quinn was so strong. Kasey licked his lips and Quinn looked down at them, lowering his head. He brushed his lips against Kasey's and Kasey groaned.

"I. Love. You." Quinn punctuated each word with a kiss.

Kasey wanted to hear them again and again. He'd never tire of Quinn telling him he loved him.

"Tell me we can work this out. I don't want to lose you, Quinn."

"I don't want to lose you either, but this probably won't be the last time I do something stupid. I ran scared. I'm sorry. I shouldn't have stopped calling."

"No, you shouldn't have and I shouldn't have made something between us turn so ugly. What I did was wrong too. So—let's get past that and get to some makeup sex."

Chapter Seven

Makeup sex. Quinn could handle that, but he had more to make up for.

"First, let's get you some food. And maybe some more water. Shoot." Quinn moved off Kasey and reached towards the tray for the forgotten ice pack. Kasey's eye still looked a little swollen.

"What—"

"Ice pack. I can't believe I hit you in the face like that." Quinn handed the ice over and kissed Kasey on the cheek.

Kasey turned and began rubbing against Quinn.

"I don't need an ice pack, Quinn. What I need is my cock up my boyfriend's ass and if the old man can get it up again…his up mine."

"Why you—" Quinn threw back his head and laughed. Really laughed. He hadn't felt this good in weeks. Kasey did that for him. Took him outside of himself and let Quinn have fun. Quinn rolled back over Kasey and pinned him to the bed.

"Now, Quinn—"

"Nope. You started it, kid." Quinn leant down and whispered against Kasey's ear. "And it's going to be my dick in your ass. I'm going to make you come so hard you'll see stars."

"Uhng—"

Quinn grinned and nipped Kasey's earlobe. He kissed his way to Kasey's injured eye and gave it the lightest grazing of a kiss. He didn't want to hurt him. Then he took his mouth again. Nothing fast. He wanted it to go slow, first licking his lips—back and forth—making Kasey whimper and open his mouth. Quinn deepened the kiss and moaned. He'd missed this and was going to savour each and every second.

He moved from Kasey's lips and scraped his teeth along Kasey's throat, making sure not to leave a mark. At least not there. He lightly bit Kasey's nipple. Kasey rocked his hips. There was only a blanket between them and Quinn wanted to see his lover's body. Stopping what he was doing, he jerked the covering off Kasey and threw it to the floor.

And there he was in all his glory. Quinn shucked his underwear before pressing his naked body against Kasey's. They both hissed at the first taste of skin on skin. Quinn went back to where he'd left off—Kasey's pretty pink nipples, all rosy and beaded up for him. He sucked hard.

"Fuck! Quinn."

"Nope…fuck Kasey." Quinn gave an evil chuckle.

"I want you inside me." Kasey clutched at Quinn's ass, moving them closer as if he could force Quinn's cock into him.

"Not yet."

"Please," Kasey whined.

"Nope." Quinn went to the other nipple, giving it the same treatment before making his way down Kasey's body.

It was a masterpiece and a painting should be done of its magnificent glory—but only for Quinn to see. God, he could look at Kasey all day and still not get enough. What the hell had he been thinking?

He reached Kasey's dick, but he wasn't going to suck it. He had to make Kasey ready because as much as he said he needed to take his time and explore, it was getting to the point where he was going to explode and he wanted inside his lover before that happened. It had been too long.

Quinn lifted Kasey's legs.

"Hold on."

Kasey grabbed his own thighs and lifted up so Quinn could see his wrinkled hole. He licked a path from Kasey's opening to his balls. He drew them into his mouth, laving them with attention before going back to Kasey's ass. He licked and sucked, making Kasey wild before he added a finger.

"More, please. Quinn."

This time Quinn didn't ignore him and added a second finger, still tonguing that beautiful hole that he was going to be inside very soon.

"Lube," Quinn grunted.

Kasey twisted a bit, but Quinn didn't stop. He added another finger and blew on the hole, watching it quiver with Kasey's need.

A condom and lube landed by his hand. Kasey groaned as Quinn's fingers slid from his body.

"Shh—soon." Quinn ran a hand over Kasey's shaking thighs and placed Kasey's legs over his shoulders. He crawled onto the bed, folding him almost in half.

Quinn kissed Kasey's calf and stroked Kasey's legs, feeling the little prickles of hair. Quinn had missed this connection. Just being this close to Kasey was going to his head. He needed inside.

"Quinn...Quinn..."

Kasey was beautiful as he tossed and turned on the bed. Quinn tore at the condom wrapper, his hands shaking as he slid it on. The lube was next and he fumbled with it before coating his cock. He rubbed the excess into Kasey's hole, his dick kissing the entrance. Kasey pushed against him, trying to take things faster. Quinn stopped Kasey's movement and inched inside.

"Quinn, damn it. Hurry."

"Shh—"

Kasey's ass clinched around Quinn's erection. He was going to come too soon.

"Kasey—slow, please. Let me—"

"Move, please, please, please," Kasey whimpered and tugged at his cock.

He was beautiful. And all Quinn's. Finally, he was balls deep and they slapped against Kasey's ass. He liked the sound and moved just a bit to hear it again. Quinn closed his eyes and counted to ten. If he didn't, he would be spent before he even began. It was taking every ounce of willpower he had because Kasey was going wild underneath him.

"Kasey, grab the headboard. Go on."

"Just...fucking *move*."

Kasey was panting now, tugging away at his dick.

"Do it or I won't move."

"Motherfucker. God, Quinn!" Kasey complained, but he listened and did as he'd been told.

Once Kasey was situated in the way Quinn wanted him, Quinn moved Kasey's legs so his lover was almost bent in half. He eased out before slamming back in again and again. Kasey wanted it fast and hard? Quinn was going to give it to him.

Kasey had his hands braced so he didn't hit the headboard. It didn't take long before he came all over his stomach. The sight sent Quinn into a frenzy. A few more pumps and he collapsed onto Kasey. He quickly rolled over, threw the used condom into the trash then cuddled Kasey to his side, both of them breathing hard. Quinn closed his eyes and put his arm over his face.

"Now that—that was really, really great." Kasey sighed.

"Yes, it was." Quinn turned towards Kasey and tugged him closer, putting one of his legs over Kasey's thighs, tangling them together. They stared into each other's eyes.

"I love you, Quinn. Don't make me chase you down again."

"Not going to happen. I love you, too. And maybe next time we have a bit of afternoon delight, we'll mean it and have some fun. Um…preferably in our own room."

"Oh my God. You don't think they—"

"Those women? I don't think they saw much, but one of them was asking all kinds of questions. She knew something was up."

Kasey buried his head against Quinn's shoulder.

"I'm sorry. You won't get in trouble for that, will you?"

"I don't think she will say anything. She was talking about wishing she'd gotten there earlier for a show." Quinn shuddered.

"What?" Kasey exclaimed.

"Yeah—didn't you know? The hotel is hosting a convention for gay romance readers or something."

Kasey snorted. "And we almost gave them real live porn." Now Kasey was laughing.

Quinn joined in. It was good.

"Thank you," Quinn whispered.

Kasey leant back to look at him. "For what?" His brow was wrinkled in confusion.

"Bringing laughter back into my life. When you're here, things are...shiny."

"There you go with that shiny crap again."

"But it's true. I'm a better person when I'm around you. So...thank you." Quinn kissed Kasey's forehead, smoothing it out.

"Okay then. I'll take it. You're welcome."

Quinn smiled and squeezed Kasey closer. They could have this all the time now.

"Move in with me."

Quinn was as stunned as Kasey looked. He hadn't meant to say it, but thinking about it—it was the right thing to do. The next big step and they were ready to take it. He wasn't going to run anymore. Kasey might deserve better, but he was getting Quinn and that was the end of it. Maybe some of the shiny would rub off.

"Are you sure?"

"Yes. This way you won't have to worry about me not calling. Right?"

"Don't joke."

"Okay, I won't. I do mean it. You have school and work. This way we can have more time together without being rushed. I have a spare room we can convert into an office for you and... Yeah, let's do this."

"Then yes!" Kasey wiggled out of the bed.

"Hey, where are you going?"

"To get my clothes. We've got things to do."

"What?"

"When do you work next?"

"Tomorrow, why?"

"Well, I have college Monday and work—uh—tonight? Yup—tonight. So let's start moving." Kasey slapped Quinn's hip.

Quinn pulled him back down onto the bed.

"Full stop there, Kasey." Quinn laughed. "I want you to move your stuff in as well, like as soon as possible, but I need to move stuff around to make room for yours and we should go through things to see what we want to keep or get rid of, right?"

Kasey sighed, but melted back into the bed. "See, that's what I mean. Grounding me. You're right. So what are we going to do today? More makeup sex?"

"You've got studying to do and we need to eat. Then we can go over and grab a few of your things for now so you can come back here after work. Hold on a second." Quinn got out of bed.

Kasey gave him a wolf whistle, but Quinn kept going until he reached the front door. He searched the bowl that he kept near there for when he came home and looked for... He knew it was there somewhere...

Ah ha!

Quinn took the extra key and headed back to the bedroom and tossed it at Kasey. Kasey leapt off the bed and threw himself into Quinn's arms.

"A week ago, I was worried we'd never get here." Kasey peppered kisses over Quinn's face.

"Thank God you brought me to my senses."

"Yeah—and we are never doing that again."

"Amen."

He tossed Kasey onto the bed and followed him down. Now he had his easy job and could come home to that cold beer, TV...and Kasey. Life didn't get any better than that. And maybe along the way, he'd get back his own optimism about the world. With Kasey in his life, it would be easier to be a man Kasey could love.

"Stop thinking and fuck me again."

"Yes, sir."

He'd have to put nooners on his happiness checklist. He chuckled as he kissed Kasey. Now this was his idea of some real afternoon delight.

SLIPPERY WHEN WET

Stephani Hecht

Dedication

To all the Renos and Bruces out there. May you find
your own HEA.

Chapter One

He finally had the chance that he'd waited over six months for. Reno was going to have an excuse to talk to the man of his dreams, Bruce McCall. The man who had all the swagger of Jagger, the cool of Bond and the good looks of David Beckham.

It was really a shame that said man worked as a lifeguard at a hotel. But then again, for all David's wonderfulness, Reno had to remind himself that David was just a normal, everyday guy. Besides, who was Reno to talk? He worked as the head coordinator for children's activities at the same hotel. At least Bruce got to actually save lives. What did Reno do? He helped kids make macaroni necklaces and finger paint pictures to show off to their uncaring parents. So, as far as he was concerned, that put Bruce steps ahead of him.

Reno held his hand up to his mouth and huffed to make sure his breath didn't stink, ran a nervous hand over his hair to smooth his cowlicks, brushed his fingers over his lips to guarantee he didn't have any pieces of leftover dinner stuck to his face then checked his fly was all the way up. He wanted to be certain that he made a good impression. Taking a deep breath to steady his nerves, he pointed himself towards the pool area.

He found Bruce in his usual location on the fourth floor where the pool was located. He was sitting in the lifeguard chair, looking as gorgeous as ever. Reno paused a moment just to stare at him. With sleek, tanned skin that covered a set of muscles to die for, dark, short hair and brown eyes that one could get lost in, he was every gay man's wet dream come true and then some. That was before one threw in the cute set of dimples and the high cheekbones — they were just the bonus on the spank-bank cake of yumminess. And, damn it, Reno didn't just want a big old slice of it. Hell, who was he kidding? He wanted the whole cake, icing and all.

It wasn't until he'd been standing there for a good five minutes that Reno realised he was stalling. Not only that, but he was pretty sure he was doing a good impression of a stalker.

Taking in another deep breath, he said to himself, "Come on, stop being a wimp. You can do this. It's not like he's going to bite or anything. At the worst, he can just treat you like you're nothing. Just like every other good looking guy in the world does. It won't hurt — much."

Making himself put one foot in front of the other, Reno closed the gap between himself and Bruce. His heart pounded harder the closer he got. His throat grew dry and his breathing became so fast it was a wonder that he didn't hyperventilate. Before he knew it, he was there. Bruce barely glanced his way before returning his gaze to the water.

Yeah, just the way Reno wanted things to start off. He could already feel himself wanting to crawl into a hole and die.

"Is there something you needed?" Bruce asked in an almost bored tone.

"Yeah, we need to touch base on the group that's coming in tomorrow," Reno said, shuffling his feet nervously.

Wow, when had his voice become so high pitched? He sounded like Peter Brady from that old Brady Bunch episode. The one where they had the singing gig and Peter's voice was going through the change. Only Reno didn't have that excuse to fall back on since he'd gone through puberty a long time ago.

Bruce curled up a lip. "Oh, you mean the 'daddy and me' one? Yeah, that one is going to suck majorly. Thanks to all the overtime they're making us work, I already had to cancel two dates. It's going to cut into our social life big time. Good thing it's only going to last a week."

Ouch, that hurt to hear. Not that Reno was the jealous type...much. Actually, he should be used to it by now. Bruce was a notorious playboy. Some might even say a slut. He went through guys faster than Taylor Swift. All the while, Reno was forced to stand by on the side lines and watch.

Not only that, but Reno had no social life to be ruined. His idea of a good night was watching old TV shows and eating Pizza Rolls. Not that he'd ever dare admit that one to Bruce. It was obvious the guy already thought he was a dork. No sense adding fuel to the fire, so to speak.

"Yeah, since I'm the head coordinator of children's activities, we're going to be working together a lot this week," Reno said. "There are going to be a lot of water activities planned and they coincide with what we'll be doing indoors. So, we should get together and decide on timing and stuff."

"Oh, yeah, I forgot that's what you do. What's your name again…?" Bruce snapped his fingers repeatedly as he struggled to remember.

Reno's heart sank to his sneakers as he said, "Reno."

Of course, why should somebody like Bruce remember a nobody like him? Reno looked down at his own clothes. He was dressed in a red polo shirt and khaki shorts, whereas Bruce wore a tight-fitting white tee and red board-shorts. They were like the Wiggles meet Baywatch. They weren't even in the same league. Hell, they weren't even on the same planet. Reno was a fool to think that Bruce would ever notice him.

"Look, kiddo. I would love to talk about all the fun activities you have planned, but I'm on duty right now and I really can't take my eyes off the water. So maybe we can do it another time. I'm sure you have all kinds of interesting things to tell me." The bland tone in Bruce's voice said otherwise.

"Okay, what would be a good time for you?"

Even as Reno asked that question, he knew he was getting the brush-off. Bruce had no interest in talking to him again or even seeing him another time for that matter. As far as he was concerned, Reno was just an annoying bug that needed to go away. The sooner, the better.

Bruce gave a shrug. "I'm sure we'll run into each other sometime tomorrow. We can chat then. Now, why don't you run off? Aren't there some kids that need to paint something somewhere or something?"

God, Reno needed to get out of there before he made a further fool of himself. He took a step back and pasted on a fake smile. "You're right. We can talk more about it later on when you're not on duty."

"Sure, sounds nice..." Bruce floundered again.

"Reno."

Damn it! It wasn't that hard of a name to remember. It's not a name one heard every day. Had Bruce been dropped on his head as a kid or something? Maybe it was true that beauty only did go skin deep. At this point, Reno didn't know whether to feel hurt, angry or insulted.

He turned around and walked as fast as he could out of there. Of course he had to hit a patch of water and slip, nearly falling on his ass. Great, he couldn't even make a proper dramatic exit. The only thing missing was a clown and a pie to the face. Or the *whomp whomp* sound-effect.

Since his shift was over, Reno made his way directly to the bar. After the exchange he'd had, it seemed the proper place to go. Isn't that where everybody went to drown their sorrows?

Technically, since he was only twenty, he was too young to be there. Because he was an employee, though, they bent the rules for him. Besides, he was pretty good friends with one of the bartenders there and he needed a good pair of shoulders to mope on.

As always, the place was packed, but Reno managed to spot an empty stool at the end of the bar. He squeezed his way through the throng of bodies and slumped down on the seat next to a guest at the hotel he'd heard Gib call Edwin.

He leaned on the bar, where Gib and Isaac were working and said, "I'll take a shot."

When Gib gave him a shot glass full of cola, Reno narrowed his eyes. "What is this?"

"You're still underage, kiddo," Edwin said.

"In that case, make it a double."

Another shot glass of cola was slid his way.

"Here, take some beer with it." Isaac snickered as he handed over a glass of root beer.

"You guys really know how to kick a guy when he's already in the dumpster," Reno groused.

"How bad can it be?" Edwin asked.

Looking into the glass of root beer, Reno confessed, "He didn't even know my name."

Reno didn't even have to tell them who *he* was. Both Gib and Edwin knew about his crush on Bruce. They both shot him sympathetic looks, which only served to make Reno feel all the more a loser.

"You really don't want to be with him anyway. Remember when I told you that I heard he's a real player. You could do much better than him," Edwin said.

"Yeah, he's a real slut and, coming from me, that says a lot. He's not the type of guy for you," Gib added.

A pit formed in the bottom of Reno's gut. "You guys never... Well you know, did...anything...sexual..."

He trailed off, unable to go on. When Gib just cocked an eyebrow, Reno held up a hand. "Forget it, I don't want to know."

He slugged back both the colas then stood up. "Thanks for the pep talk, guys, but I think I'm just going to go home and lick my wounds. Hopefully tomorrow will be better. I don't see how it could possibly get any worse than it did today."

With those parting words, Reno left the hotel.

* * * *

As Bruce went back to the locker room, he recalled how Reno had practically run from the pool area after the conversation. The guy had been so eager to get away he'd almost fallen. It was kind of cute in a clumsy sort of way. In fact, everything about the kid was cute. From his floppy blond hair, to his innocent blue-eyed gaze. It made Bruce wonder how Reno had never landed on his radar before.

It must be because Bruce was terrified of kids so he stayed away from the kids' area as much as possible. When the hotel had decided to become more family-friendly six months ago and had added that department, Bruce had wanted nothing to do with it. All he'd known was it had made his job a lot harder, but gave him more hours since they needed lifeguards all day and a good part of the evening because children were now there more often.

So, as it was, Bruce came into contact with children more than he wanted. Now he realised he'd made a big mistake in not visiting the children's centre sooner. Obviously it had been hiding someone very interesting. It had taken all of Bruce's self-control not to jump all over Reno when he'd been at the pool. The only reason he hadn't given the man more of his attention and really flirted with him was because Bruce had to keep all his focus on the kids in the pool and do his job as a lifeguard. It had become so difficult that he had finally had to send Reno away, just so Bruce could concentrate on his work. He knew that he'd come off as a jerk and he hated that.

He quickly got dressed into his street clothes then went to the bar. If anybody were to know anything about Reno, it would be Gib. He knew just about everything about everyone there.

As Bruce walked in, he found the bartender busy as usual, so Bruce took a seat and waited to be noticed. When Gib shot him a dirty look, Bruce was a bit confused. While they might not be the best of friends, there weren't any bad feelings between them, so the hostility was unfounded.

"What do you want?" Gib asked.

"I just wanted to ask you about somebody," Bruce replied.

"Who?"

"Reno."

He was shocked when a flash of anger came over the bartender's face. "What do you want to know about him?"

"I was just wondering what makes him tick, that's all," Bruce replied innocently.

"Since when do you care about anything but a guy and his ass?" Gib shot back.

"I'm just asking a friendly question. I met Reno for the first time today and I'm interested in getting to know him better."

Gib leaned his hip on the bar and gave Bruce a shrewd look. "Leave Reno alone. He's a nice guy. He's not one of your screw and dumps. You treat him that way and you'll end up breaking his heart. So, do me a favour and just leave him alone."

"What if I want him for more than just that?"

Gib laughed. "Since when have you ever wanted a real relationship with anybody?"

Bruce thought it over and realised that Gib had him on that one. But for some odd reason, he could see himself wanting to be with Reno for more than just one night. Reno seemed to be different than all the other guys. Whether it was because of his innocence or his quirkiness, for some strange reason, he intrigued Bruce unlike any guy had in a long time.

Whatever the reason, Bruce made a personal vow that whatever it took he would find a way to get to know Reno a lot better. No matter who stood in his way.

Chapter Two

The next morning as Reno went into work, he vowed that he wasn't going to let the miserable events from the day before ruin his day. Okay, so he'd found out that the guy he'd been harbouring a crush on for months was a jerk. He'd get over it. Worse things had happened. It wasn't the end of the world — really, it wasn't. He'd move on.

He went directly back to the kids' area in time to be met with mass chaos. The project at the time was hand painting and for some reason they had left Brandy in charge. While she was a nice enough girl, she had no organisational skills at all.

The kids were all running around without discipline and the only things getting painted were the walls and the carpet.

"Brandy, what is going on?" Reno asked.

"I don't know!" she wailed, her hands going to her head. "They won't listen to me at all. I keep telling them to stop, but they just won't."

She had green globs of paint hanging from her curly blonde pigtails and she had several other colours splattered all over her uniform. It made her look like she'd been attacked by a gaggle of paintbrush-wielding monsters. Which, in a way, she had been.

"You need to show them who's boss," Reno said.

Be it karma, or maybe it was just because of the way his luck had been going lately, but that's when his own words came back to literally smack him in the ass. A boy of about the age of five came running up and, with outspread, red-coated hands, pushed Reno right in the butt.

Brandy gasped. Reno groaned in irritation. All the kids burst out laughing.

Twisting to the side, Reno could see two perfectly formed handprints on the seat of his khaki pants. It was the beginning of his shift and he hadn't brought a spare pair with him either.

Great! Just great! It looked like it was going to be another one of those days. It wasn't even noon yet and he'd already been having a doozy of a bad shift.

"Personally, I think the colour looks good with the khaki," someone behind him said.

Spinning, Reno was horrified to see Bruce standing behind him. Of course, Bruce looked as stunning and paint-free as always. Reno opened and closed his mouth several times as he tried to think of a snappy comeback. Something that would make him sound clever or sexy, but all that came out was, "Thanks?"

"Well, Reeeeennnno," Bruce drew out the name, as if to prove that he'd remembered it, "I just wanted to come down and apologise for my behaviour last night. I was preoccupied and came off as a bit of a jerk."

"You came to say that you're sorry," Reno said, knowing he sounded like an idiot and wishing he could stop himself.

Why oh why couldn't he handle himself better around cute guys? It never failed. Get him around anybody that was handsome or hot and he became a modern day Jerry Lewis. Reno didn't have an ounce of charisma in him, no matter how hard he tried.

"I think he already said that," Brandy oh-so-helpfully piped in.

"Why don't you call Danny over to help you with the kids?" Reno told her.

Maybe if he got rid of her and got the kids under control he could think enough to formulate a complete sentence while talking to Bruce.

Yeah, and maybe pigs would start flying and Republicans would vote for gay marriage.

Once Brandy had scampered off, leaving behind a trail of paint droplets, Reno turned his attention back to Bruce. "Thanks for stopping by, but it really wasn't necessary."

"Well, you did say that we had to get to together and talk about next week," Bruce pointed out.

Reno gestured to the chaos around him. "As you can probably tell, this isn't really the best time."

"I thought Danny was coming to help."

"Danny and Brandy can only do so much."

"You have to talk to me sometime. You can only avoid me for so long," Bruce replied smoothly.

Reno gaped. Had he been that obvious? "Who said I was avoiding you?"

"It's pretty clear. In fact, I'd say it's as subtle as the red handprints on your ass that you don't want to talk to me."

"No, it's not."

"Yes, it is."

Reno huffed, realising they were sounded like a pair of children. "Why should I want to talk to you after what happened last night?"

"I said I was sorry."

"You don't know my name and now you want to act like everything is okay and we're best buds?"

"I know your name now."

"I'm wearing my name tag, just like I was last night. So, you don't get bonus points for that," Reno drawled, gaining some confidence.

Danny and Brandy came back at that moment and took over. Bruce grabbed Reno by the hand and dragged him into a nearby employees' bathroom, which just happened to be empty.

Pinning Reno to a wall with his body, Bruce put a hand on either side of Reno's head. "You know what I think?"

Reno's heart began to race as his senses became invaded by the spicy scent of Bruce's cologne. For so long he'd wanted to be this close to Bruce that he was hard pressed to remember that he was supposed to hate the guy. His cock sure as hell didn't hate him. It swelled to life, pressing against his zipper, begging to be set free.

"What?" Reno asked, his voice raspy.

"I think that you and I should go on a date."

Reno shook his head. He may like Bruce, but he wasn't going to be just another notch in the guy's belt, either. Bruce was going to have to work at it. "I've heard all about your 'dates' through the gossip mill. They involve a comp employee meal then a quick fuck in your car. After that, you never call the guy again. Thanks, but no thanks."

Bruce's lips curled up into a sexy smile that almost made Reno's knees give out. "No, I was thinking of a real date. I'll pick you up after work—after you change out of those shorts, into something without paint all over them. We'll go to someplace nice. If you want to fuck, that's okay. If not, that's okay, too. Then, we'll take it from there. I like you, Reno."

Reno looked up in shock. "Are you playing games with me? Trying to trick the dork into thinking he actually has a chance with the jock or something? Because, if so, you can just knock it off now. We're not in high school anymore."

Bruce leant down and ever-so-briefly brushed their lips together. "Did you ever stop to think that I may actually like you?"

"No," Reno answered honestly.

"Well, I do. You intrigue me, Reno. You're different than all the other guys. I like that about you."

"Is that the same line that you use on your other 'dates'? Or do you make up new ones every time?"

"Why don't you trust me?"

Because there is no way in hell that a guy like you could ever be interested in a mess like me. That only happens in books and movies. Not in real life.

"Gib warned me about you."

"Did he now?"

Bruce went in for another kiss. Reno strong-armed him and stopped him short. "I need to get back out there, before there's a *Lord of the Flies* moment and the kids take control."

"So, are you going to go out with me or not?" Bruce asked.

Reno ducked under his arm and dashed out without giving him an answer. Maybe that was the coward's way out, but so be it. He was too confused to react any other way at that moment.

He went over to the table and was pleasantly surprised to see that Brandy and Danny had managed to restore order. The kids were all sitting down and none of them were throwing paint anymore. Reno was half tempted to look around for Super Glue, to be sure the two hadn't pasted the kids into place.

"There's a delivery up front and you have to go sign for it," Brandy announced.

Reno's gut clenched. "Can't one of you do it?"

Danny shook his head. "No go. They said it has to be accepted by the big cheese only."

Reno put a hand to his butt as he thought about the twin handprints that were there in all their scarlet glory. "I can't go out like this. The whole hotel will see."

Brandy gave a shrug. "At least it will give everybody something to talk about."

Reno glared at her. That was easy for her to say when it wasn't her that was literally going to be the butt of the jokes. He thought about putting it off, then let out a sigh. Might as well get it over with. It couldn't be worse than sitting around and dreading it.

He left the kid's centre and made his way towards the front desk. With his luck, he wouldn't run into too many of the hotel staff. Yeah, right. More like they would all be having some sort of meeting and would get a good look at his red ass. Then he'd never hear the end of it.

Just as expected, he had only taken a few steps into the lobby when he ran into Jonah. While Reno tried to wave a quick hello and rush by, he still heard the dreaded words.

"Hey, did you know you have paint on your pants?"

"Thanks, Jonah. I'll have to check that out," Reno said as he practically ran by.

He prayed that would be the only one he ran into, since Jonah was technically just a guest. The damage control wouldn't be that bad. Reno groaned when he spotted Chris.

Reno twisted sideways, trying to hide his butt. He knew it probably made him look ridiculous and it ended up not working anyways, because he soon heard it.

"Hey, Reno! Why do you have paint on your pants?"

Reno let out a groan.

"Because some kids are the spawn of demons."

"Ah, you gotta watch out for those ones."

"I try but they always seem to find me."

He kept moving, wondering why the front desk had to be so damn far away. The next staff member he ran into was Quinn.

"What's up with the paint on your pants?"

"I ran into a kid's hands."

"You got to be more careful. Make sure that Trevor doesn't see that."

Shit! Reno hadn't even thought of that. The last thing he needed was a write-up on his record. It would be the whipped cream on his already crappy banana split of a day.

"Thanks, I'll try to avoid him."

He turned around to encounter Jayden, or at least that what the badge around his neck said. "I like the paint on your pants. I think it looks cute."

"Thanks," Reno said, wondering if he could get out of this mess without further embarrassment.

He finally made it the front desk where Esteban was waiting for him. "You have a package for me?"

"Yeah, although I didn't expect you to cause so much excitement when you came to get it."

"You know me, disaster always at my tail."

Esteban made a huge show of leaning over the counter so he could look at Reno's butt. "I can see that."

"Just give me the package so I can go back to the kid's centre and hide for the rest of my shift."

As Esteban waited for Reno to sign, he said, "I heard you have a date with Bruce tonight."

Reno looked up, shocked. "What? I never said yes or no. How can gossip travel that fast?"

"How long have you worked here? You know how people love to get into other peoples' business."

Reno took the package and walked away.

"Have fun on your date," Esteban called.

"I haven't said yes yet," Reno said.

"You will."

Chapter Three

For his entire shift, all Bruce could think about was how cute Reno had looked with those handprints on his ass. He also couldn't get his mind off how sweet that one all-too-brief kiss had been.

The work day seemed to drag on forever. All he wanted was to get it over with, so he could go on his date with Reno. Which was funny, since he'd never been this eager to be with a guy before. He couldn't help himself, though—there was just something about Reno that made Bruce want to know him better.

After what seemed like forever, it was time to clock out. He waited to be relieved from duty before getting down from his chair and heading towards the locker room. When he got there, he found his friend Kipper. Kipper worked in the bar and was just getting ready to start his shift.

"Is it true?" Kipper said by way of greeting.

"What? That you're an asshole? Yes, it is," Bruce teased.

"No, are you really going on a date with that guy from the kids' centre?" Kipper wrinkled his nose.

Bruce immediately went on the defensive. "So what if I am?"

"I don't know. He just isn't the type you usually go for."

"What's wrong with Reno?" Bruce sat down and began to pull off his shoes.

"Well, for one thing, he's a bit dorky."

"He's cute, there's a difference."

"Come on, even you have to admit he's a bit of an oddball."

Bruce could feel himself getting angry on Reno's behalf. "How can you know that? I'll bet you've never spoken more than three words to the guy."

"I just don't get why you would want to date him. You could have your pick of hot guys."

"Maybe, I'm bored with just dating hot, boring guys who have the IQ of a pea. Has that ever occurred to you?"

"Why? The sex is great."

True, but lately, Bruce had been finding that he wanted more than just a quick hook-up. He wanted — he didn't know…more.

"Sex isn't everything."

"Says the guy who probably isn't going to get laid tonight." Kipper snorted.

"Maybe I'm okay with that."

"Since when?"

"Since I realised that there is more to life than just satisfying my cock."

Kipper gave him a shrewd look. "Have you been watching Dr Phil again? How many times have I told you not to do that?"

"No, I haven't. I'm just bored of the same thing every night. Don't you ever want a real relationship?"

Kipper gave a shudder. "Hell no. That would mean I would have to commit to one person. No, thank you. I like variety in my life. Besides, if I were to pick one guy to settle down with, it wouldn't be the Mr Rogers of the hotel."

"I happen to think that Reno is cute."

"*Cute?* That's fine for puppies or kittens, but not for guys. Are you sure you didn't hit your head on the bottom of the pool or something?"

"Don't you have a shift to get to?" Bruce snapped.

Kipper held up his hands. "Whoa! Sorry, dude, didn't mean to offend you or anything. Sorry. If you want to go dork, it's fine with me."

"Don't call him that."

"Fine, if you want to go cute, it's fine with me. Is that better?"

"Yes."

Once Kipper had left, Bruce wondered why he hung out with a jerk like that. Then he wondered if that's how he'd come across to Reno. If so, then it was no wonder he was having such a hard time getting the guy to trust him. Shit, he wouldn't trust himself if he were in Reno's place.

Letting out a sigh, Bruce realised he'd have to work double-time to gain Reno's trust. Well, he'd do whatever it took, because what little he did know about the guy he really liked.

Bruce quickly got dressed, then went to the kids' centre. Reno was cleaning up the area. He looked up and seemed surprised to see Bruce there.

"What are you doing here?" Reno asked.

"We have a date, remember?" Bruce asked, hoping he wasn't about to make a fool of himself.

A smile came over Reno's face. "I never said yes as far as I can recall."

"But you didn't say no, either," Bruce pointed out.

"Where would this date be?"

"I was thinking about some pizza."

Bruce held his breath while he waited for Reno's answer. He couldn't remember the last time when a yes or a no had meant so much to him. Kipper would be laughing his ass off right now if he could see this.

Reno nipped on his bottom lip for a second before he nodded. "Okay, but we'd have to stop by my place first so I can change. There is no way I'm going out with red handprints on my ass."

Bruce laughed, both from the comment and relief. "Deal."

Reno put up the rest of the stuff and they went out to the parking lot. Reno had a little economy car, while Bruce had a higher-end luxury car that had been a gift from his father.

"Why don't I follow you back to your place, then we can take my car to the restaurant?" Bruce suggested.

"Okay," Reno agreed. "My apartment is only a few miles from here."

True to his word, the drive was less than five minutes. Reno's apartment looked like a million other complexes. Not too run-down, but not too high-end either. Reno led him up to the second story and opened the door.

"I should warn you that my roommates are probably home," Reno said.

"How many do you have?" Bruce asked.

"Just Brandy and Danny."

"The ones you work with?"

"Yeah. They're a couple so I get the second bedroom all to myself. It's pretty cool."

Reno opened the door and let them in. Danny and Brandy were sitting on the couch, cuddled up in front of the TV. They smiled until they saw Bruce.

"I guess you caved and went out with him after all," Danny said with a sigh.

Bruce wanted to fire back with, *'No, I just followed him home like a puppy'*. But he didn't want to make any waves, so he just settled for a smile.

"Be nice," Reno said. He turned to Bruce. "Just give me a minute and I'll be right back."

He then took off and left Bruce alone with the two bulldogs.

"So, where are you taking him? To the hotel restaurant for a comp dinner and then your car?" Brandy asked with a snide look on her face.

Yeah, she really wasn't a fan of his.

"No, we're going out for pizza. As for what we do after, I haven't decided yet," Bruce replied smoothly.

She got up and whispered in his ear. "If you fuck and dump him, I will eviscerate you. Got that? He really likes you. I don't want you to break his heart."

"Message received, but you don't have to worry," Bruce whispered back. "Believe it or not, I like him too."

The look on her face said she doubted him, but she went back to the couch and sat down. An uneasy silence fell upon them while they waited for Reno. After what seemed like a millennium, Reno came out.

Bruce sucked in a breath. In regular clothes, Reno was nothing short of stunning. He'd traded his uniform for a pair of skinny, worn jeans and a tight-fitting light blue T-shirt. It moulded to his body and showed off every one of his assets to perfection, from his rounded ass to his tight stomach.

"You look great," Bruce said, surprised at how husky his voice sounded.

A blush crept up Reno's cheeks. "It's just an old outfit I had, nothing big."

"Learn to take a compliment," Brandy called.

"You ready to go?" Bruce asked.

The sooner he got away from Brandy, the better. He held out his hand and was pleased when Reno took it. The simple touch sent a jolt of electricity down Bruce's arm and went straight to his cock. He gave it a silent *calm down*. He wanted this date to only be about getting to know Reno, nothing else. If they were going to have sex, it would only be when the time was right. They weren't going to rush into it. Bruce wanted it to be special, because Reno wasn't just some other guy.

They went downstairs then Bruce unlocked the doors. As they got into the car, Reno ran a hand over the dash. "This is nice."

"Thanks, my dad got it for me for my birthday."

"You're lucky. My dad got me a savings bond and a gift card to McDonalds." Reno laughed.

Bruce turned on the ignition and Reno's eyes grew wide. "Wow, it even starts on the first try. Now, I'm really impressed. I usually have to crank my engine three times and talk sweet to get it going."

Bruce felt himself getting a bit self-conscious that he had it easy when others had it so hard. He had an apartment, too, but he didn't have to share it with any roommates. And he sure as heck didn't know how it felt to drive a car that was on its last breath.

"Yeah, like I said it was a gift from my dad, otherwise I would be stuck driving something like you have. The pay from being a lifeguard isn't exactly that good."

Reno looked up from under his lashes. "There's no need to act apologetic. I love the car. Now, let's go get some pizza. I don't know about you, but I'm starved."

"I guess running after kids all day must work up a pretty good appetite."

Reno laughed. "You have no idea. I had two escapees today and it took five minutes to track them down. I found them trying to sneak into the bar. When I asked them what they thought they were doing, they said they wanted to get a pack of smokes. They were six years old."

"That young and they wanted to take up the habit?" Bruce chuckled.

"They thought it would make them look cool and help pick up chicks." Reno shook his head. "Here I thought all boys that age thought girls had cooties. Guess I was wrong."

"Maybe it's just the gay ones who think that."

Reno smiled and it took Bruce's breath away. "Could be. I never thought of that. So, how was your day?"

"Pretty uneventful. There was a group of teenage girls that kept trying to flirt with me. They were wearing bikinis that were so small I would have had a heart attack if I had been their father. The things were like dental floss."

"Guess they didn't have any gaydar."

Bruce pulled out of the parking lot and onto the road.

"Nope, it was broken or non-existent. They kept finding excuses to walk by me. It got to the point where it was almost funny."

"You should have broken into *YMCA*, maybe then they would have gotten the point."

"Or I could have started singing *It's Raining Men,*" Bruce suggested with a smile.

They went back and forth, suggested more songs, each one getting more outlandish than the last. By the time they pulled up to the restaurant, they were both laughing so hard they had tears streaming down their cheeks, and Bruce's stomach hurt.

They got out and went inside. It was a nice little Italian place he'd discovered a while ago, but he'd yet to take a date there. It was decorated with old, vintage pictures from Italy, had the typical red-checker tablecloths and drippy candles. In other words, it was romantic perfection and he was happy to be sharing it with Reno.

"Wow, this place is great," Reno said, a happy smile covering his face.

For some reason that sent a warm thrill through Bruce. It made him happy to know that he'd pleased Reno. Which was weird because he'd never given a damn if he impressed any other guy before. But Reno's opinion meant a lot to Bruce.

They were seated in a booth and made their order. As they waited for it to come, Bruce asked Reno, "So, what made you decide to work in the kids' centre of all places?"

A light blush came over Reno's face. "Promise you won't think I'm a dork."

I could never think that of you. "Promise."

"I'm going to school to become an elementary school teacher, so I thought it would be a fun way to get a head start on my future job."

"Do you like working there? It seems like a pretty hectic job to me."

Reno tilted his head to the side. "You don't like kids, do you?"

Bruce's gut clenched, wondering if he told the truth, would it make him look worse in Reno's eyes? "Not very much. Is that a bad thing?"

Reno shook his head. "No, it isn't. A lot of people are afraid of having to deal with children. It just makes you human."

Bruce let out a sigh of relief. At least he'd passed one test. "Not that I don't think it's great that you do. In fact, I admire you for your patience."

"I admire you for yours. I could never do your job. The first time I saw somebody drowning, I'd probably panic and drown right along with them while trying to save them," Reno confessed.

With the walking disaster Reno was, Bruce could see that happening. He let out a chuckle. "It's not as hard as it sounds. Most of the time, I just sit there. It's actually quite boring."

"What made you decide to do it?"

Bruce winced. Reno would have to ask that.

"At first, it was because my dad insisted that I find a job. He thought it would build character if I worked instead of just living off him all the time."

Looking back, Bruce realised what a spoilt little brat he'd been and he wasn't proud of the old him. All his life had consisted of was partying, fucking and not working a day in his life. The sad thing was, had it not been for his father's intervention, he'd still be doing it. What kind of person did that make him?

"And how do you feel about it now?" Reno pressed.

"I really like it. After I took my first responder course, I realised that if I could, I would like to take it further. Maybe get my paramedic licence and work in that field. I know the pay isn't that good, but I don't care. I would love to do that for the rest of my life."

Wow, that was the first time Bruce had admitted that aloud. It felt good, too. Especially when Reno gave him a proud smile.

"Then you should do it," Reno said.

"Maybe I will," Bruce said.

He reached across the table. Reno slid his fingers so that they held hands and they talked about mundane things until the pizza came.

They continued to chat through their meal and after, even talking until the place closed. Bruce found that he couldn't get enough of Reno. From the way his nose scrunched when he was telling a funny story, to the way his face grew pensive when he was serious. He could have gone on all night just so he could watch him.

When it came time to take Reno home, Bruce was disappointed. He wanted to spend so much more time with Reno. As he walked Reno up the steps, Bruce was reluctant for the evening to end.

They paused at Reno's door, and Reno seemed just as unwilling for the date to be over. He jiggled his keys from hand to hand as he got that awkwardness about him again.

"Well, thank you for dinner. It was really nice," Reno said.

"Yeah, we'll have to do it again," Bruce replied.

"I'd like that."

"Soon."

"Yeah."

"How about tomorrow night?" Bruce suggested. He then gave Reno a deep, lingering kiss, just as he'd been dying to do all night long. Reno moaned and leaned closer, his lips parting. Bruce slipped his tongue in.

Reno tasted of basil and tomato, but underneath was a lingering sweetness that Bruce knew was unique to Reno. While Bruce's cock demanded more, Bruce forced himself to pull away after the one kiss. He reached out and brushed the back of his knuckles against Reno's cheek.

"I think I'm falling for you, Reno," Bruce confessed.

"Really, you're not just saying that?" Reno asked, his voice slightly breathless.

"No, I wouldn't play you like that."

With those parting words, Bruce turned around and walked away.

Chapter Four

"So, he didn't try to get frisky with you at all?" Brandy asked for what had to be the millionth time.

Reno gave a pointed look to all the kids around them and said, "No, he didn't. We just got some pizza. We talked for several hours and he took me home. Then he said that we had to go out again some other time."

She shot him a sympathetic look. "Sorry."

Irritated, Reno slammed down a box of crayons harder than he intended. "For what?"

"He obviously wasn't that into you. Otherwise, he would have...well, you know."

For the first time since Bruce had left him, Reno felt a flicker of doubt. Sure, Bruce had said that he was falling for him, but what if that had just been his way of letting Reno down easily? Could he have not liked Reno? Maybe their date hadn't gone as well as Reno had thought?

He swallowed hard as he realised that idea hurt him more than it should have. They'd just gone on one date, for Pete's sake. It wasn't like they'd been going out for months and were engaged or anything. So, it shouldn't feel like somebody had just ripped out Reno's heart and stomped on it.

That's what he got for getting his hopes up. He should have known better. There was no way some rich jock like Bruce would ever go for some poor dork like him. Reno had been an idiot for ever allowing himself to think otherwise.

Strong arms came up from behind him and wrapped him in a brief hug. He let out a yelp of surprise and jumped, nearly falling to the ground. Turning around, he was shocked to see that it was Bruce.

"What are you doing here?" he asked.

Bruce flashed that winning smile of his. "I realised we forgot to set up the details for our date tonight."

"Tonight?" Reno echoed stupidly.

"Yeah, don't you remember?"

"You said soon. I didn't realise you meant this soon. I thought you were kidding."

Bruce shoved his hands into his pockets and actually blushed. A new one for him. It made him all the more endearing. "Yeah, well. I can't wait to see you again."

A feeling of elation went through Reno. Even though he knew it was childish of him, he couldn't help but shoot a triumphant look in Brandy's direction. Brandy, for her part, appeared so stunned that she was frozen in place.

"I'd love to go out again tonight. What do you want to do?" Reno asked.

"I know it sounds crazy, but I was wondering if you want to check out that new putt-putt place that just opened up."

Reno got so excited he almost jumped up and down like one of his kids. "Are you kidding? I've been trying to get Brandy and Danny to go there with me forever and they refuse. I would love to go."

"Okay, I'll meet you after work. We can go to your place so you can get changed and we'll leave from there like we did last night."

Reno nodded. "That sounds great."

"Okay, I'll see you then."

As soon as he was gone, Reno turned to Brandy. "See, I told you he likes me."

Brandy had a dumbfounded look on her face. "I owe you a major apology. He does. I never thought I'd see the day, but Bruce has actually fallen for somebody and it's you, of all people."

"Hey," Reno exclaimed, slightly hurt.

"I didn't mean it that way, but you do have to admit, you guys are the exact opposite of each other."

"Maybe that's what he likes about me," Reno suggested.

"It just could be. That doesn't mean that if he hurts you, I'm not going to rip him apart."

"Has anybody ever told you how vicious you can be?" Reno asked.

She gave a sweet smile. "What can I say? I protect those I love."

* * * *

The day dragged slowly, but soon Reno's shift was over and Bruce was there to pick him up. This time when they went to the apartment, thankfully, Brandy and Danny weren't there.

Reno leaned in and gave Bruce a kiss, fully aware that it was the first time that he'd initiated the contact. The kiss turned into another, then a third, until soon,

Reno was pinned against the wall, a panting mess as they made out.

"You know we could always stay in. We don't have to go out," Reno suggested, hardly believing how forward he was being.

Bruce stepped back, but just one step. "Not yet. I want you to know that you mean more to me first."

"What is that supposed to mean?" Reno asked and he could have sworn his aching cock echoed the question.

"I don't want you to think that you're just like the other guys. I don't want to rush things between us. When we do make love—and we will make love, don't have any doubt of that—I want you to know it's because I consider you special and not just another notch in my bedpost."

"Brandy said it's because you really don't like me."

Bruce took Reno's hand and held it to his hard cock. "Does this feel like I don't want you?"

Reno sucked in a breath. Damn, but Bruce felt huge and it was all for him. "No, it doesn't."

"Now, go get dressed, so I have a few moments to compose myself."

Reno did, but not before he gave Bruce's cock a playful squeeze. He decided on another pair of skinny jeans, since Bruce had seemed to like them so much the night before, and paired them with another T-shirt, this one red. He styled his hair then ran out to meet Bruce.

Bruce had changed at work, and he looked great as always. He wore a pair of black jeans with a dark blue button-down top. The jeans made his already great ass look all the better. His dark hair was styled so it went slightly to the side, almost as if he didn't have a care in the world.

"You ready to go?" Bruce asked.

"Yup, can't wait to beat your ass at putt-putt," Reno teased.

Once they got to the course, they picked their coloured balls and began to play. It soon became apparent that neither one of them was any good at it. So they just got goofy and decided to see who could get the worst score. Much to Reno's shock, Bruce 'won' at that game.

After, they went to a local hot dog stand and ate. When they were finished, they sat on the nearby bench and talked for a while, much like they had the night before. They spoke mostly about how their families reacted when they'd come out.

Bruce's parents had been shocked but supportive. Reno's parents hadn't been surprised in the least and it had been so anti-climactic that it had almost had been a disappointment.

"At least they could have gasped or acted stunned or something," Reno said. "All they did was shrug then went about their day."

"What did you want, drama and hair pulling?" Bruce teased.

Reno scrunched up his nose as he thought it over. "I guess you have a point. It was better it went down the way it did."

"You ready to go? It's getting pretty late and I'm getting eaten alive by the mosquitoes."

Reno let out a sigh. He hated for the date to end, but Bruce did have a point. "Yeah."

They got back in the car and Reno took a steadying breath. What he was about to say would make for either the best or worst night of his life, but if he didn't go for it, he would regret it forever.

"I want to go home with you."

"Sure, we could watch a movie or something."

"Not to watch a movie. I want you to fuck me."

Reno's hands shook as he waited for Bruce's response. He didn't know what expression Bruce wore, because Reno was too afraid to look over to see what it might be. If it were disgust or pity, he didn't think he could take it. Sure, Bruce acted like he was attracted to him, but there was still a small part of Reno that wondered what a great guy like Bruce saw in a dork like him.

Bruce reached over, grasped Reno by the chin and gently turned his head so they were gazing at each other. What Reno saw wasn't disgust or pity—he saw lust and longing, something that no other man like Bruce had ever shown when looking at him.

"Are you sure? We don't have to do this if you're not ready. You're worth waiting for," Bruce said.

"I've wanted this from the first moment I saw you," Reno confessed. "It was my first day at work and they were giving me a tour of the place. I walked by the pool and you were on duty. I saw you sitting in your chair and I knew right then that I wanted you, even though I realised that I would never have a chance with a guy as hot as you."

Bruce ran his thumb over Reno's bottom lip. "You need to give yourself more credit. You're pretty damn hot yourself. You just need to have a little more self-confidence and you'd have guys all over you."

Reno gave a half-laugh. "Somehow I doubt that. Guys tend to look through me. Take you, for example. How long have we worked together? And you just now realised who I am."

"That's because I'm an idiot. Now that I do know who you are, I'm not letting go any time soon."

Reno cocked an eyebrow as a jolt of shock went through him. "That's an interesting thing coming from you. Especially since this is only our second date."

"Well, what can I say? You're an interesting guy." Bruce then leaned in and lightly feathered their lips together. "Now, let's get going to my place."

The entire drive there, Reno was a jittery mess. He was worried that he wouldn't live up to the standards of all the men that Bruce had been with. On the other hand, there was no way in hell Reno was going to back out. Not when he'd been waiting for this moment for so long.

All too soon they were pulling into an apartment complex that made his look like a dump. Then again, he had to remind himself that Bruce's dad was probably supplementing his income, because there was no way that he could afford this on the salary that the hotel paid.

They got out of the car and Bruce led him to the door.

"Damn, this isn't an apartment—it's a townhouse," Reno exclaimed as he examined the outside.

It was two stories tall and even had an attached garage. The landscaping was top-notch too and the lawn furniture was all high-end. There was no blue-light special plastic crap here.

Bruce just gave a shrug as he unlocked the door. "My mom picked it out and decorated it for me. I would have been happy with anything."

"You should consider yourself lucky. At least you don't have to listen to Brandy and Danny go at it every night," Reno said as they walked inside.

The interior was just as nice. The décor looked as if a woman had done it. The colours were all earth tones, but the curtains and everything were soft and had a finished touch to them. The couch was huge and so was the flat screen TV that was mounted to the wall.

A kitchen was off to one side and it had everything a foodie could want and then some. Not that Reno was much of a cook, but it would be fun to make breakfast in there with Bruce. Both of them glowing in the aftermath of a good night of fucking.

Whoa there, boy! Don't get ahead of yourself. He may just fuck you then take you home. He's not exactly inviting you to grab your jammies and toothbrush and have a sleepover. You're here for one thing and one thing only. Don't forget that.

"So, what do you think of the place?" Bruce asked.

If Reno didn't know better he would have sworn that Bruce was nervous, which was crazy. He was the one that was supposed to be the cool and suave one here, not the other way around.

"It's really nice," Reno admitted honestly. "Although, it's awfully big for one person."

For some reason, he wondered if Bruce ever got lonely being here all by himself. While Brandy and Danny might be annoying at times, it was nice to have somebody around, even though it was so much smaller. The thought of being the only one in such a large place seemed so…stark.

"Can I get you something to drink?" Bruce asked.

"A cola would be great, thanks."

Reno followed him into the kitchen. Bruce went into his massive fridge, got the drink and handed it over. During the exchange, their fingers brushed. They froze and their gazes locked. Reno swallowed hard as desire shot through his body.

"You know what? On second thought, I'm not so thirsty after all."

Chapter Five

Bruce took the can of cola and sat it down on the counter. He then grabbed Reno by the waist and hauled him closer, crushing their lips together for a heated kiss. Reno let out a whimper of surprise, but soon caught on, twining his arms around Bruce's neck.

"Want you," Bruce said between kisses.

"I want you, too," Reno replied as he pressed in closer. It was as if he were trying to climb up Bruce.

"Then let's take this to the bedroom." Bruce pulled back and held out his hand.

"That sounds like a good idea to me."

In their eagerness, they began kissing again halfway up the stairs. Reno tripped three times and would have fallen had Bruce not been there to catch him. Finally, they safely made it to the top. Bruce slammed Reno into the wall and they made out for a few moments, Reno grinding his cock into Bruce's hip. Bruce was pretty sure Reno wasn't even aware of his action or else there would be a pretty blush on those cheeks of his. As for Bruce, he loved the wanton display of need.

They made it a few more steps before Bruce tackled Reno and took him down. Reno fell with a giant *oomph*. Bruce took the opportunity to nibble and bite on Reno's neck, loving how soft and smooth the skin felt under his skin.

Reno wiggled out from under him and got back to his feet. He stumbled a few steps then gave Bruce a warning look. "Bedroom."

"Bedroom," Bruce agreed with a sigh.

That still didn't stop him from coming up behind Reno, reaching around and feeling him up through his jeans. Damn, for such a little guy, he felt huge. Bruce gave him a few gentle squeezes before leading him the rest of the way to the bedroom.

As they went inside, never had Bruce been so happy that he had an oversized king bed. That made for plenty of room to play and he had so much in mind when it came to Reno. Bruce knew they both had the next couple of days off and if he had his way, they would be spending those two days in the bedroom doing nothing but screwing.

Bruce reached into his dresser and got the supplies then tossed them on the bed. When Reno saw that he'd grabbed a whole strip of condoms instead of just one, he cocked an eyebrow. "You either have amazing stamina or you're expecting me to be here for a while."

"Since we both have the weekend off, I was hoping that you'd stick around for a couple of nights."

Bruce's mouth grew dry with nerves as he waited for Reno's response. Then Reno gave a sweet smile and all the heaviness that had been weighing Bruce down was suddenly gone.

"I'd love to."

Bruce grabbed the hem of Reno's shirt. "Well, then let's get this weekend started."

Reno nibbled on his bottom lip, but there was a hint of a smile, too. He stood still, not helping at all as Bruce took off his shirt then tossed it to the side. Once he had Reno's chest bared to him, Bruce ran his fingers over it. "Who knew that you had such a perfect body hiding under that polo shirt?"

He leant down and took one of Reno's nipples into his mouth, sucking on it. Reno let out a hiss of pleasure as his body swayed. For a second, Bruce thought he was going to fall, but Reno grabbed onto his shoulders for support.

"That feels so good," Reno said with a moan.

So Bruce moved onto the other nipple, giving it equal treatment.

Soon, Reno was making small whimpering noises. Bruce smiled to himself. If Reno was already getting this vocal, he couldn't wait to hear how loud Reno was once things really got started. It was a good thing he had thick walls, or they would be giving his neighbours an earful.

Bruce began to kiss his way down Reno's toned belly. He stopped long enough to swirl his tongue around Reno's navel, because it was just too cute to ignore. When he reached the top of Reno's pants, Bruce slowly unbuttoned them and pulled down the zipper.

Reno had on a pair of dark blue briefs and there was already a wet spot in the front from pre-cum. Bruce licked at it before he gradually lowered them and the pants only to realise that he was hindered by both Reno's shoes and the tight fit of the pants' ankles.

Reno let out a small chuckle. "Here, let me help."

He sat down at the edge of the bed and undid his shoes, taking off the rest of his clothes then tossing them to the side. He made to get up again, but Bruce put a hand to his chest and stopped him.

"Just lie back so I can look at you," Bruce ordered.

A blush came over Reno's cheeks, but he obeyed, stretching out on the bed. Bruce looked down, desire crashing over his body as he gazed down at what had to be the most amazing sight in his life.

Reno's toned body was a work of art—there was no better way to put it. He didn't have an ounce of fat on him anywhere. Yet, he wasn't too skinny either. He had sleek lines of muscle right where they should be. His cock was thick and long, curling up towards his tight stomach.

It was all Bruce's, too. At least for the weekend.

And if he had his say, it would be his for a lot longer than that.

Still staring at Reno, Bruce began to undress. He toed off his shoes and kicked them to the side, along with the rest of his clothing. He was so quick about it, that he worried he was coming off like some overeager high-school boy. Once he was nude, Reno let out a gasp.

"Wow, I thought you were hot before, but I had no idea *how* hot you really were. You must think I look like Gumby's paler, skinnier younger brother," Reno said.

Bruce crawled up onto the foot of the bed. "When are you going to realise just how amazing you are?"

"Probably never," Reno admitted.

"If I didn't find you attractive, do I think I would do this?"

Bruce leant down and ran his tongue over the tip of Reno's cock, collecting the droplets of pre-cum that had formed there. Reno let out a hiss, his head tipping back, exposing the expanse of his throat.

"I wouldn't think so," Reno admitted in a shaky voice.

Bruce made another pass with his tongue, spearing it into the slit on the head of Reno's cock in an effort to get more of his essence. It tasted sweet, yet salty at the same time. Much like Reno himself.

"Damn, you're good at that," Reno said.

Wanting to please Reno even more, Bruce parted his lips and took all of Reno's cock in. He was so big that Bruce gagged a bit, but it was worth it when he heard Reno's cry of pleasure. Hollowing out his cheeks, Bruce pulled back until only the head of Reno's cock remained in his mouth. Bruce swirled his tongue over it again before he sucked him in once more.

Bruce continued that routine for several minutes until he became aware of Reno struggling to get up. Pulling back so Reno's cock slipped from his mouth, Bruce asked, "What are you doing?"

Cheeks flush with passion, Reno said, "It's not fair that I get all the attention. I want to please you, too. Show me how."

Damn, but Bruce was falling hard for this guy and fast.

Turning his body so his cock was now hovering over Reno's mouth, Bruce said, "Now you can suck me off, while I do the same to you."

"I like that," Reno said, his hand already wrapping around Bruce's aching cock.

Bruce let out a moan. He was so jacked up that the simple touch almost made him come. It was by sheer will that he stopped himself. Then he felt the first tentative licks and he knew he wouldn't last long.

Since he wanted to come inside Reno's ass, not his mouth, Bruce reached out and grabbed the lube.

He squirted some of the gel on his fingers then ordered, "Spread your legs some more for me."

Once Reno had obeyed, Bruce began to suck him off again. Only this time, Bruce began to circle Reno's hole before slowly sliding the finger into Reno. Reno let out a groan and the vibrations shot up Bruce's cock, making him moan in return.

Yeah, he needed to get to the fucking and soon or he was never going to make it. He added another finger, thrusting them in and out, wanting to stretch Reno out as quickly as possible, while at the same time not hurting him.

Reno meanwhile was proving to be a master at giving blow jobs—what he did with his tongue was amazing. Several times Bruce had to stop and take several deep breaths just to regain his composure. Reno also didn't seem to possess a gag reflex—he had no problem taking all Bruce's dick in his mouth. While Bruce wasn't huge by any means, he wasn't small either. So that said a lot.

Finally, Bruce was able to get in a third finger. He worked them in and out several times until he was certain that Reno was ready before he pulled them out and got up.

Reno let out a small whine. "I wasn't done yet."

"I need to fuck you now, baby, or I'm going to come in your mouth."

Reno blinked innocently. "I don't mind."

"I do. I want to finish in your ass."

Reno got on all fours and wiggled his ass. "Well, then take it. It's all yours."

Bruce chuckled. Leave it to Reno to joke around in the middle of hot sex. There was no other guy around that could even compare to him. Bruce grabbed the condom, ripped open the package then slid the latex on. Just to be sure, he added some extra lube before lining his cock up with Reno's hole.

Grabbing Reno's shoulder with one hand, Bruce used the other to guide his cock as he slowly thrust inside. He closed his eyes in bliss. Reno was tight—so tight, and so damn hot. It was the best feeling ever.

"Move, please," Reno begged.

"Who would have thought that you would be so bossy in bed?" Bruce teased, but he did as Reno had requested and began to thrust in and out.

Since he was so close to the crest, it didn't take long for Bruce to feel the tell-tale tingle at his spine that told him that he was about to have an orgasm. Determined not to be the first one to come, he reached down and began to stroke Reno off.

Reno let out a garbled sound as he came, his cock shooting off long streams of spunk that covered the sheet. Only then did Bruce allow himself to let loose. Throwing his head back, he let his orgasm wash over him.

It hit him harder than any other orgasm in his life, sucking all the breath from his body as his cock filled the condom with cum. He swore he saw stars—it went on for so long. The entire time he held onto Reno, his only anchor to the earth.

When he could finally breathe again, Bruce rolled off Reno and lay on his back. Reno rolled to the opposite side, panting for breath. It was nice to know that Bruce wasn't the only one who'd had the wind knocked out of him.

"That was..." Bruce waved his hand as he floundered around for the right word.

"I know," Reno replied.

"Shower?" Bruce asked.

"Yes, please. But, only if you take it with me."

"Hate to break it to you, but there was never another option."

Reno laughed. "I would make some cheesy comment about how it wouldn't be safe for me to go near the water without a lifeguard, but I don't want to ruin the moment."

"Thanks, I appreciate it. I get enough of those kind of lines at work as it is."

"Don't complain. At least you don't have to put up with snot and boogers."

Bruce shuddered. "Okay, you got me there."

He sat up and got rid of the condom in a nearby wastebasket before grabbing Reno by the wrist and hauling him to his feet. "To the shower we go."

When they went in and Reno's gaze fell on the huge shower that had multiple showerheads his eyes went wide. "That's it—I've died and gone to heaven. Great sex and now this!"

Bruce turned on the water and adjusted the temperature. "If you're good, I may even wash your back for you."

Reno blinked those baby-blues at him. "Please?"

"Like I could ever say no to you. Get in there."

Reno got in and, as it turned out, they both took turns washing each other. It ended up being a very sensual experience, the soap making for the perfect lubricant for their hands to glide over each other's skin.

Even though he hadn't thought it possible so soon after having sex, Bruce found himself getting hard again. More so when he looked down to find Reno was too.

Reno looked up from under the fringes of his wet bangs. "Do you want to go for another round?"

"Just give me one second."

Bruce dashed out, not even caring that he was getting water all over the place and grabbed a condom. He came back and ripped open the package, putting it on in record time.

"God, you make me hornier than hell," Bruce said right before he pinned Reno face first against the wall of tile.

Since Reno was already stretched out, Bruce plunged right in. Reno let out a cry of pleasure, tilting his head back to rest on Bruce's shoulder. This time there was no nice and gentle about it. Bruce pounded hard into Reno and damn if Reno didn't seem to enjoy every second of it. He even came untouched, his spunk painting the tile in front of him.

As Bruce found his own release, he bit down on Reno's shoulder. The sensations became too much to take and he nearly fell to his knees.

As he came back down from his after-sex high, he could hear Reno chuckling. "This is going to be one hell of a weekend."

Chapter Six

The next Monday at work, Reno could hardly stop smiling the whole shift. All he could think about was the amazing weekend he and Bruce had shared. They'd spent almost the entire time making love, only getting up long enough to eat or take a shower.

Sure, it made sitting a bit hard for Reno, but the pain was well worth it. So much so that he was already ticking the days off until the next weekend. And there would be a next weekend. He and Bruce had already made plans for that.

"Ugh," Brandy snorted. "Will you get that look off your face?"

"What look is that?" Reno asked.

"The 'I'm in a new relationship and I'm just so happy' one. It's so sweet that it's sickening."

Reno playfully stuck his tongue out at her. "You're just jealous because you and Danny have been together for so long that you're beginning to sound like an old married couple."

"So, are things really getting serious between you and Bruce?" she asked.

"It's looking that way. We already have a date for tonight and we plan on spending next weekend together."

"Wow, then I would say things are really, really serious. Who would have thought it?"

"Thought what?"

She gave a slight shake of her head. "That my sweet, little Reno would be the one to bring Bruce to his knees. I love it."

Danny came running up. "Hey, boss, they have a delivery up front for you."

Reno let out a sigh. "Oh well, at least I'm not covered in paint this time."

He left the children's centre and started to make his way up front. He was nearly there when he was waylaid by one of the waiters. While Reno had never talked to the guy, he did know his name was Kipper.

Come on! Who names their kid Kipper? What were his parents on when they picked that one?

"Hey, Kipper. How is everything going?" Reno said, trying to be friendly.

There was just something about the guy that had always rubbed Reno the wrong way. Kipper always had this *I'm better than you* kind of attitude about him, be it to a hotel maid or management. For the life of him, Reno couldn't figure out how the guy had managed to keep his job for so long, because frankly his attitude sucked.

"I'm doing great since I won the bet," Kipper said with a smug smile.

"What bet is that?"

"We all had a bet going on over how long it would take for Bruce to get into your pants. I said that it would take at least two dates. Not that I blame you for giving in so easily – the guy is an animal in the sack. I had a blast fucking him. Maybe now that he's done with you, he'll give me another go."

Unwanted images of Bruce fucking Kipper flashed before Reno's eyes and Reno began to feel his blood boil. Turning away from Kipper—which was still a stupid name, damn it—Reno walked outside.

He needed some fresh air to clear his head. It was either that or punch Kipper's lights out. Since Reno wanted to keep his job, he chose to go with the former. Besides, Reno wasn't even sure he could make a proper fist. Knowing his luck, he'd probably end up breaking his thumb or something.

On his way out, he passed by Bruce. Bruce called out his name, but Reno gave him the finger and kept on going. He couldn't talk to Bruce. Not while he still had those images fresh in his head. Reno knew it wasn't fair of him and he'd apologise later. Right then he just needed some alone time so he could regroup and forget about the whole conversation he'd had with Kipper.

Bruce watched as Reno stormed out, a look of pure rage and hurt on his face, which was something he'd thought he'd never see on the easy-going guy's mug. Turning, Bruce found Kipper standing there with a smirk on his face. Bruce groaned. *Shit, this can't be good.*

"What did you say to him?" Bruce demanded.

"Why do you assume it was me?"

"Because I know how you work. You love to stir things up more than anybody."

"I was just teasing him. It's not my fault he can't take a joke." Kipper shrugged.

For the first time ever, Bruce had the desire to punch his friend. How could Bruce not have seen what an asshole he was before? It looked like Bruce had been blind to a lot of things. Thank god meeting Reno had opened his eyes. Or else he would have just been another jerk like Kipper.

"What did you say?" Bruce repeated, this time more firmly.

"I told him that we all had a bet going on about how long it would take you to get into his pants. I then told him that I hoped once you were done with him that you would give me another go, because you're so great in the sack."

Bruce had to take a couple of steps away and run his hands through his hair so he didn't give in to his rage and punch Kipper's face right in the middle of the lobby.

"I tell you what, Kipper. You are a real piece of work. If you ruined my chances with Reno, I'll never forgive you."

Kipper laughed. "What? You don't actually like the little dork, do you?"

"Yes, I do—a lot. He's the first guy who's every meant anything to me and now you may have gone and destroyed any chance I had with him."

Kipper shook his head. "What has happened to you? Guys like us don't lower ourselves and date guys like him."

Bruce got right into Kipper's face. "No, guys like us are lucky if we find a guy like Reno to give us a chance. There's a huge difference. Maybe one day you'll be lucky enough to wake up and realise it."

Bruce then ran out to find Reno. He only hoped he wasn't too late. Part of him wanted to hold Reno close and tell him that none of it was true. The other part wanted to yell at Reno for thinking that Bruce would ever be part of such a bet. That he would ever think so little of what went on between them. When was Reno going to realise that Bruce liked him just the way he was?

Bruce found Reno standing next to one of the nearby benches, his shoulders hunched over and a forlorn look on his face. He looked so sad that it felt as if somebody had ripped Bruce's heart out and stomped on it. Then kicked it to the side for good measure.

He walked up to Reno and put a hand on his arm. "You and I need to talk."

"I'd rather not at this moment, if it's all the same to you."

Anger surged through Bruce and he spun Reno around so they were facing each other. "Too bad. It's the least you owe me."

Reno snorted. "The least I owe you. That's rich coming from you."

"Do you honestly think I would take part in that stupid bet? I thought you realised what we had together meant more than that. What in the hell do I have to do to prove to you that I really like you, Reno? Do I have to go into the lobby and publicly flog myself? I really care for you, but I don't know what else I can do to prove it to you. Help me out here, because I'm at a loss."

Reno stared at Bruce a few moments with a confused expression. "That's not what has me so upset. As soon as Kipper mentioned the whole bet thing, I knew that you weren't a part of it. In fact, I never doubted you for a second."

Now it was Bruce who was confused. "Then why are you so upset and mad at me?"

"Because you slept with him."

"That was a long time ago. Way before I met you."

Reno sighed. "I know, but when he mentioned what a good fuck you were, all I could think about was you two together and it made me so angry and jealous. I kind of lost it, I guess."

Bruce could see where Reno was coming from. Just thinking about his lover being with anybody else would make him jealous, too. Pulling Reno into a tight embrace, Bruce said, "I'm sorry about my past. If I could change it, I would. Just know that from now on, it's just going to be you. I care about you a lot, and I don't want to be with anybody else."

"I feel the same way about you."

They shared a long, deep kiss before Bruce pulled back and took Reno by the hand. "Come on, let's go in and get to work. We can finish this on our date tonight."

"Just promise me it's not putt-putt again," Reno teased.

"I think it's a given that we both suck at that. Although you have to admit, it was fun."

They walked inside and passed through the lobby. Bruce was just about to start towards the kids' centre when Reno gave him a tug on the hand and led him to one of the employee bathrooms.

"What?" Bruce asked, already intrigued.

"Just come with me," Reno replied, a wicked grin playing on his usually sweet lips.

This particular bathroom only had one stall, so they were able to lock the door and have total privacy. Reno tested the door before he turned to Bruce and dropped down on his knees.

Bruce let out a gasp of shock. "Are you crazy? My shift starts in five minutes."

Reno gazed up from under his lashes. "That gives us plenty of time, plus I owe you an apology for going off on you earlier. What better way to say I'm sorry than a blow job?"

For the life of him, Bruce couldn't come up with a valid argument to that one, so he just stood there as Reno lowered his shorts and let his cock free. Reno grabbed it with both hands and licked the tip.

"Mmm…you taste so damn good," Reno said with a moan.

He gave the head another lick before parting his lips and slowly sucking Bruce's length in, acting like he had all the time in the world. Bruce wanted to remind him that they were on a schedule, but it felt too damn good. So, instead he let his head fall back and released a groan of pleasure.

Reno sucked in, pulling back at the same time, then bobbed his head down until he had all of Bruce's cock in his mouth again. He set up an easy, gentle rhythm that had Bruce both gasping for more and never wanting it to end.

In between, Reno would occasionally pause to do a twirly thing with his tongue on the head of Bruce's cock that nearly drove Bruce mad. Several times, Reno brought Bruce to the brink of an orgasm only to pull back at the last minute.

"You're such a fucking tease," Bruce accused, his voice husky with need.

Reno let Bruce's cock slide out of his mouth and spat into his hand. "Just wait until you see what else I have planned."

Before Bruce could ask what he meant, Reno began to suck him off again. Damn, Reno's mouth was a gift from heaven. Bruce knew that sounded cheesy but there was no other way to put it. He somehow managed to make it rough, yet gentle at the same time.

Then Bruce felt it, the tentative press of Reno's finger against his hole. So, that's what the spit had been for. To slick up his digit so it wouldn't be dry. How thoughtful of Reno. Bruce didn't object, and Reno must have taken that as permission because he thrust it in.

The intrusion threw Bruce over the edge. Crying out Reno's name, Bruce came, his cock filling Reno's eager mouth. Reno took him in, his throat working as he swallowed every drop. He even licked his lips after he pulled back, like he didn't want to miss any of it.

"Okay," Bruce panted, "apology accepted."

They laughed and washed up, then left the restroom. As they walked out they got knowing looks from Chris and Esteban, but since they were also smiling at them, Bruce wasn't worried that they would get into any trouble.

They went to the kids' centre, where Brandy and Danny already had the children working with some finger paints.

"It's about time you got here." Brandy looked up at the clock. "You've been gone forever."

"I had some other things to take care of," Reno said.

Smirking at Bruce, Brandy quipped, "I'll just bet you did."

A little boy came running up behind Reno and smacked him on the butt. Reno turned around to see that he had two handprints on the seat of his pants, only this time they were bright green.

"Not again," he groaned.

They all laughed.

Bruce gave him a great big hug. "Babe, I hate to tell you this, but you have paint on your pants."

OUT OF SERVICE

Devon Rhodes

Dedication

For Jared.

Yes, I had to do it, and you said I could!

I'm very fortunate to have you in my life and can't wait to see you again!

To my partners in crime—Carol, Amber, TA, Jambrea and Stephani—thanks for liking my crazy idea and for all of the extra work that went into combining our characters.

As Jambrea said, at least now readers won't have to ask for the secondary characters' stories—they're already done!

Chapter One

Jayden couldn't believe he was actually there at the Meliá Hotel. He shifted his shoulder bag, which seemed to be growing heavier by the minute, yet again as he waited in line in the lobby for check-in. He finally shrugged it off and rested it on the top of his rolling bag.

Excitement warred with nervousness in his gut, leaving him wishing he'd taken the time to grab a bite from one of the dozens of fast-food restaurants he'd passed before he'd eventually made his way through Atlanta's airport to the transportation area to catch the shuttle.

He hadn't done much travelling before... Well, to be honest, he hadn't *ever* flown before. It had been a huge step for him to leave his podunk little town to come all the way to the East Coast to attend a conference where he didn't know a soul. Registering had been an impulse, and once that had been done he'd faced the realisation that he was going to then have to buy a plane ticket, reserve a hotel room and actually get there. The planning hadn't been as bad as he'd thought—it had been kind of fun to imagine being at the event—but that had been last winter and it had seemed so far off at the time.

Soon the day had come when he'd had to pack then drive himself to Denver for his flight. It had taken him way longer than he'd thought to get through security, so he hadn't had time to eat in the terminal before his flight—it had already been boarding when he'd reached the gate.

He'd vaguely expected that there would be a meal served on the flight like they always showed in the movies. Instead, they'd been offered some undersized and insanely high-priced snack options for purchase. Hell, he could've picked up ten at the grocery store for what one would have cost him. In the end, he'd ignored his growling stomach and passed, savouring the free pretzels and going for juice instead of pop.

Now things were really getting dire, and he was feeling a bit lightheaded from lack of blood sugar. He wished the line would hurry up and move before his damn stomach decided to go on a rampage and eat all its neighbouring organs. He eyed the long counter with several computer stations...and one person working.

Seriously? One?

Jayden tried to be patient and looked at the people around him, seeing if he could pick out any other GayRomLit attendees. He didn't know anyone who would be there other than a few people he had 'online friendships' with. A few small clusters of people stood here and there, but he had no way of knowing if they would be with the retreat or were just random travellers.

There was a sudden, piercing squeal as a petite blonde woman appeared out of nowhere to his left and grabbed the long-haired woman in front of him in a crushing hug.

"You're finally here!" She grinned at her friend then met Jayden's eyes briefly before scanning the rest of the line. "Have you been waiting long? There's usually, like, four people working the desk."

"Yeah, we've been here forever. My luck, they have a staff meeting or something right when I get here." She laughed, sounding happy in spite of her words. "At least I'm standing up. My flight was lo-ong."

He could relate.

The already-checked-in lady grabbed one of the other woman's suitcases decisively. "Come on. Let's go up to our room. We'll come get your key and do the credit card thing later when there's not a line."

"Hell yes."

Jayden stepped back a touch to give the lady in line room to manoeuvre her bag. She gave him a bright, hang-in-there smile before she followed her roommate away towards the elevators, chatting all the way.

Lucky her. To not have to wait...and to have a roommate she knows.

As if she'd blessed him with her luck along with her smile, there was a sudden flurry of movement as three employees came through a door behind the front desk area. They took up their stations and waved the next people in line forward. He mentally counted and realised it was finally his turn, so he headed towards the beckoning man at the far end.

He almost stumbled as he reached the counter and finally got a good look at just who had motioned him forward. Probably only the hottest guy he'd ever seen in person, smiling at him.

Jayden immediately averted his gaze then mentally smacked himself. This wasn't like back home, where checking a guy out could get your ass pounded…and not in the good way. He tried to cover his instinctive reaction by pretending to look for something in his bag. He squared his shoulders and made himself look up directly at the man, meeting his ice-green gaze. He imagined he saw a slight spark of return interest, though the desk clerk maintained his professional smile. Those light eyes, though. *Wow, what a combo.* They were amazing with that caramel-coloured skin. He had full lips and rather high cheekbones. It was really difficult to tell just what ethnic background he might be from — maybe a combination…

"Can I help you, sir?"

"Oh…yes. Sorry. Long flight," he offered weakly to…Esteban, according to the name badge pinned to his suit jacket lapel. "I have a reservation. Jayden Yates."

Esteban immediately looked down as he began to type. "Welcome to Atlanta. And where did you come in from today?"

"Well… I flew from Denver, but I live in Wyoming. Kinda middle of nowhere." He cut himself off before he could start babbling. Esteban was obviously just making polite conversation, not really interested. Already his welcoming expression had faded as he tackled the computer system with one staccato burst of typing after another.

"That's Yates. Y-a-t-e-s, correct?"

"Yes," he confirmed, starting to get an uneasy feeling as Esteban continued to periodically type then scan the screen, a small frown puckering his brow. "I, um, have a confirmation I printed out." He began to rummage in his bag in earnest now, feeling his face warm. He wasn't sure exactly *why* he was embarrassed — that was just the way he reacted when any kind of interaction hit a snag. Especially in the face of such a good-looking, articulate guy.

"Good, then I can look it up by the confirmation number." Esteban offered him a reassuring smile as he patiently waited. Jayden nearly panicked then suddenly there was the folded sheaf of papers with all of his various reservations and registrations for the trip.

"Got it," he said unnecessarily, waving them as he set his bag down then fanning the pages out on the counter.

Esteban reached into the assortment and immediately plucked the correct paper out with his long, capable-looking fingers. "Logo," he explained. "I spotted it right away."

"Great. Um, thanks." Jayden began to relax now that things seemed to be moving towards a key and a room and a place where he could stash his stuff then go get some real food.

Except...Esteban didn't look any happier with the information on his screen than he had before. Jayden watched him look back and forth several times between the paper and the computer. An expression of comprehension crossed his face before he raised a sympathetic gaze to meet Jayden's.

Uh-oh. "Is there a problem?"

"Mr Yates, I'm afraid your reservation is for the sixteenth of *November*." He stressed the month, and Jayden's jaw dropped before he grabbed his paper up from where the desk clerk had it turned on the counter to face him. Sure enough, there was the evidence of his idiocy in black and white.

He'd made the reservation for the wrong fucking month. *Stupid drop-down boxes...*

Jayden's stomach roiled as he looked up at Esteban, praying for luck. "I— If there's a price difference, I'll gladly —"

"I'm sorry," Esteban gently interrupted, looking genuinely sad at having to be the bearer of bad news. "We're completely booked through this weekend."

Hearing what he'd already read in the man's expression confirmed aloud sent the blood pounding in his ears, drowning out the sounds from the lobby. He stared at Esteban, whose lips were moving, though Jayden couldn't seem to make out what he was saying.

See? His father's voice seemed to mock him. *I knew you'd fuck it up just like you fuck everything up. Go ahead and go. Atlanta, Jesus. Fucking fairy. And why don't you just stay there? You don't belong here.*

The memory of how excited he'd been, even in the face of his dad's derisive dismissal of his plans, was tarnished now by his mistake. Now what was he going to do? Everything was happening here at this hotel and now he had to try to find another? And no way would it be as inexpensive as the rate he thought he'd booked. He started to panic, feeling slightly hysterical.

He gripped the handle of his rolling bag for balance. Suddenly Esteban was beside him and he was being led through a small half door then back into an office and farther back past a sort of break room and into a private office.

Esteban closed the door behind them, urged him into a seat then grasped the back of his head, shoving it down.

"Whoa," he managed, sounding like he was talking through cotton balls. "Jus' met you...but s'okay. You're pretty hot."

"What...? Oh!" A huff of laughter. "No, I'm just making sure you don't pass out on me."

Jayden absently processed that as he revelled in the feel of Esteban's strong grip on the back of his neck, holding him down. Then the hint of amusement penetrated the fog, or maybe he was just getting some blood back in his brain.

Ouch. Rejected.

He knew it was silly to have actually *wanted* this beautiful, perfect god to have dragged him back into his workplace for an on-the-spot, dub-con blow job...

But an insane part of him would have gone for just that.

Wishing the floor would open up and swallow him whole, he struggled against Esteban's hold. It gentled as he stroked Jayden's neck, sending little shivers through him, but he didn't let him up right away. Jayden finally stopped fighting and simply enjoyed the feel of another man touching him, even under these innocent circumstances.

"Sorry," he apologised, happy to hear that his voice sounded almost normal. "I haven't really eaten today, and then hearing about not having a room..." Saying it aloud brought back his panic at not knowing where to stay or how much it was going to cost him. He didn't have much available credit left on his card, and cash? He had to conserve what little he had.

At that, Esteban let go. "Sit up slowly if you can, okay? I'll be right back."

With his forearms braced on his knees, Jayden watched Esteban's lower legs as he walked to the door, opened it and left the room. Nice shoes. Probably cost more than his plane ticket.

Your grand adventure is off to a great start, Jay.

"Here."

He jumped a bit, having missed Esteban's return. He looked up to see a cardboard box half full of doughnuts being offered to him. *Pride be damned.* Jayden grabbed two doughnuts and polished the first one off in ten seconds flat. There was the sound of a can being opened.

"Drink some juice, too."

Orange juice and doughnuts didn't exactly go great together, but beggars couldn't be choosers. He slugged back most of the can then ate the other doughnut at a slightly more polite pace.

Evidently reassured that Jayden wouldn't be passing out on the floor, Esteban retreated to sit behind the desk as though he had every right to be there. That was when the brass name plaque on the front of the desk caught Jayden's eye. *Esteban Parks, Front Desk Manager.*

Jayden was slightly and probably inappropriately turned on that he was in the sharply dressed guy's office with the door closed. *Get a grip!* The combination of lack of blood sugar, shock and too long a period of celibacy was really doing a number on his imagination.

"Are you feeling better, Mr Yates?"

He grimaced, as that reminded him of his dad. "Call me Jayden, or Jay, please. And yeah, I guess I just really needed some food." Starting to feel a bit self-conscious, and aware that he was going to need to figure out where the hell he was going to stay tonight, he shrugged. "I'd better get out of your hair. I don't suppose you know any hotels nearby that might have rooms...that aren't too expensive?" he finished, a bit embarrassed that he'd had to admit he needed a cheap hotel. A rash hope in a city like this, but hey, it didn't hurt to ask.

Esteban regarded him thoughtfully. "I'm afraid not, at least not nearby."

Jayden tried not to appear too disappointed since he'd expected that to be the case.

"However," the manager continued slowly, "I might have another solution... If I can trust you to be discreet, and keep it just between us."

Jayden's heart began to pound as his imagination ran wild, images of what might require his discretion playing in his fertile mind like a porn video preview.

"I... I can be discreet. Sure. Anything."

Esteban gave him an enigmatic smile, as though he could read every thought flashing through his head. He stood and walked around the desk, and as Jayden rose, his mouth went dry at being the focus of those striking eyes.

"Perfect." Esteban's voice was like a caress. "Grab your things and come with me."

Chapter Two

Trying not to second-guess his decision, Esteban led the pretty young man through the lobby then back to the service elevator, where he nodded hello to a couple of housekeepers as they held the elevator doors for him. One of them was Quinn Nelson, an ex-military guy who was a damn hard worker, even though he didn't exactly fit the mould of a typical housekeeper with his muscular build, buzz cut and serious demeanour.

Seeing Quinn headed off shift reminded Esteban that he was going to have to call Gib, one of the bartenders, who would probably be just coming on his. He hated to have to tell Gib he was giving away 'his' room, but hopefully Gib didn't have any...dates lined up for this weekend. Jayden had sat there in his office, looking so embarrassed and defeated about his reservation error and the subsequent fallout of not having a place to stay... Esteban had just had to do something to help him.

The young man was a paradox, with his obvious naïvety about some things against that dick-hardening comment he'd made when Esteban had forced his head down. His shy admiration. A few glimpses of determination. And overall, a sort of air as though he'd deep down expected the worst, while contrarily shooting for the moon.

Jayden stood next to him in the elevator, and they could see themselves reflected as they rode up to The Level, the concierge floor. Jayden didn't spare a glance for himself, though. His gaze was on Esteban's image the whole time, and the weight of that regard did funny things to Esteban's insides.

The doors finally slid open, dispelling the building tension somewhat. He again took the lead, this time wondering whether Jayden was checking him out. An urge came over him to spin in his tracks and catch him at it. He smiled to himself as he pushed the impulse aside and paused in front of the room. After using his pass key to open the door, he gestured for Jayden to enter. A moment's pause, then Jayden crossed the threshold. That slight hesitation seemed to ratchet up the sexual awareness between them once again.

Shaking his head at his wayward imagination, he followed Jayden into the room and let the heavy door close behind him. There was enough light to see by, but he flicked the light switch anyway out of habit.

Jayden looked around the room, a pleased expression on his face, then his expression fell.

"Wait. I know I didn't pay for this nice a room. I'm...not putting someone out, am I? I mean, you're full and..." He trailed off uncertainly.

Time to explain. "The reason I asked for your discretion is because this room is one that I keep out of service for when...someone I know needs a place to stay. It's not exactly common knowledge, though a few people will need to know you have permission to stay here. The rest of the staff isn't aware that this is a useable room, so..." His gaze flicked to the bare space where the flat-screen TV should have been. He'd had maintenance cannibalise it to replace one in a different room, then not requested a replacement. At least that way, it was immediately obvious to any curious staff members who might come in that it wasn't saleable.

He ran his hand over his hair, a bit tense at the unexpected situation. Last thing he needed was Trevor, the GM, finding out about his little deception. "I'd like to offer you this room to stay in. However, you can't tell anyone what room you're using. Especially any staff. It wouldn't be good for me if you did."

Jayden's eyes had grown wider and wider during his explanation. "I don't want you to get in trouble for me." His worried expression lit up at a thought. "Oh! Why can't you just check me into this room? Like, for real? I'll still pay and everything."

Esteban briefly considered it, but knew the risks would be even greater then. He sighed and found himself explaining, even though Jayden probably wouldn't know what the hell he was talking about. "The problem with that is, if I take it off OOS, there is a special part of the nightly folio recap that is automatically generated and shows up for every change of status. And that goes to the GM, and maintenance, and housekeeping..."

And everyone. Then it wouldn't be off the radar anymore, and he'd not only have to explain why it had been out of service to begin with, but also how it had become rent ready without anyone's help or any maintenance orders being fulfilled... In short, it would be a mess. Once done, he'd never be able to use it again. And as long as Gib kept up his dangerous moonlighting—though Esteban was ever hopeful of eventually talking him out of it—he needed a safe place to bring his men, and nothing could be safer than a public hotel on the concierge level with a camera practically pointed at the door.

"Crap." Jayden looked like he got the dilemma. "I feel like a heel. I mean, I really, *really* want to stay here, but I would hate it if you got caught doing something you shouldn't because of me." He took a couple of steps closer.

From a respectable distance, Jayden looked to have brown hair and eyes. But as he closed in, Esteban could see specks of gold shot through his sherry brown eyes, which were almost the same colour as the glint of auburn in his just past shoulder-length hair.

"I promise I won't let on to a soul. And I don't need housekeeping. I can reuse my towels and make my own bed."

Esteban smiled, relieved by his sincerity. "Well, I can still get service for you. That male housekeeper we just saw by the elevator? Quinn's one of the few who know about this room and the reason behind it. He cleans it when I let him know it's needed." He paused. "The concierge also knows, and I'll need to let him know you're in here. And, of course, my friend who usually uses it."

"That was a housekeeper? I thought he was, like, a security guard. Housekeeper...huh." Jayden seemed stuck on that part.

"Probably best to just not mention what room you're in to anyone. Okay?" he checked.

"Not a word to a soul. Um, except I'll need a key."

Esteban started laughing and Jayden joined him. His eyes crinkled up a bit around the corners, and dimples he hadn't noticed before popped out on his cheeks.

Damn, he's a knockout. It blew Esteban away that he didn't seem to be aware of his appeal. Of course, he might not be gay, or out. Though the fact that he'd put in the comments of his botched reservation that he'd registered for the GRL conference was probably a strong indication of his bent...

And I have no business caring either way. He mentally smacked himself.

"I need to get back downstairs. Why don't you settle in, then stop by the front desk when you come back down? I'll have a room key ready for you. If I have to step away, I'll leave an envelope for you."

Jayden looked down at his chest then back up. He was about four or five inches shorter than Esteban, which meant that the action had him looking up as though from under his lashes. Esteban swallowed against another inappropriate pulse of desire.

"Thank you, Esteban." Jayden rose to brush a quick kiss on his cheek then abruptly stepped back. "This is about the nicest thing anyone's ever done for me. *Ever*," he stressed.

Esteban hoped that was just a sentiment and not actually the case. The thought of this genuinely nice young man being seldom on the receiving end of acts of kindness made him sad. He had a renewed sense that he'd done the right thing.

"You're welcome. I'll see you downstairs in a bit." Esteban was reluctant to leave, but forced himself to head to the door. As a sort of karmic punctuation, a text hit his phone just then, and the sound indicated it was a staff member. Yep. Time to get back to work.

He turned as he went out of the door and gave Jayden, who was still standing in the middle of the room, a quick wave before the closing door cut off his view of him. Another text.

"Okay, okay," he muttered, pulling the phone from its case on his belt.

It was from one of the front desk clerks on today.

We're ten deep. Need help.

He hurried his pace a bit, making a mental note to text Gib and also touch base with Quinn and Chris to let them know about Jayden.

Jeez, relax about the kid already. He's here for four nights then he's gone forever.

The mental reminder that they were ships passing in the night didn't do much to dissuade his interest, but those four days would go by in the blink of an eye.

Time would take care of things. It always did.

* * * *

The next morning, Jayden made an attempt to get into the spirit of the retreat. He really did. He managed to find the registration area and was handed a huge envelope full of papers and a lanyard. The smiling volunteers behind the table helped him to get his name badge in the window of the lanyard and even attached a few pieces of bling so it didn't look so plain.

He thanked them for their help and moved out of the way so others could take their turn. Not wanting to look like a noob digging through his packet right there, he decided to head back up to his room to go through it all and figure out the schedule... After a little 'detour' by the front desk...

He was so focused on getting to the front desk area that he almost ran into a slim blond man who was sidling along almost backwards. Jayden stifled a laugh when he saw what he was obviously trying to hide—a set of kid-sized red handprints square on the ass of his khakis.

"Make sure Trevor doesn't see that," someone was saying to him. An employee, maybe?

The guy mumbled a response then turned and his panicked blue eyes met Jayden's.

"I like the paint on your pants. I think it looks cute," Jayden offered, trying to cheer the guy up.

It seemed to work a little. "Thanks," the guy replied, looking grateful, though he didn't stop moving sideways towards the front desk. Jayden looked past him to scan for his favourite employee.

Damn. Esteban was nowhere to be seen. Feeling a bit down about being so fixated on the guy, as well as his lack of participation at the event so far, he got on the elevator to go back to his room.

The night before had been a complete fail. As though he'd used up every reserve he'd had between travelling and his encounter with Esteban, he just couldn't force himself to be social. But that had to change. He didn't want this trip to be a waste. He pressed his lips together in determination and tore into the registration packet to figure out his plan of attack.

It was nearing noon when a knock sounded. Jayden's head jerked up from where he'd been sorting through the contents of the registration package spread out all over his bed. It was hard to tell if it was his door or not. Jayden paused to listen.

A harder knock, definitely his door. "Housekeeping."

He froze, remembering Esteban's warning about not letting anyone know he was in the room. But it had sounded like a male voice.

Maybe it's Esteban.

Wouldn't he use a key, though? Maybe not. He seemed like the type to respect one's privacy.

He quietly crept towards the door and leaned in to peek through the peephole. It looked like the male housekeeper they'd seen at the elevator the day before.

"Come on, man, I saw you duck in there. Open up before you get us both in trouble."

The deep rumbling voice had him obeying instantly.

When Jayden finally had the door wide open, the man gave him a once-over, not looking particularly impressed with what he found, and grabbed a stack of towels and a cleaning caddy off his cart. He stepped forward and Jayden hastily jumped back out of the way as he strode in the door without pause, letting the door close behind him. He began to clean the bathroom. Jayden felt a bit weird just watching him, so he retreated to the main part of the room and stood around idly, trying to think of something he could do while the guy was cleaning.

A sound from behind him had him jumping around. The housekeeper opened the door to set the caddy back on the cart and toss used towels somewhere, then passed him as he came into the main area of the room.

"So why the hell are you up here and not downstairs grippin' and grinnin'?"

Jayden's jaw dropped as he watched the man—Quinn, that was it—start collecting his piles of papers from on top of the bed. "What do you mean?"

"I mean, you're about the only person in the hotel who's in their room right now." He set Jayden's paperwork on the desk and began to efficiently remake the bed. "You paid good money to be at this conference or meeting or whatever. You flew all the way here from somewhere out West. So why are you holed up in here fiddling with your papers instead of being downstairs?"

"Well, the events don't really start until —"

"Bullshit," Quinn interrupted succinctly. He finished perfecting the bed then, to Jayden's surprise, laid all the items he'd had back out on the bedspread again, in exactly the same places. "You want me to vac?"

Jayden's head was spinning at the abrupt change of subject. "What? No. It's fine."

"All right. So grab your stuff and go. You need anything at all, just find me or Esteban. He's downstairs in his office right now. Texted me that I should come do my cleaning since he saw you down at the retreat reg table not long ago and figured you'd be out of the room for a while."

Jayden warmed at the mention of Esteban and hoped Quinn hadn't noticed, though he figured there wasn't much that got past the man. He also got the impression that Quinn wasn't going to budge from the room until he left too.

He sighed. Quinn was right. It was tougher than he'd thought to just join in when he didn't know anyone, but he certainly wasn't making any progress up here. He stuffed a few things into the handy compartments of his retreat lanyard then looked around the room, grabbing his phone and the room key he'd picked up last night. He'd hoped to see Esteban then too but he hadn't been there, though he'd left the envelope for Jayden as promised. That had been a let-down, so instead of going to the bar like he'd planned, he had come upstairs after a quick bite to eat, written a journal entry and dinked around online.

What a wasted night. He only had three left until he had to go home, and he was going to make the most of them.

Quinn walked out of the door first, looked down the hall then gave a jerk of the head for Jayden to come out.

After the door had closed, Jayden looked at Quinn, who had a bit of a smile on his face now. "Thanks."

"Don't mention it. Now, go on. Have fun. Jesus, wish I was that young again. I wouldn't be sitting around in a hotel room, that's for damn sure..." Quinn's muttering trailed away as he pushed the cart down the hall and stopped in front of another room.

Jayden was waiting at the elevator doors when he got a call. He didn't recognise the number. "Hello?"

"Hi, Jayden. It's Esteban."

Immediately the day looked brighter. The doors thankfully opened to an empty car then. He stepped inside and took a deep breath. Something about Esteban just did it for him. "Hi, there. Thanks for the housekeeping."

"You're welcome. I wanted to see if you have any plans for lunch?"

The door opened, but not on the main floor. A group of five women, all wearing lanyards like his, boarded the elevator and smiled at him. He spoke softly as they began chatting among themselves, "No, no plans."

"Good. I'd love to feed you again." Esteban chuckled and the sound rolled through him, leaving a pleasurable ache in its wake. "Meet me down at the registration desk. We can eat in my office, unless you'd rather go out somewhere?"

The elevator arrived at lobby level and he let the other occupants depart first. "No, your office sounds perfect. I'm just getting off the elevator." He quickly strode in the direction of the front desk. When he caught sight of Esteban with a cellphone to his ear and their eyes met, he laughed and they both hung up.

He continued to walk towards Esteban, feeling incredibly self-conscious as the older man watched him approach. When he reached the desk, Esteban indicated a door to the side and Jayden walked around to meet him.

He knew he'd been through here before, but he'd been so out of it that he barely had any recollection of his first trip back to Esteban's office. A bit lost in his embarrassment at the memory, he nearly walked right into Esteban as he stopped and held out an arm to indicate that he should precede him.

"Sorry," he apologised. Jeez, could he be any more of a clown?

"That's all right," Esteban reassured him with a smile.

God, he was just a beautiful man. Jayden watched him surreptitiously as he strode around his desk and, without sitting down, pulled a menu from a drawer then held it out to him.

"Why don't you choose something from the room service menu?"

"Sure." Jayden accepted it and glanced through the listings, trying to mentally calculate how much he could spend on lunch today and still have money for something before bed. He supposed he could put charges on his credit card, but he really hated the thought of the slippery slide into debt, so he only ever charged as much as he knew he had in the bank to pay off right away.

When he didn't reply immediately, Esteban gave him an understanding look and picked up the phone.

He dialled and listened for a moment. "It's Esteban. Busy?" He laughed in response to whatever the person said. "Yes, well, one day I might get a different answer. Can I get some lunch sent to my office? Yes, whatever soup, salad and sandwich combo you want to put together, for two people. And some fruit," he added with a glance up at Jayden.

At yet another reminder of his ridiculous episode the previous day, Jayden blew out a frustrated breath, not sure exactly what he was even doing there. He stood abruptly.

Looking concerned, Esteban wrapped up his call. "Everything okay?" he asked as soon as he'd hung up.

"I'm fine," Jayden snapped, knowing he was blowing things way out of proportion but somehow unable to stop the drama. "I seriously don't go around passing out all the time. Yesterday was the first time, in fact, so you needn't worry about a repeat performance."

"I'm not worried. Please sit down... Not because I think you'll fall at my feet, but because I'd like you to stay and have lunch with me." Esteban's lips quirked as though he was fighting back a laugh.

He should probably take offence at that, but he somehow knew that he wasn't being laughed at. Esteban seemed too classy a guy to out-and-out make fun of someone. But maybe he was a bit of a tease. Jayden decided he liked that thought. He wished he'd had a bit of practice in flirting, but no time like the present to gain some.

"I don't put my head between my knees for every guy I meet, you know." He paused and thought about what he'd said. "Hmm, that didn't come out like it sounded in my head."

"Oh, it came out just fine." Esteban narrowed those piercing, light green eyes and Jayden swallowed. He might not have been the most experienced guy in the world, but there was no mistaking the interest in his gaze or his tone of voice.

"So, how are you liking the retreat so far?"

The change of subject was both welcomed and a disappointment. Jayden found himself telling Esteban about his conversation with Quinn. "He had a good point about not hiding out in my room, but... It's just hard when I don't know anyone."

"I understand completely." Esteban leant forward, bracing his elbows on the desk. "One way to look at it is, no one here knows you. So you can be whoever you want for three more days. Fake it." He shrugged. "Everyone is here because they have a similar interest—gay romance. And honestly, so many of the participants are women—you're definitely in the minority. I'll bet they'd love to spend time with and talk to a gay man. I know I'm enjoying it."

Jayden's heart beat a little faster at the deep tone of the last few words, and how casually Esteban referred to Jayden as being a gay man. He'd been publicly denying it for what seemed like his whole life, though he'd been forced to privately admit it to himself almost ten years ago. At home, even a hint of 'gayness' was not tolerated, either in his family or in the community he'd never really felt a part of.

A part of his inner defences crumbled as he thrilled to finally experience what had always been his fantasy—living in a place where he could be himself, with other gay men as friends.

That brought him up short. Friends? That was overstating things a bit.

Get a grip, Jay-boy.

Esteban looked about ready to speak again, but then a knock at the door had him smiling ruefully instead. "To be continued," he said as he rose. "Come in," he called out.

A young woman opened the door and smiled at Jayden and Esteban then wheeled in a cart with a few covered items on it. With an air of long practice, she went directly to a round table near the wall and began to set out the plates and two rolled napkins with utensils.

"Thanks, Lucia."

"You're welcome. Enjoy." With one last smile, she left and closed the door behind her.

Esteban walked around the desk until he was standing so close that Jayden could feel the heat radiating from him and smell his tangy aftershave. The warm scent was like an aphrodisiac to Jayden's senses, and when Esteban placed his hand on Jayden's back, his cock began to harden.

Then Esteban's whisper came against his ear. "Let's eat first. Then we'll share dessert."

Chapter Three

Jayden remained half hard all through the meal after Esteban's tease. They'd finished their lunches while sharing a bit about their backgrounds, which weren't exactly dissimilar, even with the obvious differences of their cultures—Jayden from his small town in Wyoming, while Esteban was from Miami, his mother a Cuban immigrant. Esteban said he barely remembered his father, a thin black man who had died before he was in school, and whose build was about the only thing he'd inherited.

Both had been raised in conservative, religious families, but while Esteban had lived in an urban area where he could find a place to fit in, Jayden hadn't known of any other kids at his small high school who were gay, although statistically speaking, it was unlikely he had been the only one. By the time Jayden had gone to college, he'd just found it easier to stay in the closet and under the radar. He explained he was still working towards his degree, paying for it by doing web design and search engine optimisation. He'd found that working on the Internet came easily to him, and also provided an escape from the real world.

He admired Esteban, who had come out despite the disapproval of his family and what he wryly described as his mother's dire predictions of being bound for hell. By doing so, he had lost that familial connection, which was why he'd moved to Atlanta — to gain a bit of space and start fresh somewhere that didn't hold the memories of what he'd lost. Now Esteban had a second family in his friends and co-workers at the hotel, and his face lit up when he talked about a few of them.

"I can't believe how many guys who work here are gay," Jayden commented, a bit jealous of the camaraderie he sensed.

Esteban shrugged. "No more or less than any other hotel I've worked at. But the guys here are solid. We work well together. And their being gay isn't the defining factor for our friendship. Not even close."

"Oh." Jayden was somewhat abashed. "I didn't mean that. I have friends, but never anyone I've been really close to, at least not one that knew about who I really am, much less accepted it."

"You know, you might be surprised. How do you know they wouldn't support you?"

"Well, the things they say and joke about..." Jayden trailed off, trying not to second-guess his self-imposed solitude.

Esteban moved his chair closer and leant forward, elbows on his knees, almost touching Jayden. "I get it. But some of them might not do it if they knew they actually had a 'fag' in the room who was their good friend. Then again, only you can decide what you're comfortable with. For me, there was never any doubt that I needed to own who I was and live my life openly, the way I chose."

He must've read Jayden's discomfort with the topic because he stopped speaking, reached out and pulled him into a hug.

Jayden closed his eyes as he accepted the embrace, relishing the scent of Esteban's aftershave or cologne and the feel of his strong form against him. He let his hands settle on Esteban's back, loving being able to touch him at will. Esteban was in a dress shirt, without his jacket, and the cotton was warm beneath Jayden's hands as he ran them from the middle of his back up to his broad shoulders.

Before he even realised his intent, Jayden stood then straddled Esteban's lap. Esteban didn't even blink, merely cupped his hands around Jayden's ass and helped him to settle closer until he was sitting on his lap, pressed up against Esteban's groin.

He was tired of living tentatively.

Carpe diem.

Esteban leaned in, loving the contact that seemed to signal a big green light. "Time for the dessert I mentioned." He knew he was pushing the boundaries of propriety, but something about the way Jayden looked at him, like a starving man at a buffet, went straight to his libido. And honestly, that just never happened to him. He'd seen employee-guest 'romances' over the years, but he'd always played far away from work.

A strong believer in fate, Esteban had the sense that everything that had happened to put Jayden in his path had been for a reason. It had been too long since he'd felt the kind of pull he had towards the younger man. And not just sexually. Jayden was interesting and a great listener. Esteban had even enjoyed watching him dig into his lunch with the appetite of someone whose metabolism was still in high gear.

And if Jayden was willing, Esteban would be more than happy to satisfy whatever else he was hungry for. To hell with his self-imposed rules.

There probably wasn't a clearer message that he was willing than Jayden crawling onto his lap.

Esteban claimed his mouth in a light kiss. He rotated his hips and Jayden groaned, parting his lips, rocking back against him in a sort of roll that made Esteban suspect he was a good dancer. To test that theory, he set up a rhythm and Jayden matched and countered his every move until they were panting together into kiss after kiss. The rub of Jayden's hard cock against Esteban's through all their layers of clothes was maddening.

He pulled away from Jayden's eager mouth to glance at his closed office door. Did he dare…?

"Everyone knocks here, right?" Jayden murmured against his neck, not letting up on the pressure against his cock.

"It's still unlocked, though. Maybe— Oof!" Esteban grunted as Jayden pushed off him as he climbed off his lap to quickly cross the room. He twisted the lock then turned and palmed his hand over his erection as he walked towards Esteban.

Instead of crawling back into place on his lap, Jayden dropped to his knees between Esteban's spread legs.

Esteban leant back and tried to get his breathing under control. The mere sight of Jayden there, looking flirtatiously up at him, sent a shot of pure need pulsing through him.

Jayden ran his hands along Esteban's inner thighs, up and down a couple of times. It seemed the shyness and uncertainty that had seemed a major part of his personality until now had taken a back seat to this sexy, confident man. Esteban waited, allowing Jayden to keep control if that was what he wanted, though his fingers itched to wrap themselves in that silky-looking hair and tug.

Jayden tucked his fingers inside his waistband, and Esteban sucked in slightly to allow him the room he needed to undo his belt and hook then slowly pull down his zipper.

His pulse raced as Jayden fished inside his boxer briefs to move his cock upright then settled the waistband below it so it was exposed. The warm pressure of his hand felt like heaven on his overheated cock. His lips parted as Jayden's gaze dropped to his hand and he gave Esteban's erection a couple of light strokes.

Jayden bent and ran his tongue along the sensitive underside of his cock from near his balls up to the ridge then gave a light flick before following the same path again. The juxtaposition of having the cool air on his saliva-slicked skin while being dressed for work and on the clock caught Esteban in the gut. He'd never messed around at work before, much less in his office.

Finally the teasing licks stopped as Jayden took mercy on him and enclosed the warmth of his mouth around the head of Esteban's erection. He fought the urge to thrust into that perfect heat and held himself in check by sheer willpower as Jayden used his tongue and suction to pull him closer and closer to the brink.

This is crazy. He opened his eyes, which he hadn't even realised he'd closed, to look blankly at his office wall. He was a bit of a control freak, he knew, and it shocked him how easily Jayden had managed to break the compartmentalisation of his love life from work life. Actually, he had a tendency to isolate all parts of his life—it had been part of the lesson learned young when he'd had such a negative reaction to telling his family he was gay.

The only people who had broken through before had been his friends here at the Meliá. And now this gorgeous young man…who was going to get a mouthful any moment now.

He finally succumbed to what he'd been wanting to do since he'd met Jayden—he thrust his hands into the long, fine strands of his hair and wrapped his fingers into it, taking gentle control of his movements. Jayden glanced up at him and smirked as best he could with his lips stretched around his cock.

That look and that change in the angle of his mouth were just enough to pierce Esteban's control. He tried to tug Jayden off, but Jayden refused to relinquish his suction and without pulling hard enough to hurt him—which Esteban wasn't willing to do—he was helpless under Jayden's mouth.

"I'm there," he warned on a groan and Jayden slid his hands around under Esteban's ass, actually encouraging him as he arched his hips and came, biting his lips to keep from shouting out his completion. Jayden stroked his hands along the hollows of his hips then down his thighs, holding him in his mouth until the aftershocks had ceased and the sensation became too much.

He realised that he still had his hands entangled in Jayden's hair. "Shit, I'm sorry. I didn't mean to—"

"It's fine." Jayden's voice was slightly hoarse. "I liked it. Trust me—I would have said something if I didn't want you to grab it." He ran his hands down over the bulge at the crotch of his jeans and Esteban smiled.

"Fuck...your mouth." Jayden groaned, his gaze directed at Esteban's lips. "You are too gorgeous to be real, you know that?"

"Do you want to?"

Jayden frowned slightly. "Want to what?"

"Fuck my mouth."

Jayden's eyes went wide and his lips parted. He grabbed himself firmly. "Oh God, you can't say things like that."

Esteban tucked himself back into his briefs and fastened his pants and belt, then rose and held his hands down to tug Jayden to his feet. "Want to do this in here or up in your room?"

Jayden looked down between them then back up at Esteban. "I can't walk through the hotel like this, especially coming out of your office..."

"Okay, here it is then." Esteban spun around and eyed his desk. He did some creative rearranging of what was on top of it until there was a Jayden-sized space bare. Then he made short work of Jayden's jeans, pushing them and his briefs down his thighs. His erect cock was a pleasant surprise, smooth and somewhat pale, even engorged as it was, but long and thicker than his frame might have indicated. Exposed to the air, it eagerly rose from his pubic area, which was in its natural state—no manscaping there and that was fine with Esteban. He liked his men to look like men.

"Lie back," he ordered then helped Jayden settle onto the flat surface. He noted that the desk was at a decent fucking height, but put that from his mind. It was one thing to exchange quick blow jobs in his office—quite another to go for it and fuck. That he would want to do in Jayden's bed…

Not a one-off, his brain translated and he agreed. He definitely wanted to make the most of the brief time they'd have together. There was a spark between them that he hadn't experienced in a long time—if ever—and he wished fruitlessly that they didn't live thousands of miles apart. *Fuck my luck.*

He reached out to learn the heft of Jayden's cock with his hand, and began a slow rhythm—not about rushing to the finish but meant to draw out Jayden's arousal. He loved the responsive, sexy sounds Jayden made as he arched his head back in abandon, totally giving himself over to Esteban and whatever he wanted to do to him.

Unfortunately, time was marching on and, while his staff was very respectful of his office door being closed, it was growing more and more likely that something would need his attention asap.

He moved in closer, between Jayden's somewhat trapped legs, still half clad in his jeans, and ran his hands up Jayden's slim torso underneath his shirt before drawing them back towards him. Jayden's cock jumped a bit as his hands glanced past it without a direct touch.

Esteban smiled and used a grip at the base to hold Jayden's cock upright for him to sink his mouth over the tip.

"Oh my…God…" Jayden groaned and thumped his head a couple of times against the desk.

His response was to increase his suction and press farther down until he'd reached the easy limits of his mouth then withdraw before settling into a firm, bobbing pattern. He lightly jacked from the base of his cock to make it up to the length not passing between his lips.

When Jayden came it was with a stifled gasp and a smack of his hand against the desk as he pushed upwards. His ragged breathing was the only sound in the room for a minute afterwards as Esteban stood to look at the decadent sight of Jayden sprawled on his desk, panting, cock still half hard and glistening with saliva and cum, resting towards his hip bone.

He wished he could take a picture.

"Wow, that was intense." Jayden finally opened his eyes and sat up partway, propping himself up on his elbows. That pose was no less stimulating and Esteban had the urge to say 'fuck it' to work, take Jayden back up to his room and spend the rest of the day learning every bare inch of him.

"It was," he agreed, his voice husky even to his own ears, and Jayden shot him a smirk.

"You, um…" Jayden hesitated then rose to stand and pull up his pants before continuing. "If you don't have any plans later, maybe we could meet up…?"

Esteban nodded, unable to help the smile curving his lips. "Or we could just call it a definite date and I could find you before this evening's social event."

Pleasure lit Jayden's eyes as he asked, "You want to come as my date? Is that allowed?"

Esteban shrugged. "I don't think I would really have a problem getting in, being staff, but I'd rather do it right and ask the organisers if they mind. Somehow I think they'll be okay with it. As for it being allowed by the hotel, as long as I'm not on duty, I can socialise here, provided I don't reflect badly on myself or the hotel." He moved closer and took Jayden into a light embrace. "So is that okay with you? If I ask permission to come as your date?"

Jayden tilted his head to a flirtatious angle, looking slightly up at him from close range. "That sounds great" — he grinned — "really great. I have a date. Cool."

"Cool," Esteban repeated then gave Jayden one last squeeze. "And thanks for having lunch with me."

"My pleasure." Jayden coloured slightly before adding, "In more ways than one." He walked towards the door and Esteban followed, reaching past him to open it. He let Jayden precede him down the hallway towards the front desk, then out of the side door into the lobby. He remained in the staff area and lifted his hand in farewell.

Jayden walked backwards for a few steps until he almost ran into someone then turned and apologised. He looked back at Esteban and matched his grin before walking off in the direction of the elevators.

Esteban waited until he was out of sight then closed the door.

A text hit his phone. He pulled it out and looked at the screen — it was from Gib.

Cute kid. Have a nooner with the guy who stole my room????

He snorted on a laugh and walked back to his office while texting.

Not exactly a kid and none of your damn business.

LOL, you dog. Good for you. 'Bout time you loosened up.

Esteban raised his eyebrow at that. Gib thought he was uptight? Well, he wasn't the only one messing around with a guest at the moment.

So how was the Sono Suite?

After couple of minutes there was still no reply from his friend and he laughed, sending a second text.

Now who needs to loosen up?

Touche.

Good humour firmly in place, Esteban settled down at his desk — still in disarray from his rearranging it — to get some tasks checked off his 'to-do' list. But before he got started, he added a couple of things as urgent, including *Check with GRL on OK to come as date tonight.* He wasn't ashamed of his interest in Jayden and wanted to own the fact, as well as make the most of their remaining three days.

He sobered at the thought of Jayden flying home on Sunday and not seeing him again. He hated thinking that this was just a 'conference fling', but really, what more could it be? With all that distance between them and just barely knowing each other, there really wasn't more they could be, no matter how well they seemed to fit together.

Esteban shook his head at his luck. Finally, a man he enjoyed being with and he lived in freaking Wyoming of all places.

Fates, you just don't seem to want to give me a break, do you?

Chapter Four

Jayden's body was humming from the low-level state of arousal he'd been in for hours now. Esteban had been as good as his word, and had secured permission from both the GRL organisers and his GM, Trevor, to be able to attend this evening's function as his companion. His attentive proximity had been playing havoc with Jayden's control all night.

It hadn't helped that the evening event involved dancing and even some half-naked eye candy. He was far from the only interested onlooker in the place but he was, gratifyingly, one of the few people in the room who seemed to have a date. He'd been worried that Esteban might feel constrained or cautious about being seen with him. However, that had turned out to be the furthest thing from the truth. He'd stood in line to get Jayden drinks, cosied up close while taking in the entertainment and danced pressed up against him — so close that he could feel his partial erection rub against his own.

Jayden couldn't get over the fact that there would obviously be photographic evidence of their date, too.

For some reason, while they had been out on the dance floor together, mobs of women had kept taking their picture. Through it all, Esteban had taken everything in his stride, being gracious enough but basically ignoring the outside distractions, focusing entirely on Jayden. And Jayden had happily followed his lead.

He'd finally met and talked with some of the other attendees and had even managed to connect with a couple of people he 'knew' online. They seemed so happy to meet him, and for the first time since he'd planned to come, he finally felt one hundred per cent sure about being there. They'd talked about the following days' offerings and even made plans to meet up at a few events. Between that breaking of the ice and Esteban's charismatic presence, he was just about floating as they said their goodnights and headed to take the elevator down to The Level.

Esteban watched him with hooded, sexy-as-fuck eyes, toying with his fingers in a loose hold while they rode the short distance to his floor. When the doors opened, they clasped hands naturally and held them all the way down the hall to his door.

Jayden's hands were trembling just a bit when he fumbled with his lanyard, trying to find his room key. Esteban beat him to it, using evidently his pass key to open the door.

Not sure why he was suddenly so nervous after being so confident and happy all day since their encounter at lunch, Jayden strode into the room ahead of Esteban. The sound of the door closing didn't come when he expected, and he turned to the door. Esteban was still in the doorway, holding it open.

"Can I come in? Or…?"

He met that increasingly familiar peridot gaze across the room and felt badly for perhaps ruining the mood. "Yes, please do. I'm sorry. I'm not sure what's wrong with me. I just... When we got back here, I wasn't sure what you expected."

Esteban frowned, appearing to think for a moment, then stepped inside and let the door close behind him. He didn't come any closer, though. "I don't expect anything, Jayden. I enjoyed our time tonight, as well as earlier today, but there are no expectations, so don't worry."

"I'm not worried." He ran his hand through his hair roughly. It snagged a bit as it was still slightly damp from working up a sweat dancing. He blew out a frustrated breath. Had he really thought anything negative would come after how great Esteban had been so far? What had he thought would happen? If everything tonight had been foreplay, then the most logical conclusion—sex—wasn't something he should be nervous about.

At least it wouldn't be if he wasn't a virgin.

He'd already made up his mind that if the opportunity arose, he couldn't think of a nicer, sexier, more thoughtful guy to take that final step with than Esteban. So why the jitters?

He looked at Esteban's slightly enquiring look, marred only a bit by a concerned frown. His body language was open and relaxed and he hadn't come any farther into the room than enough to close the door.

Basically, he was letting Jayden set the pace and was obviously willing to back off if that was what he wanted.

Of course, that cemented in his mind that Esteban leaving him chastely at the door was the *last* thing he wanted.

Before he could stop and think too hard about what he was doing, Jayden reached to grasp his shirt then pulled it over his head. In the brief time that he'd been separated from Esteban's gaze, Esteban's expression had changed to one of increasing heat and interest.

Heartened, Jayden undid the top button of his jeans, then the next and so on until his fly was open. He switched gears then and walked to sit on the side of the bed in order to take off his shoes and socks. Then he stood and shucked the clothing off his lower half until he was standing bared for Esteban's perusal.

He cocked an eyebrow in challenge and waited as Esteban traced every inch of him with his gaze.

"Very nice," he finally said. "I take it that means you're really not worried any longer?"

"Yes," Jayden answered and felt it with all sincerity. He was ready to have this night be about firsts, for him as well as for them. He put aside all thoughts of what the end of the weekend would bring, and waited impatiently for Esteban to catch up with him.

"Good." Then Esteban was crossing the room in several long strides. He pulled Jayden up against him and the erotic contrast of being naked pressed against Esteban's fully clothed form went straight to his cock, which hardened unbelievably quickly. Esteban pressed a deep kiss to his mouth, stealing his breath before tracing his lips along his cheek and down to his jaw line. He slid his hands along Jayden's bare back to cup his ass and fit him more closely against him.

They began a slight movement against one another that mimicked the dancing they'd been doing earlier, only this time Jayden felt free to unabashedly grind up against Esteban. Esteban grasped his ass in a rhythmic kneading that occasionally separated his cheeks. The light teasing touch that finally came against his hole was so incredibly good, and he wanted it so much, that a huge moan escaped him and he could feel a bead of pre-cum well out of his slit.

Panting, he wrenched himself away from a startled Esteban.

He gestured at Esteban's clothing. "I don't want to get you dirty." And he took himself in hand, running his palm over the tip of his cock and giving the head a circular rub.

"Very thoughtful, but I have no qualms about getting dirty with you."

"Naked would be better, though."

"All kinds of better," Esteban agreed and started stripping.

When he was finally as naked as Jayden, he took him in his arms and began a slow, seductive kiss that ignited a warmth in Jayden—not just in his libido, but within his chest. The caring he was being shown was so at odds with his usual interactions with people, and yet it felt so necessary to his continued well-being.

It was going to be brutal leaving this behind.

"If this is going where I really would like it to, I'm hoping you have supplies," Esteban half whispered in his ear. His breath sent shivers down him.

"Under the pillow closest to the lamp," he admitted. He hadn't liked the sight of them sitting on the bedside table.

"Good." Esteban pulled the comforter from the bed, folded it and set it on the chair, then turned down the sheet and blanket.

Jayden had to grin at the care he showed. It was probably hard to turn off when you were immersed in the hotel business.

"Bring that sexy smile over here."

He walked over to the bed and joined Esteban as they lay down together and resumed their kissing and caressing. It didn't take long for them to rebuild the feverish need that had been banked since their last encounter. Jayden couldn't get over the warm, smooth feel of Esteban's firm body against his. He hooked his leg over Esteban's hip and as though that had been a signal—maybe it had—Esteban immediately ran his touch down to Jayden's crack. He delved lightly between his ass cheeks as he kissed Jayden deeply, and began to run his fingers over his entrance.

Jayden had never felt so possessed, so needy in his life. He reached to grab the lube and thrust it pointedly into Esteban's hand, all without breaking the kiss or his explorations of that smooth, caramel-coloured skin. Esteban chuckled into his mouth then pulled back slightly in order to see what he was doing with the small tube.

In no time at all, his slickened fingers were back at Jayden's hole, giving it a rub before disappearing briefly then returning with more cool lube. He very slowly stroked the skin there then pressed until he had one finger inside him.

"Oh God."

"This okay?"

"Yes... Fuck yeah." Jayden squirmed, trying to get more, his hard cock running along Esteban's abdomen. He wasn't a stranger to ass play, but damn, it was completely different when it was someone else's fingers there. Different in an amazing way.

He protested slightly as Esteban moved away then manoeuvred him until he was on his stomach, legs spread to accommodate Esteban's kneeling form. "I want to see," he explained, and that was fine with Jayden, as long as he kept up what he was doing.

The slight sting of increased stretch softened and melded into pure pleasure the longer Esteban spent on him, and Jayden could feel his cock leaking onto the sheet below him. He couldn't stop moving and rubbing against the sheet, rocking back and forth between the welcome pressure of the mattress and the possession of Esteban working his fingers inside him.

"You're killing me," he groaned. "Come on, already."

"I want to make sure you're stretched."

"I'm stretched, and even if I wasn't, can you just finish stretching me with that gorgeous fucking cock?"

Esteban laughed and withdrew his fingers, then reached past him to grab the condoms. The rustling sound behind him was music to his ears.

More lube then, finally, the blunt and huge-feeling head of Esteban's cock was touching his grasping hole. Esteban teased over his entrance a few passes before aiming it at the right angle and pressing down as Jayden arched back and up, tilting his hips, making his hard cock drag along the sheet.

The head popped in and Jayden was grateful as Esteban paused. *That* stretch was more sting than pleasure at first, but a few measured breaths later, it began to ease and change into an incredible fullness as Esteban pressed forward slightly, then retreated.

He did that repeatedly until he had sunk all the way into Jayden, filling him, possessing him, and oh God, the feeling was incredible.

"Please. Move, damn it."

"Oh yes," Esteban whispered, his voice hoarse, and a wave of pride swept over Jayden at having been the one to wring that reaction from this sexy, sexy man.

Esteban began to thrust deep before pulling out almost to the brink, surging into him over and over. Jayden met his rhythm and then some, leaving passivity behind and participating with equal demand and fervour until he had no more control over his actions. The pleasure was driving them both and they worked towards the summit together.

Jayden could feel his climax barrelling down his spine and managed to get a hand worked under him. Esteban sat back, almost pulling out, and Jayden gasped when his hips were grabbed and yanked up and back so that he was on his hands and knees. Then Esteban began pounding into him with intent while reaching around to stroke him in time with his thrusts.

Only a handful of motions later, Jayden's pleasure broke over him. "Ah! Oh fuck..." Esteban was there with him a moment later, as though his climax had pulled his lover's from him. They soon collapsed together in a heap, and, rather than feeling squashed by Esteban, Jayden relished the feel of his weight and damp skin against his.

All too soon, Esteban had to deal with the condom and Jayden mourned the loss of him inside him. He lay there without moving while Esteban went into the bathroom. He might have been inexperienced but he knew enough to know that the connection and chemistry between them didn't happen for every two lovers.

Suddenly he was thinking about changing his life to have this all the time. A typical reaction to losing virginity? Or knowing what he wanted and doing what was necessary to get it?

He didn't know the answer right then, but he knew he'd need to figure it out within the next three days or so.

Chapter Five

Sunday morning came so quickly, the time that passed might as well have been in the snap of a finger. Not wanting to waste any time together, whenever Esteban hadn't been working over the past two days, he'd spent his time with Jayden. He'd even gone so far as to pack a bag and bring it here with him the morning after their first night together. He'd been living out of Jayden's room, so he hadn't actually left the hotel since Friday morning.

Now it was Sunday, and he was sitting up against the headboard, fully dressed, watching as Jayden packed his bags. Things had been quiet between them ever since they'd woken up. The impending separation was evidently having an effect on both of them.

This morning, they'd awoken and begun to make love without a single word between them. It had been hot and bittersweet at the same time, and Esteban's chest ached at the memory.

He had no idea what was going through Jayden's head. More than anything, he wanted to tell Jayden to please just stay, but how could he do that? Jayden had a life and a family—intolerant though it was—back at home. They'd only known each other for four days, and those had been spent in an unreal atmosphere. It was pretty foolish to think that they could make a lasting relationship from a holiday affair, passionate though it was.

If he was honest, it wasn't just about the passion between them. He really liked Jayden and had enjoyed their time together. They could talk about anything and everything, and he felt truly comfortable with him. The spark they shared was an amazing bonus to a camaraderie and connection that couldn't be faked.

Fuck.

Jayden's expression had been nothing but solemn all morning. Even the brief smiles he offered Esteban didn't really reach his eyes. Like the one he was giving him now that his last bag was zipped shut.

"So..."

Esteban repressed a sigh. *Here we go.* "So. Your shuttle should be here in about twenty minutes." He glanced at the hatefully fast clock. "We should probably go down to the lobby." Repeating his offer of the night before, he asked, "Are you sure you don't want me to drive you to the airport?"

Jayden shook his head. "I don't want to say goodbye to you in public." He clenched his jaw.

Esteban's throat tightened and he couldn't stay quiet any longer. "What are we doing? How can we just let this end like this? Am I the only one feeling this way?"

Jayden swallowed. "How do you feel?"

Esteban was sure his heart was in his eyes as he held Jayden's gaze. "Like I'm being ripped in two."

"Fuck," Jayden muttered. He looked up at Esteban, and the resolute sadness there caused almost a physical pain. "I have to go."

"I know." Esteban dropped his gaze to his legs stretched out in front of him.

"But I'll be back as soon as I can."

Esteban froze then slowly raised his head. "What?" he managed.

A smile slowly spread across Jayden's lips. "I'm coming back. If... If you want me to."

He didn't even know he was moving until he was off the bed and taking Jayden into his arms. "Of course I want you to, but... Are you sure?" he demanded. Now time was standing still and holding its breath along with him as he waited for Jayden's answer.

Jayden cupped his face in his hands. "Yes. I've never been more sure about anything. There's nothing for me back there. Everything I want is right here. If you were able to move to Atlanta and start over without knowing anyone, I can do it knowing you're here waiting for me."

Esteban let out a whoop of sheer happiness and relief then picked Jayden up and spun him around. He felt Jayden's legs go round his hips and he held on, grinning so widely that he thought his cheeks might cramp.

Jayden leaned in to kiss him thoroughly. It was only a knock on the door that brought them back to the here and now. They both stiffened and their gazes met.

"Who do you think that is?" Jayden whispered. Esteban lowered him to the floor.

The knock came again. "Housekeeping."

Relieved, Esteban moved towards the door, not letting go of Jayden's hand, tugging him along in his wake. "Just Quinn, thank God."

He opened the door with a greeting on his lips only to freeze at the sight of his general manager Trevor standing there. His stomach immediately began to roil at the prospect of losing his job over this. Jayden refused to back down and stood firmly at his side.

Trevor entered the room and looked around at the mussed bed and packed bags with one eyebrow raised. "Well? What exactly is going on here?"

Esteban let out a sigh. "I can explain. I know I shouldn't have, but when Jayden — I mean, Mr Yates — made his reservation, he accidentally booked the wrong month. So, since we were full, I offered to let him stay —"

"Yes, yes, I know all that part." Trevor waved an impatient hand at him. "What I mean is, you're not going to just let him fly away now, right?"

Esteban gaped at his boss, unable to process the fact that he somehow knew about this room after all. Did that mean he'd known about it with Gib? And how had he found out about —

Jayden slid his arm around Esteban's waist. "I do have to fly home, sir, but I'll be back as soon as I can drive here."

"Ha!" The exclamation from near the door startled them all. Esteban looked up to see Gib and Quinn hanging out in the doorway, huge grins on their faces.

"Pay up, guys. I had him driving back here after keeping his flight." Gib looked as smug as hell.

Quinn shoved him rudely and looked at Esteban in disgust. "And you're not flying back with him? That's just lame. Thanks a lot." He turned and left, muttering on his way down the hall about how chivalry was dead.

Trevor grimaced at Gib, then looked at Jayden. "Are you sure you don't want to take a later flight?"

Shaking his head, Jayden explained, "Sooner I get home, the sooner I can pack and get on the road back here."

Esteban couldn't fault that logic. "Sounds like a great plan to me. But I'll come with if you want me to."

"I'll be fine. I wouldn't want to expose you to the idiots I'll have to deal with anyway. You just stick to your schedule"—he lowered his voice to a whisper just for Esteban's ears—"because once I get back here, I'm not going to let you out of bed for a week. You can take the time off then."

"As I said, great plan." He kissed Jayden, not caring that Trevor and Gib were there watching.

Jayden pulled away reluctantly then gasped. "My shuttle!"

He moved to gather his things and the others helped however they could. As they walked towards the door as a group, Esteban asked Trevor, "Am I in trouble for the out of service thing?"

Trevor looked over at Gib, who smiled wryly. Then he shook his head. "No one's in trouble for anything. *But*," he stressed, "now that no one needs to use it anymore, I want this room rent ready by mid-week. It's been out of service long enough. And now that apparently every gay guy on the staff is out of circulation, maybe we can get some work done."

The three of them laughed as they followed Jayden in a rush down the hallway to the elevator.

A thought struck Esteban and he hurried to catch up. "Jayden! Don't you dare forget to eat." He reached him and gave him a side-hug as they waited for an open car. "I don't want you falling at the feet of anyone else ever again."

Jayden relaxed against him. "I'll take care of myself. And you do the same until I'm back and we can take care of each other."

Nothing sounded better to Esteban than that—a lifetime of caring for Jayden... And he'd start with that week off Jayden had mentioned.

About the Authors

Carol Lynne

An avid reader for years, one day Carol Lynne decided to write her own brand of erotic romance. Carol juggles between being a full-time mother and a full-time writer. These days, you can usually find Carol either cleaning jelly out of the carpet or nestled in her favourite chair writing steamy love scenes.

Amber Kell

Amber is one of those quiet people they always tell you to watch out for. She lives in Seattle with her husband, two sons, two cats and one extremely stupid dog.

T.A. Chase

There is beauty in every kind of love, so why not live a life without boundaries? Experiencing everything the world offers fascinates TA and writing about the things that make each of us unique is how she shares those insights. When not writing, TA's watching movies, reading and living life to the fullest.

Jambrea Jo Jones

Jambrea wanted to be the youngest romance author published, but life impeded the dreams. She put her writing aside and went to college briefly, then enlisted in the Air Force. After serving in the military, she returned home to Indiana to start her family. A few years later, she discovered yahoo groups and book reviews. There was no turning back. She was bit by the writing bug.

She enjoys spending time with her son when not writing and loves to receive reader feedback. She's addicted to the internet so feel free to email her anytime.

Stephani Hecht

Stephani Hecht is a happily married mother of two. Born and raised in Michigan, she loves all things about the state, from the frigid winters to the Detroit Red Wings hockey team. You can usually find her snuggled up to her laptop, creating her next book.

Devon Rhodes

Devon started reading and writing at an early age and never looked back. At 39 and holding, Devon finally figured out the best way to channel her midlife crisis was to morph from mild-mannered stay-at-home mom to erotic romance writer. She lives in Oregon with her family, who are (mostly) understanding of all the time she spends on her laptop, aka the black hole.

All of the above authors love to hear from readers. You can find their contact information, website details and author profile pages at http://www.total-e-bound.com.

Total-E-Bound Publishing

www.total-e-bound.com

Take a look at our exciting range of literagasmic™
erotic romance titles and discover pure quality
at Total-E-Bound.

Lightning Source UK Ltd.
Milton Keynes UK
UKOW04f0105051113

220439UK00001B/43/P